Blue
Haven

Blue Haven

Lisa King

The Story Plant
1270 Caroline Street
Suite D120-381
Atlanta, GA 30307

Story Plant hardcover ISBN-13: 978-1-61188-320-6
Fiction Studio Books e-book ISBN-13: 978-1-945839-58-0
Story Plant paperback ISBN-13: 978-1-61188-355-8

Visit our website at www.TheStoryPlant.com

First Story Plant printing: May 2022
First Story Plant paperback printing: October 2023

Printed in the United States of America
0 9 8 7 6 5 4 3 2 1

For my husband, Dave, with love.

"I looked but I couldn't see anything
through its dark-knit glare;
yet don't we all know, the golden sand
is there at the bottom,
though our eyes have never seen it,
nor can our hands ever catch it."
—from *Bone*, by Mary Oliver

Also,

What doesn't kill you.
Can.
In fact.
Still kill you.

Chapter One
Day One

Less than twenty-four hours earlier, Aloe Malone was sitting on a tattered couch, a distinct eagerness coursing through her veins. She shivered; ßher radiator was on the fritz again, sputtering from one side, cackling, rendering her tiny bachelor apartment bone-cold uncomfortable. She curled into a sweater, still freezing, slowly succumbing to the chronic, aggravating chill.

And then she laughed, her breath puffy with condensation. She'd worked her last shift at the diner, and said her meager and limited goodbyes—except the one owed to her crummy apartment.

"Sayonara, shithole," she whispered under her breath.

Now, she squinted into the radiant sun: hot but not fierce, a tempered warmth that was perfect and satisfying. She pressed her feet into the fairy dust sand and gave her toes a wiggle. She'd never felt sand like this before: white, delicate, possibly otherworldly, like it'd been manufactured in a laboratory or harvested from another universe. Like someone had broken one million hourglasses to populate this beach.

She turned to her personal concierge, Amir. "Is this … *real* sand?"

Surely, it couldn't be.

He nodded. "Real indeed. One of the many reasons we chose this location."

This location: a mysterious venue somewhere on planet Earth. She'd love to know the actual coordinates and considered asking (for the third time) but confidentiality was part of the deal. If you wanted to live in the world's most lucrative beachfront community, secrecy was paramount.

Still, she dug her toes deeper into the cushy grains. *What part of the world produces sand like this? Aruba? Somewhere in South Asia? The Philippines?*

She stared skeptically at Amir. His natural tan and dark features were clearly exotic. And his name, *Amir. Was that Arabic?*

"Aloe?" He touched her arm. "Are you feeling okay? You look a bit dazed."

Her mind floated back. "Yeah, sorry. Still a little groggy."

"That's a very common side effect," he replied. "Rest assured, you'll be back to normal in a few hours at most."

She nodded, somewhat attuned to the aftermath of drugs slugging through her arteries. The whole "going under" aspect had been daunting: a white mask, followed by slow, deep inhalations; *counting down from ten*, as requested; waking somewhere new and unknown— though it made good, logical sense. How else were people supposed to fly to a top-secret paradise without discovering its whereabouts?

Besides, *look at this fucking view.* The oceanfront, steps away, was a prism of blue light. Turquoise lapped at the shoreline, fading to a sumptuous cerulean. The sky was a lovely robin's egg, swept with long, lazy clouds. Her eyes found the horizon. There was nothing in the distance, no islands, shorelines, or glimpses. Just pure, unadulterated space.

Aloe turned to the billowing palm trees swaying in her periphery. Not an imposing number, just enough to provide a calculated amount of shade. Unlike other beaches she'd visited, Blue Haven's was devoid of human life; and that, was its true appeal. No sandcastles or shoddily impaled umbrellas or squawking birds begging for scraps of potato chips. Blue Haven was a stock-grade computer background that didn't exist in real life—except it did, to her absolute astonishment.

"*Paradise*," she looked at Amir and smiled. "Y'all weren't lying."

"We aim to please," he replied. "Go ahead, test the water. Dip your toe in. We've installed top-of-the-line thermoregulators to ensure the perfect temperature. Always."

"You're heating … *the ocean?*"

"Only as required."

"Wow," she replied, stepping forward.

A wave drifted over her toes, warm as bathwater, and she instantly unwound. A salty gust of air filled her lungs, causing her chest to lift.

And just like that, the unshakeable sense of irresolution that'd been following her for years was suddenly gone. All that mattered was here and now—this moment.

"How's the temperature?" Amir asked.

She returned to his side with a lightness in her step. "Perfect."

"Excellent." He tucked a fuchsia hibiscus behind her ear, and for some reason this motion summoned a pang of guilt. Her stomach lurched, and the weight of her body returned.

Did she really deserve this new life?

The answer was clear and undisputed. *Of course not.* No cognizant, twenty-five-year-old could honestly admit otherwise. She'd simply gotten lucky.

Then again, who was she to contest the force of luck?

"Are you ready to continue with the tour?" Amir asked.

She took one last glance at the ocean, nodding. The view was dreamy, glorious, enchanting—beyond any adjective she'd ever learned. Maybe she didn't deserve this life, but it had found her. The only choice now was acceptance.

Even if Blue Haven seemed too good to be true.

Chapter Two

Aloe followed Amir up the white cobblestone path that twisted through Blue Haven like a vine. "We kept the design very straightforward," he explained. "This path is a series of loops that weave throughout the condominiums, ultimately leading here, to the *Hexagon*."

He stretched his arms, showing off the massive hexagonal structure before them that ventured forever into the sky—the tallest building, *by far*, that Aloe had ever seen. It was entirely composed of dark-tinted windows that glinted in the sunlight. She cranked her neck to the point of discomfort staring up—and up, and up, feeling more like a speck of dust than a human being.

"Twenty-eight hundred feet exactly," Amir stated proudly. He nudged her arm. "That's taller than the Burj Khalifa in Dubai."

"Isn't the Burj Khalifa the tallest building in the world?"

His mouth pinched at one corner. "*Was* the tallest building in the world."

"Incredible," she replied. A set of grand, brass-clad doors opened to a reception lobby, and a gasp fled her lips; the architecture was literally breathtaking: dramatic arches and slanted windows with swirls of turquoise bleeding throughout. Warm sunlight blazed through circular skylights, landing on her happy cheeks. Everything seemed suddenly brought to life: gold embellishments blossoming in corners, boxy white tiles speckling with diamonds, a crystal chandelier the size of a city bus. She reached toward the glimmering prisms, the number of tiers uncountable.

"Stunning," she whispered.

"We employed several world-class architects to design this space," Amir said. "I think it turned out alright." He winked.

"I'll say."

Seconds passed, stark with silence. Aloe stepped further into the room. The lack of movement and sound in such a large, elaborate space was striking; her guts twisted with unease. Part of Blue Haven's appeal was its sparsity—they'd made that abundantly clear during the interview—but this was next level desertion. A nervous tick came and she tapped her toe against the glossy, oversized tiles. "Where is everyone?"

Amir glanced at his watch. "Sleeping, I imagine. It's only nine in the morning. The pace here is very slow, very calm—as intended. Residents enjoy a relaxing start to the day."

"Sure," Aloe replied, instantly more at ease. She hadn't realized the time.

"Speaking of residents," Amir added. "You can find the Directory here." He pointed to a wall-length slab of marble etched with rose-gold cursive.

Her eyes traveled down the encompassing list. The facilities and services were endless, and she couldn't surmise a single missing amenity. The so-called Hexagon had everything, apparently, from restaurants and spas to podiatrists and chiropractors.

Everything except for occupants.

She found her name at the bottom, under Residents.

Aloe Malone, Number Five.

She was last on the list, which meant only five condos in this sprawling, spacious paradise were taken.

In a sense, she'd expected only a small number of neighbors: the invitation was exclusive and the facilities were new. But *only five people*? That was a little … *odd*? Wasn't it? She closed her eyes and drew a breath, trying to escape the dull pull of meds still weighing down her thoughts.

"Let me guess," Amir said. "Right now, you're bothered by the eerie sense of vacancy."

Her stomach unwound like a spool. *Thank God. I'm not entirely off base.* "Yeah, if I'm being honest, only five residents is a bit weird, no?"

Amir gave an understanding grin. "Of course. And I think you'll find solace in knowing your peers had similar first impressions. We're relatively new, as you know, and we like to stagger admittance. But there's also an adjustment period that comes with living in a facility like Blue Haven. It's meant to feel vacant. You're from downtown Chicago, correct?"

Aloe nodded. "Yes, Pilsen area, Lower West Side."

"Right, so you're accustomed to congested, densely populated busyness. *This*," he flashed his arms, "is the opposite—by intention. Here at Blue Haven, we've created an atmosphere that caters to a person's need for tranquility, relaxation, stillness, and pleasure. Such outcomes are difficult to achieve in an environment with …"

"People?" Aloe suggested, not sure if that was the right word, but it seemed appropriate.

"Sure." Amir smiled. He had a warm smile that matched his approachable demeanor. "Any other questions for me at the moment?" he asked.

She mulled for a second. "Not really. I'm sure I will. I mean, this is all incredibly overwhelming—in a good way."

"Of course. Just let me know. That's what I'm here for." He flashed another retail smile. Amir had a way of calming her nerves, and she appreciated his soft aura and soothing voice. Everything about him was level and paced, like a yoga instructor in a crisp, white pantsuit. Though, she couldn't help but wonder what sort of person Amir was after hours, when he wasn't her "personal concierge." He was young, late twenties, early thirties at most. Did he drink on the weekends with his buddies? Watch football at sports bars? Graze communal nachos?

Then again, what sort of person was she underneath it all? Did she really want to know? Did *anyone*?

After a few lingering moments of standing and staring—there was little to do in the massive lobby besides stand and stare—she met Amir's gaze, and his dark eyes lit with excitement. "Are you ready to see your condo?"

"*Am I*," she replied, a smile pushing at her lips.

Months ago, she'd been searching for a place (in Chicago at the time) when a real estate acquaintance with a tip-off for new luxury condo developments reached out. After checking out the photos, she'd never been so amazed, instantly hooked by the modern glass-front exterior and ocean view. But even more so, the feeling in her soul of belonging—that she'd finally be a somebody, among other somebodies.

To think, all it took was several applications, a multitude of security checks, a stack of book-thick legal documents, one passed-out plane ride, and twenty million dollars.

Ha!

"Follow me," Amir said. "You're actually just around the corner. Perfectly central—not that any residence isn't perfectly central. Part of the loop-around design, naturally."

He paused and smiled again. "I think you'll find we've thought of everything here."

Chapter Three

They merged back onto the cobblestone path, flanked by aromatic plants birthing ripe, tropical flowers. Aloe drew in their sweetness. She'd never smelled anything so enticing, not that she had much experience with flowers or plants, being the sort that couldn't remember pesky watering schedules. The last of her botany adventures ended with a crispy brown skeleton, tossed in the trash.

They stopped beside a white concrete exterior with large panes of tinted glass. The design was sleek and ultra-modern, unlike anything that existed anywhere else: clean lines and smooth curves, bold angles and sharp contrast. Aloe's heart welled. *This is freakin' gorgeous.*

NUMBER FIVE spanned the door in thick, stylish typeface—hard to miss.

"Love it," she said. "I absolutely love it."

"Wait until you see the view," Amir replied, pressing his finger against a small round button. "It's fingerprint activated, by the way."

"Do I need to …?" Aloe trailed off, not knowing what sort of technological lingo completed the rest of that sentence. Regardless, she wasn't looking forward to any set up. "I'm allergic to technology," she said, causing Amir to laugh.

"Don't worry," he replied. "We've preprogrammed everything for ease. Here at Blue Haven, your life will be devoid of those annoying, ficklesome tasks we all hate. Also, just so you're aware, the only people with access into your space—besides yourself, of course—are staff members."

Amir slid open the door and gave her a nod. *After you.*

She stepped inside, welcoming a blast of cool air.

The space was a living, breathing version of the photos she'd seen initially—though they'd hardly done the place justice. She focused on the floor-to-ceiling beachfront view, drawn to the bold colors of the water, so bright and unmuted she had to shake the surreal cloud of doubt from her thoughts. *This is truly happening. This is your life now.*

"We're facing west?" she asked.

Amir nodded. "Indeed. You're in for some incredible sunsets."

"Fantastic." She recalled her south-facing Chicago apartment, closely nestled between other buildings. The view in every direction was some exterior facade: gray concrete, melancholy yellow brick, pale siding—not even a glimpse of sky. In hindsight, of course she was mildly depressed. *She couldn't even see the damn sky.*

Her feet danced across the soft, pale hardwood. The open-concept design allowed a universal sightline: everything all at once. She liked the exposure—the freedom—of such a large airy space, unbound by useless walls.

The furniture choices were sleek and tasteful, exactly her style. A large white sectional spliced through the middle like the letter "C," resting adjacent to a circular glass table with glossy, high-back chairs. Behind the living and dining arrangement was an all-white kitchen with tall, lustrous cabinets and sparkling countertops.

The walls were mostly windows, slightly tinted with massive peaks and valleys. And then her eyes were drawn up—*and up*, until they met an arched ceiling, at least twenty-feet in height.

"Everything's so … perfect," she said, hardly believing she would call this place home.

She glanced inside the main bathroom—a behemoth of a bathroom, noticing a button on the outside wall, positioned at light-switch height.

"What does this do?" she asked.

Amir gave a permissive hand swing. "Go ahead and find out."

She pressed her finger against the cool metal, watching in amazement as the main stretch of ocean-facing glass simply vanished. *Poof.* A gust of balmy air arrived, followed by a rolling echo of waves. She approached the water.

"Holy shit," was all she could manage. "Somehow, my expectations have been exceeded."

Amir's face scrunched into a giddy, childlike smile, and then he passed her a watch, or something similar: a slim electronic bracelet. "Oh yes, before I forget. This is your device."

"Device?" she asked.

"Yes, think of it as your personal, round-the-clock on-call button. Anytime you need me, just tap the surface. It's very straightforward, and can also be used to make phone calls. As you know, all other types of personal electronics are prohibited. For our sake—and your sake."

She nodded. "Right."

Exterior communication in Blue Haven was essentially banned, save phone calls to a vetted list of contacts. In today's day and age, confidentiality would be impossible to achieve otherwise—so they'd explained, which made sense. Luckily, Aloe didn't care much about losing Google or Facebook. Social media platforms, like anything else that involved the word social, didn't really appeal to her. Friends were hard to come by.

She took a few strides toward the water, stopping as her feet reached the sand. Her arms outstretched, long and sturdy. The ocean, feet away, lapped against the shoreline—a sound so lulling she barely registered Amir's receding footsteps. By the time she turned, he was half-way out the door.

"Didn't want to ruin your moment," he said. "I'll let you get settled. Remember, I'm literally a tap away."

Her stomach dipped—just slightly, like a ripple in still water. "Wait," she said. "What am I supposed to ... *do*?"

There it was again, that smile. "Easy," he replied. "Live your best life."

So simple, it was almost complicated.

Chapter Four

Aloe reached into a fully stocked fridge and selected a pre-assembled plate of creamy cheeses and ripe tropical fruits. She popped in a slice of mango, taking a moment to savor the burst of sweetness before venturing into the master bedroom: a soft and breezy space with brazen white linens and bamboo furniture. The windows were once again astounding, creating a vast, boundless sightline. Skylights carved through the ceilings, dramatic and interesting. Whoever designed Blue Haven had architectural prowess, for sure.

She sat on the edge of her new bed—a roomy California King—and ran her fingers over the puffy comforter. She imagined slipping beneath the buttery linens, and seriously considered a nap. But the tiredness in her bones was starting to fade, replaced by a jittery energy.

She stood and tapped on the so-called device, now secured around her wrist. Amir's voice instantly materialized. "Aloe, hope you're settling in well. What can I do for you?"

"Wow that was fast," she replied.

"Here to please."

A guilty smile met her lips. She was hardly the type of woman who enjoyed being waited on hand and foot. She liked independence, and never shied from hard work, aspiring to blaze a well-earned path in life.

Then again, that was before an incredible path just showed up.

"I really appreciate you, Amir," she said. *There.* That felt better. "Anyway, I won't keep you long. You said I can make phone calls on this thing?"

"Absolutely—pending the number is listed on file and the contact has been vetted."

"Of course." She recalled how pathetic her three measly contact numbers had looked on a multi-page spreadsheet: Gram, Aunt Patty, and Tess from book club. It had been one of those abrupt, self-shattering moments people avoid acknowledging. *I'm just an introvert*, she'd said to herself. Which sounded a helluva lot better than, *I have no friends*.

"Can I call Gram?" she asked.

"Of course," Amir replied. "I'll put you through right now."

She grabbed a slice of brie cheese. "Great, thanks."

As ringing sounded from the other end, she stared at the deal-sealing view, thinking of ways to adequately describe it. The ocean was an electric aquamarine that seemed almost contrived in the dazzling daylight—the type of color that only existed in nail-polish bottles.

"*Beatie here. Can't take your call right now. Leave a message and we'll chat soon.*"

Beep.

"Hi Gram. It's me, Aloe. Just wanted to let you know I've made it safely to Blue Haven. So far, it's *absolutely* incredible. Can't wait to tell you all about it. I'll call again soon. Hugs and kisses."

She tapped the device—assuming that's how a person ended a call—and entered the walk-in closet, where a wardrobe of new, designer clothes awaited. Her eyes landed on a pink string bikini with sparse material. She lifted off her T-shirt and pulled down her leggings, then slipped the bathing suit over her small frame.

Her reflection in the mirror was striking and took her by surprise, almost viscerally, though she wasn't sure why. The bikini was skimpy but tasteful: a skin-exposing lack of material she'd typically shy away from. It took a solid minute for her to realize the crippling sense of self-awareness that followed her like a shadow was—miraculously—missing.

She smoothed her hands down her tiny waist; she'd always been thin, God-given and almost boyishly thin, save a perky set of breasts that showed up in sixth grade, unwelcomed. They'd been hidden ever since. Maybe *she'd* been hidden ever since.

As she met her own reflection, the strangest sense of division arrived. A wavering of sorts, flimsy and static-like. Her hands began to tingle.

Something is wrong.

Panic came like a burst of lightning.

Then *zap!* The moment was over before she could even dwell, and she felt completely fine.

She lifted her brutally pale arm toward the light, hoping the sun would take mercy for once. She had her mother's Irish bloodline to thank—not that she remembered much about the woman. According to Gram, they looked alike: the same strawberry-blonde hair and small, bright blue eyes. Based on photographs, Aloe disagreed; their resemblance was weak, distant relatives, at best.

She forced her gaze back to the windows, to the ocean, where there wasn't room for the contortion of anger and sadness her mother evoked. At this point, the heartache had become generalized, untethered to a single instance. Instead, a hollow sense of desertion veiled over her childhood like a net. Such were the ripples of abandonment: not one memory, but all of them, in a way.

She closed her eyes, trying to let go.

Besides, her mother was long dead.

Chapter Five

Aloe rose up from the warm water with slick, dripping hair. A gust of air—the same temperature as the ocean, or close to it—charged across her skin. She stared down at her fuchsia-painted toenails, noting the chip on her pinky toe. The water clarity was incredible.

She assumed a starfish position and buoyed for a while, the hot sun beaming off her face. Elation lifted in her chest. This sort of carefree life was unfamiliar, and almost uncomfortable. She wasn't used to having everything taken care of, no groceries to get, or laundry to do, or late-night shifts at the diner. Absentmindedness used to beckon worry—*When is rent due again? How do I fix a radiator? What the hell am I supposed to do with my life?* Now though, her mind drifted away, with nothing pressing to stop it.

After a while, she stood and waded to the shore. Amir was waiting with a plush white towel and a glass of cucumber water. *God*, he was good.

"Here you are, Aloe."

She thanked him and dried off, then took a swig of ice-cold freshness. "*Ahh*," she moaned. "Hits the spot."

"How was the water temperature?"

"Spectacular."

He smiled, squinting into the sun. "Perfect! So the thermoregulators are performing well. If it's a smidge too cold or warm, please let me know, and we'll adjust accordingly."

"You'd change the whole ocean just for me?"

"Of course!" He beamed. "You're worth it."

Her heart swelled at the thought, and she couldn't help but look away. *You're worth it.* When was the last time she felt worth much of anything? She stared at her feet, trying not to tear up, then her skin tightened with control. *No crying in paradise!*

Amir rested a soft hand on her forearm. "Have a lovely rest of the morning. I'm just a tap away."

"Thanks," she replied, smiling as he left.

She took a moment to compose herself, letting the words sink in. *You're worth it.*

Her shoulders straightened and chest extended. *I am worth it, aren't I?* Maybe she didn't believe it fully, but a small part resonated. She stared at the sweep of white-stucco condos spiraling the monstrous glass Hexagon with a belly full of gratitude. This was her present—her future, and what a sight it was. Urban advancement meets exotic utopia. An odd mix, but somehow it worked.

She strolled up the beachfront, heading home (*home*—as if this place was home!), when suddenly a man emerged from the condo next door: Number Four. He was young, approximately her age, with dark skin and a physique that held her eye: ridged muscles, tended and grooved, veins bursting. She'd always been attracted to the nerdier sort, but there was no denying this man was incredibly attractive. He propped his hands on his hips and turned his face toward the sun.

She found herself suddenly hurrying toward him. Never had she been so happy to see another person—let alone a stranger. When she was only steps away, he gave a lopsided grin. "Hello." His voice was quiet and tender for such a burly guy, an unexpected peek of shyness coming through.

"Hi," she replied, trying not to stare at his immaculate abs.

He offered his hand and she gave it a shake; he was tall, six foot five, at least. "Welcome to the neighborhood. I'm Westley—Westley Young."

"Aloe Malone," she replied. "I can't tell you how nice it is to meet another human being. I was beginning to think I was the only *actual* person here besides my concierge, Amir."

Westley laughed, feather light. "Yeah, there aren't many of us."

A moment passed and Aloe clicked her fingernails together, trying not to overanalyze the situation. Typically, a lull in conversation sent her brain spiraling. She was too perceptive for her own good, dissecting the smallest eye veer or flat-mouthed sigh as a sign of disinterest—rejection. Her mind tended to create unfavorable narratives.

But that was before.

Blue Haven was a fresh start, an opportunity to become a different person. Someone with confidence. Someone with friends. Someone who was less skeptical and … alone.

She drew in a breath. Her nerves were going haywire, but she wasn't going to let them stop her—not this time.

"Hey," she said, trying to sound casual. "I know you just stepped outside, but would you like to come over for a drink? I'm right here," she pointed, "in Number Five."

Westley gave a shy nod, and she wondered whether he was employing a similar personal philosophy: stepping outside of his own comfort zone. She didn't know this man, of course, but they seemed cut from the same cloth: two people unsure how to be people.

Westley motioned ahead. "Lead the way."

Her lungs exhaled. "Great."

She took a few steps and he followed. The thrum of nerves in her chest was subsiding—slowly, but thankfully.

Maybe, becoming an entirely different person was far less complicated than her brain made it out to be.

Maybe, it was as simple as one foot after the other.

Chapter Six

They entered Aloe's condo through the front, still open and exposed to the shoreline. Feet away, the eternity of ocean frothed against the pale white sand. A faint breeze lingered.

It was *literally* the perfect day.

She motioned Westley toward the couch. "Please, sit."

He did, and she proceeded to the kitchen with an antsy swirl in her gut. Playing hostess wasn't a role that came naturally. In her old apartment, she never had people over or entertained guests. The place was downright embarrassing, first off. And who would she even invite?

A cool blast of fridge air perked her chest—a stark reminder she was only wearing a string bikini. Normally, this sort of realization would have prompted a quick cover-up, but she forced away the thought. *This is paradise. Time to stop caring so much.* If Westley Young wanted to ogle, what was the worst that could happen?

She turned back to Westley. "I'd offer you a beer, but ... you know."

He smirked, followed by an eye roll, "Oh, I know."

Alcohol was prohibited in Blue Haven—a near deal breaker for Aloe, personally. She loved to guzzle a few wine coolers after work. But it all made sense in context, and she'd ultimately come to accept her sober fate. Blue Haven wasn't a resort, and it wasn't a party; it was a place to live in contentment and abundance. Here, a person was supposed to enjoy life in its purest, most unadulterated form—or something like that. Being drunk was a false sense of elation, *apparently.*

"Sparkling lemonade?" she suggested, and Westley nodded.

She grabbed two cans and returned to the couch. They popped their tabs at exactly the same time, making a synced phush—which drew a chuckle from Westley. She'd decided long ago not to judge a book by its cover, but was surprised by Westley's gentle sense of reservation, like he was entirely oblivious to his extraordinary good looks. That sort of humbleness was hard to find in a man.

"So, Aloe Malone," he said. "That's a nice-sounding name. Very flowy."

"Thanks," she replied. "Westley Young: not a terrible combination of letters and sounds, I'll admit."

"Actually, Westley Young isn't my given name; it's my dad's name. He died in a car accident over a decade ago, and my mom, who had early-onset Alzheimer's, constantly mistook me for him. I made the change official before I came here. In honor of my pops."

Aloe frowned, touched by the gesture. She lifted her drink into the air. "To your pops."

Westley joined and their cans clunked. After a moment passed, he offered a small grin. "Thanks for that."

"You're welcome." She took a sip of tart lemonade, preparing a topic change, something less heart wrenching.

"So, what did you do before this?" she asked.

"I played football."

"Oh," she replied, expecting model or actor. "Very cool."

When he didn't elaborate, she decided to pry. "Like, professionally?"

He nodded.

"What position?"

"Running back."

"Which team?"

"*Umm*," he looked uncomfortable. "The Dallas Cowboys."

Her body tensed with shock. "The Dallas Cowboys? No way. That's incredible."

"It was—until my knee injury." His smoky black eyes winced. "Talk about ending your career in less than two seconds."

"Jeez, what happened?"

"Honestly? I barely remember. A bad side tackle, I'm told. Happened during practice and knocked me unconscious. Sent my tibia straight into my fibula. Hasn't healed properly since."

26

She glanced at his leg, trying not to stare. It looked normal, but on second thought, she'd noticed his gait was a bit off on the walk over. A subtle jerk to his step.

"That's awful," she replied. "I'm so sorry that happened to you."

He shrugged. "I've come to terms with it. Besides, I always dealt with performance anxiety on the field. My body liked the sport, but my head ... not so much." He broke eye contact to glance at the ocean. "This is my happy place."

"Ditto," she replied. The hush of waves echoing throughout her condo was surely the adult version of a lullaby.

"So, what's your story?" he asked.

"Well," she paused, deciding how much of her story was appropriate to disclose. "If you're wondering where the money's from, I won the lottery."

"Wow, lucky gal."

Lucky indeed. And yet, she sometimes wondered: if a small girl was abandoned by her drug-addicted mother, then shuffled through foster homes all her life, abused and forgotten, was it *luck*, or universal retribution?

"Someone's gotta win," she said, deciding not to horrify Westley with her past. "Before coming here, I lived in Chicago, Lower West side. When I wasn't working as a waitress for my aunt's shabby diner, I wasted plenty of time contemplating my purpose in life—and proceeded by doing nothing about it, obviously."

She smiled to signify her sarcasm, even if it saddened her a little. She'd spent so much time thinking about what she wanted to be when she grew up, she missed the part where she ... *grew up.*

"Ahh." Westley waved his hand. "Doing's overrated." He lifted his lemonade and smiled. "To doing less."

She reached across the couch, nudging her can into his. "To doing less."

Westley struggled to rearrange his legs on the chaise—the right leg, specifically, though it was clear he was trying not to draw attention. Aloe pretended to fuss with a cushion, seemingly preoccupied.

She took a few more sips of fizzy lemonade, averting her attention and giving him space. She liked Westley. He was easy to like: sweet and soft-spoken and humble. A gentle giant. He seemed like the type of person she could easily befriend—even as a recovering introvert with a few suitcases of emotional baggage, and a wrought-iron fence around her heart.

"*Crap*," Westley said, glancing at his device. "I'm late. Bob and Franny invited me over for brunch." His eyebrows arched in an inviting way. "Do you want to join?"

Nerves sparked in her chest, suddenly on high alert. *Bob and Franny? Who are they? A couple? You hate couples—double the conversing. Why don't you just stay here and—*

She rose above her chattering brain. "You know what?" she said, pausing to set her lemonade on the side table. "I'd love to."

Chapter Seven

Franny and Bob Jennings lived in Number Three, beside Westley. All too suddenly, Aloe found herself standing at their doorstep, which looked exactly like her doorstep, save a few billowing tropical plants flanking the entrance. Westley rapped on the door and she took in the medicinal, almost minty scent coming from the bright evergreens, trying to maintain calm.

"Come in!" a voice called from inside. Westley led the way, confidently enough to suggest he was comfortable with these people.

Aloe's flip-flops snapped against the hardwood—*thwap, thwap, thwap*—much like her heartbeat. The interior was a striking resemblance to her own place, with only a few subtle differences: the couch was gray instead of white, the quartz countertops a shade lighter. Otherwise, the two condos were identical.

The sameness put her at ease. *Mi casa es su casa.* Literally.

A woman approached in a crisp white pantsuit, like Amir's. Her loose blonde curls and clear blue eyes reminded Aloe of someone she couldn't place—someone with similar blue eyes: fierce and crystal.

"Hi, I'm Tiffany," the woman said. "Bob and Franny's concierge. Can I grab you something to drink?"

"Sure," Aloe replied, the weird sense of familiarity fading.

"What would you like? Something hot? Something cold?"

Caffeine. The word struck like a bolt of lightning. "Coffee would be great."

Tiffany beamed. "Coming right up!"

As she headed to the kitchen, an older couple emerged from the bedroom—Bob and Franny, presumably—in matching tropical button-ups. Both shirts were fluorescent yellow and covered in miniature palm trees.

Franny stepped forward and did a small spin, showing off her outfit. "*I know, I know*. We're adorable." She pulled Westley into a hug and kissed him on each cheek. Afterwards, she turned toward Aloe with a massive grin.

"Hello dear, I'm Franny."

Before Aloe could respond, Franny ambushed her into a tight squeeze. Being voraciously opposed to hugs, she tried not to flinch, which wasn't that hard; the embrace was surprisingly comfortable. Franny had a thin-boned fragility and palpable warmth, like a grandmother—not *her* grandmother (Grams was more a chain-smoking, swearing-at-the-bingo-hall sort), but a stereotypical one.

"I'm Aloe," she replied. "Nice to meet you."

Franny pulled back and sighed—a full, happy sigh. She had large sunken eyes the color of taffy and tight gray curls. "Welcome darling. We're really glad you're here."

We're really glad you're here.

The sentiment caught Aloe off guard, and her cheeks took on a fireside warmth. Surely, this was the first time anyone was glad she was anywhere.

And then Bob swooped in, with his filmy green eyes and brilliant bald head. The buttons on his shirt were undone just enough to expose a forest of curly white chest hair. He half-hugged Westley, more of a headlock, then took Aloe's hand and gave it a single, solid shake. "Bob Jennings. Pleasure to meet you."

"The pleasure's all mine," Aloe replied, cringing at the trite response. But it was the truth. "Thanks for the warm welcome. I really appreciate it. Honestly."

Bob and Franny gravitated toward each other, smiling. Their teeth were uncommonly white (veneers or something), and Aloe had a feeling that Mr. and Mrs. Jennings had traveled the world before coming here. They both had the tight, leather skin of professional vacationers.

"Coffee's ready, Aloe," Tiffany called from the kitchen. "How do you like it?"

"Here," Aloe replied, heading over. "Let me, I don't mind." As much as she appreciated the service, it still felt odd to be waited on. Normally, that was *her* job.

Over at the counter, she scooped in a spoonful of sugar, followed by a drizzle of cream. She circled her spoon around and around, watching the light and dark come together, timidly at first, before melting into one solid color.

"So," Bob said. "Shall we brunch?"

"Aren't we waiting for Bibs?" Westley questioned.

Bob waved his hand. "*Nah*, you know Bibs. He's always late."

"Who's Bibs?" Aloe asked from the kitchen.

Franny smirked. "*Oh*, Julian Bilbo. You'll know him when you see him—or should I say hear him."

Aloe shrugged, not sure what that meant. Still, her stomach whirred at the thought of another new face. *Three people. Less than an hour.* She was practically a socialite. For better or worse, she was putting herself out there: attempting to make legitimate connections with other human beings. It was an odd sort of liberation from her previous life. Terrifying really—though she refused to show it.

She straightened her shoulders and lifted her coffee when suddenly a billowing sound exploded, loud as a fog horn, causing her to jolt. Coffee sloshed from her mug, burning her lip and landing on the hardwood. She searched frantically for the source, heartbeat skyrocketing.

When she found it, her jaw dropped.

Chapter Eight

A booming, operatic voice shattered the silence: "*FA-LA-LA-LA-LA!*" followed by a large man skidding through the doorway, cradling a pineapple.

"Sorry I'm late, kids. I was busy." He laughed explosively. "That's a lie. But I am sorry. I bear offerings of tropical fruit by way of remorse."

He tossed the pineapple at Bob, who caught it reflexively, while Tiffany skirted over and sopped up the coffee Aloe had spilt on the floor with a paper towel.

"Thank you," Aloe whispered, dumbstruck by the man in front of her. He'd entered the room like a cannonball, loud and boisterous and bright, and her heart was still recovering. He was wearing a tight, fluorescent pink tank top and everything about him was round: full belly, plump cheeks, wide bulbous nose, droopy earlobes. He had slick, theatrical sideburns, like an early Elvis Presley (though the rest of him was more of a later-years Elvis).

Bibs made eye contact almost instantly. "You're new," he blurted, and then he rushed over and pulled Aloe's hand to his lips. The kiss he left was surprisingly dainty, like the flap of a butterfly wing. "Julian Bilbo, retired opera singer, ex-Broadway performer, and your chummy new best friend. People call me Bibs. You'll find me in Number Two."

"I'm Aloe Malone," she replied, still baffled.

Julian Bilbo—or Bibs, apparently, seemed to have the sort of personality that directly opposed her own. Still, his eyes were gentle: espresso and fanned by dark, dense eyelashes, like a calf.

Westley leaned closer. "Charisma for days," he said.

32

"*Charisma,*" Bob said jokingly. "If that's what you want to call it."

Julian trotted over and slapped Bob on the shoulder. The pair appeared to have a joking relationship, the sort that involved a lot of teasing.

As the group came together, making small chat, Aloe tried to find a safe space in her head. Being the new girl brought with it an all too familiar sense of shrinking. Like there wasn't room for her, as she was. Normally, in these sorts of situations, she'd conjure up an excuse to leave. *Hold that thought—I have to pop back for a sec,* and then never return. But against her inner urges she stayed put: smiling and nodding and listening.

After a few moments, the urgency to leave dissolved, and an unexplainable calm swept through her like clean, lovely vapor. Where this came from, she wasn't sure.

Change, she decided. *Change the circumstance, and you change the person.* This seemed contrary to what she knew about personal change—inner work, wasn't it?—but how many people had experienced such a dramatic shift in scenery? This place, Blue Haven, made everything different—better.

She stared at the sapphire ocean, unfolding in every direction like a giant hug. Such a stark departure from the view in her old living room: industrial gray concrete, splashed with smog. She imagined what she might be doing otherwise, if not for Blue Haven: probably just waking up—chilled, groggy, a headache forming, her back stiff. After a sloppy stretch or two, she'd stumble to the fridge—temples throbbing, skin prickled with goosebumps—only to find it nearly empty: a few wine coolers; a leftover pastrami on rye, cold and stale. The day would pass, slow with boredom and loneliness, and then suddenly it would be four in the afternoon, her sliver of freedom gone and wasted. Back to the diner she'd go for another tenuous night shift, serving people cheap hamburgers and flat beer and fake smiles—for next-to-nothing wages and tips.

These memories seemed faraway now, further than they should be. She was happy enough to forget the past, but couldn't dismiss the fuzzy quality of her thoughts, like an underdeveloped photograph.

Strange.

Or maybe not.

Either way, as brunch arrived, all was forgotten.

Chapter Nine

"Think I'll sit beside the new girl," Bibs said, thumping down beside Aloe.

She took in his spicy cologne. The dark, deep notes of his scent reminded her of motor oil, in a good way, and she sipped her coffee as Tiffany placed a silvery tray filled with fresh fruit and pastries at the center of the table.

The choices were overwhelming: Danishes with jam-filled centers, thick slabs of pineapple, puffy donuts coated in icing sugar, dragon fruit and papaya wedges on kabobs.

She hovered her hand like a spaceship before dropping down to grab a croissant.

As the pastry hit her tongue, the flaky crust melting in her mouth, she gasped. "Jesus H. Christ. This is insanely delicious." In twenty-five years, she'd never tasted a croissant quite so delicate.

Bibs loaded his plate with a handful of cannolis and some purple grapes. "Indeed, the food here is *damn* tasty. They make sfogliatelle that puts my nonna to shame—bless her soul." He brought his hand to his forehead, and then across his chest in remembrance.

Westley, to Aloe's left, took a slice of carved papaya with frilly edges. "Yeah, if you like food, you're in the right place. Rumor has it, Gordon Ramsay will be cooking at Allure tonight—that's one of the restaurants here."

A *pah* of disbelief fell from her lips. "Gordon Ramsay? Like, *the* Gordon Ramsay?"

Westley nodded. "Yep, *the* Gordon Ramsay."

Tiffany set down glasses of freshly squeezed orange juice while Aloe choked in disbelief. She loved the Food Network, and watched Gordon Ramsay plenty on television, but never imagined actually tasting his food in real life.

Bob stood abruptly and raised his drink. "I'd like to propose a toast," he said. "To our new friend, Aloe. Welcome home."

The group stood and glasses clinked. Aloe's bottom lip began to tremble—in a good way. If only she could freezeframe this moment, print it out and hold it in her hands. *A personal toast.* She'd never been celebrated before, and had no idea how to react, besides bursting into happy tears.

"How long have y'all been here?" she asked, fighting the urge to cry.

"*Hmm*," Westley replied. "Well, I've been here for a few months. Bibs is the founding father of our crew. You've been here what, a year?"

Bibs shrugged. "About that. Who's counting?"

"We've been here for almost six months," Franny replied. Her smile drew long, wavy creases that encircled her features like a fine pencil. "The best retirement a couple could hope for."

Bob leaned over and kissed her on the cheek. "Forty-five years in the making. Me and this lovely lady met when we were twenty. Worked together for forty. Sold the family business for two tickets to paradise and haven't looked back since."

"What was the family business?" Aloe asked.

"Oh, nothing much," Bob replied, waving her away.

Franny smirked. "Don't be modest, dear. Bob is a famous inventor. He's sold patents for devices all over the world, haven't you darling?"

Bob blushed and Franny leaned onto his shoulder. Aloe held in an *aww*. Gosh, they were adorable. Her stomach leapt at the idea of finding love like that one day—not that she was in any rush. She needed time to focus on herself, to become someone worthy of being loved like Franny. If you build it, they will come—as the saying went.

Tiffany arrived then, distributing plates of eggs benedict from a large tray.

Aloe leaned into the heavenly aroma before sinking her knife into the egg's center. She marveled as the yolk seeped out, drenching her plate in a deep, buttery yellow.

"Something special, isn't it," Bibs said, pointing to the smear of liquid-gold across her plate. "That's the good life, right there."

It was a simple but accurate conception of the good life: a perfectly poached egg.

"Actually," Bibs said. "You know what this moment is begging for—on all-fours, with a look of desperation in its eye?"

Westley spoke through a grin. "Oh boy. *Here we go.*"

Before anyone could respond, Bibs stood and broke out *O Sole Mio*, probably the only opera song Aloe knew off hand. His voice filled the room with depth and soul and wall-shaking vigor. The man had a serious range, and Aloe found herself momentarily transported to another dimension, where there was only sound—and a three-hundred-pound Italian man.

When he was finished, they all clapped.

"That was incredible," Aloe said.

Bob's face cinched together in fake seriousness. "*Whoa, whoa, whoa.* I thought you were taking a break from the spotlight."

Bibs took a long, dramatic bow, and then he sat. "The great Julian Bilbo will never concede. I'll be here all night."

All at once, and to her absolute astonishment, Aloe acknowledged she was completely and utterly at ease in the company of human beings she barely knew. She drank in the strange and lovely nothingness of it. *Is this what life feels like for everyone else?*

Is this what life is supposed to feel like?

"Okay," Westley said, pushing his empty, yolk-smeared plate toward the center of the table. "Nap time."

"Agreed," Bob said, taking a stretch.

Franny stood and pushed in her chair. The table was a flurry of scattered pastries and sloppy egg bits. Forks lay jagged and haphazard. Glasses half drunk. Tiffany swept in to collect the mess.

The mood suddenly flopped, full and drowsy. Aloe liked this communal napping agreement, like they were a class of kindergarteners. Her muscles softened just thinking about it, and she could already see the routine unfolding: lengthy sleep ins, a bout of hot sun, late brunches, afternoon siestas.

"It's been a slice," Bibs said, heading for the door. "See everyone around six?"

"Six?" Aloe asked.

"We usually do dinner as a group," Westley replied. "You in?"

"Are you kidding me?" She laughed. "There's no way in hell I'm missing out on Gordon Ramsay."

§

On the walk back, she began flipping through her mental wardrobe for something fitting—*that little black number with the cinched waist?*—until suddenly she was standing at her doorstep, waving goodbye to Westley as he ducked inside his condo. Only then did she realize a sound vibrating against her lips: O Sole Mio.

I'm humming!

She had to laugh, never pegging herself as the humming sort. Then again, maybe she was. After one glorious morning in Blue Haven, she'd become a hummer.

Back inside, she pressed the button that separated the interior from oceanfront, summoning a large pane of glass from thin air. She pressed her face against the partition, watching the water. It was still now: flat and radiant as an ice rink beneath the glowering sun. She imagined walking across it, wondering where she might end up. *Somewhere in Europe? Indonesia? Australia?* And then she turned, weighted with exhaustion and quickly losing interest. She had no idea where she was. But what did that matter?

Paradise was paradise.

Chapter Ten

*B*eep.
Aloe leaned closer to her device. "Hi Tess, it's me. Been a while. Just wanted to see how you were doing." She unscrewed a tube of mascara and swept the black wand over her blonde eyelashes. "You'll never guess where I am right now." She paused. *Wait, I don't even know where I am right now.* "Anyway, my new place is incredible. I can't wait to fill you in. Hope you're well. Chat soon!"

She took a step back, admiring how much larger her eyes looked with noticeable eyelashes. Her skin was still buttermilk pale—probably the first time she'd escaped a wicked sunburn in twenty-five years, all thanks to some incredible ray-blocking technology that intercepted harmful UV. "All of the sun. None of the burn," as Amir had put it. No need for sticky, greasy sunscreen that smelled like hot plastic. Not in Blue Haven.

Frankly, she couldn't believe it worked. After a typical day at the beach, her cheeks would be flushed and forehead crimson.

She tousled a cloud of mousse through her thick, strawberry-blonde hair, encouraging her curls to behave, then she slipped into a flowy, black, ankle-length dress, enjoying the light brush of material against her skin (cotton-chiffon: dressy, but not too dressy). She glanced in the oversized mirror, hardly recognizing herself without a pair of sweats and saggy hoodie, or her hair in a literal top-*knot*.

She'd never admit it out loud, but more days than not, she longed to disappear. Not that she'd do anything dramatic about it; she was stuck here, bottom line. But the idea came to her like a vacation: the urge to find a quiet place, unbothered and invisible; to fit inside a great and wondrous pause.

Tonight though, she actually wanted to be seen. For the moment at least, her self-esteem dumpster fire had smoldered to embers.

She was cautiously approaching the word *beautiful*—trying it on for size.

After one last glance in the mirror, she was off to meet Westley. Her stomach gurgled with excitement. This was—quite frankly—the most exciting night of her life. Dinner with new friends in the world's tallest structure. Gordon freakin' Ramsay. *Actual* paradise.

Westley was waiting outside in a baby-blue dress shirt, a lovely compliment to his dark skin. He'd undone just enough buttons to reveal a raised, muscular collarbone. He smiled when he saw her.

A few steps later, her heels sunk into the sand, so she slipped off her shoes and hung them from her pinky. The grains were cool, refreshing—just like night air: a touch enchanting.

She waved. "Hi."

"Hey," Westley replied. "You look gorgeous."

"Thanks," she replied, certain she was blushing. "Not too shabby yourself."

"You ready for your first dinner out in Blue Haven or what?"

"Absolutely, I haven't been out in ages." Unless, of course, one counted sitting at the diner solo, scarfing down a post-shift burger on a stale bun. Hardly *dinner out*.

A few steps later, they arrived at Bob and Franny's. The window partition was up, exposing the interior. Bob was leaning over the coffee table, peeling a boiled prawn.

"Aloe!" he said, plunging the shrimp into a bowl of cocktail sauce. Another button-down shirt was draped loosely around his body, solid green this time, but still the same turf of curly chest hair, rising up.

"You like seafood?" he asked.

"I do. Very much so." Even if it were a recent love story. Her old server's salary didn't jive well with ocean-fresh produce—or anything fresh, really.

He pointed to the spread. "Then have at 'er."

She grabbed an oyster, trying not to look like a starved cat, then added a squeeze of lemon before tossing it back. The briny, salty goodness slipped down her throat.

"Damn, that's fresh."

Westley tipped a shell and slurped, licking his lips afterwards. "*Mmm hmm.* Here, try the crab." He passed over a massive, pre-shucked claw—the circumference of her wrist.

She gripped it like a club. "Holy shit. This is basically a weapon."

Westley laughed as she soaked the meat in butter, then took an overzealous bite. "That's the meatiest crab I've ever tasted," she said, blown away by the sweet, unctuous flavor.

Westley nodded. "I know right? The crabs around here are basically on steroids."

Franny breezed in from the back bedroom wearing a cute maroon dress with matching lipstick. Her gray curls were pulled back into a slick bun.

"*Oooh*, look!" She pointed. "Here it comes."

Aloe followed her finger to the ocean, where the horizon was awakening. The descending sunlight left a wisp of lilac and tangerine that flowed up through the sky like drapes on a clothesline. A dark, brilliant teal crept through the gaps, surrounded by cotton-candy clouds, thin as steam. Skeletal palms curved in the foreground, nearly blackened by shadow.

"Now *that's* a sunset!" The voice was unmistakably Bibs, wandering up from the beachfront. His thin black hair was practically varnished to his scalp, and he was wearing a tight tuxedo T-shirt that was entirely unforgiving but in the spirit of irony was a true success.

He gave Aloe a quick hug and pecked her on the cheek, the same to Franny.

"*Bellissimo*," he said, and then he leaned in Bob's direction. "That means beautiful, for the less cultured among us."

Bob gave him a chummy thwack on the shoulder. "Coming from the guy wearing a tuxedo T-shirt."

Aloe tossed back another oyster, turning toward the sunset. The brightness was quickly receding, leaving leftover folds of illumination across the sky. It was hands-down the most extraordinary sunset she'd witnessed firsthand—naturally. This was Blue Haven. She was coming to expect as much.

"Is it always this beautiful?" she asked Westley.

"Always." He stretched out his arms, taking in the night. "But never the same kind of beautiful." A breeze stirred, warm on the cusp of cool.

"And do we typically go out for dinner together?"

We. She hoped she wasn't being too presumptuous, already including herself in the group.

"Most nights, yes," Westley replied.

"Doesn't everyone get tired of eating at the same spots?"

He laughed, still staring at the sky. "Bibs has lived here for almost a year, and he's never been a repeat customer. *That's* how many restaurants there are. So no, we don't get tired of eating at the same spots, because we've never had to."

Aloe leaned forward, just enough to glimpse the Hexagon. Soft light filtered through the tinted windows, glowing faintly as darkness invaded. She was struck with awe, but also a sudden wave of doubt that flipped her stomach.

The tallest building in the world.

A secret location.

Wasn't the Hexagon a giant landmark, screaming *"Come find me!"* into the abyss?

Someone's arm slung around her shoulder; the other landed around Westley. She turned to find Bibs, wedged between them like a hamburger patty.

"Hey kids, what do you say we go savor the esteemed culinary renderings of a foul-mouthed English bloke?"

Westley grinned. "I say *hell yes*. What do you say, Aloe?"

She glanced up at the illuminated tower, wishing the skeptical part of her brain would just die already. This was so *like* her, to ruin a perfectly nice moment with a splash of paranoia. One step forward, two steps back.

"I'm ready," she said, refusing to let her anxiety take over. "Let's do this."

Chapter Eleven

The group merged onto the cobblestone path, veering toward the Hexagon. Night had nearly settled; only a faint trace of light lingered along the horizon, like a dying bonfire.

Aloe loved the ambiance, cast somewhere between Shakespeare's *A Midsummer Night's Dream* and an episode of *Survivor*. Poetic, yet primal. Tiki torches burned high in the sky, casting thick plumes of smoke; the path itself shone with periwinkle orbs and dangling Edison bulbs, everything tangled in greenery.

She walked beside Franny, passing condo after condo, hardly visible at dusk. *So many empty buildings.* Maybe it was the lack of visibility, or the sudden rush of shadows, but she couldn't deny a feeling of unease passing through her, twisting like a vine. Based on everything she'd seen so far, Blue Haven was extraordinary; yet one after the other they came, the sad and silent condos, inexplicably unoccupied.

Don't people want to live here?

She drew a breath, knowing there was a logical explanation for all of this: the high price tag, staggering residential entry, some intended aura of absence "by design," or whatever Amir always said. Regardless, these excuses were incapable of stifling the obvious fact that left her tense and slightly on edge: *This place is a fucking ghost town.*

"Hey," she said to Franny, struck with realization. "If I live in Number Five, and Westley lives in Number Four, and you and Bob live in Number Three, and Bibs lives in Number Two, who lives in Number One?"

Franny shrugged. "No one. It's empty."

Empty? That got her heart thumping. Why would Number One be vacant if the others were occupied? She wiped her moist palms along her outer thighs, cinching the material like a hand towel.

"That's strange, isn't it?" she asked.

"Strange?" Franny replied, her small face crinkling together. "I never thought so. I just assumed Number One was the model condo. That's usually how it goes, isn't it?"

"*Oh,*" Aloe replied. "Right, of course."

An arm looped around her waist, and Franny pulled her close, just for a second. "Don't be nervous, darling. The first time I met a celebrity chef, I was practically vibrating. But you'll get used to them—they're a regular perk around here."

"Thanks," Aloe replied, glad Franny attributed her silly worrying to something less ridiculous. She took a deep breath, getting her nerves in check. Those trigger-happy nerves may have gotten the better of her previously, but that was then. She refused to let them take the lead—not with paradise at stake.

Westley stopped, a few paces ahead. They'd reached the Hexagon in all its glory. The grand, brass-clad doors opened automatically, revealing Amir.

"Guests!" he said. "Please, right this way."

The monstrous lobby stretched before them, now transformed. Prisms of rainbow-colored brightness cast up the walls like Northern lights, coming together in the center of the room, where an ice sculpture of a thirty-foot dolphin (at least) was frozen into a bow. Static, icy waves splashed at its fins.

"Wow," Aloe said, admiring the impressive detail. "I've never seen anything like that before."

Bibs stepped forward and tossed her a wink, then he casted his arm toward the ceiling.

The peppy background music was immediately overpowered by his lovely and roaring voice, and Aloe found herself leaning forward, drawn to the sound. There was a juxtaposed quality to it: heavy yet light, tragic yet joyful. It made her want to laugh and cry, simultaneously.

When he was finished, she found herself applauding with vigor.

Bibs took a bow, "Thanks folks. The acoustics in here are too good to ignore."

"True talent," Amir said to Bibs, and then he ushered them along. "This way, please."

They loaded into a shiny metallic elevator and traveled seventy-two stories up. The ride was quick, and just as Aloe's stomach began to twist with movement, the doors opened and a gust of awe lifted through her chest.

She understood instantly why the building was all windows. In every direction, stars splashed across the sky, the sort of galaxy view one might acquire through a high-powered telescope. Dots of light twinkled in every direction, layer after layer, millions and millions of specks. She crept forward, her legs unconvinced they'd meet solid ground; being up there was like standing in outer space.

"Holy shit," she said, barely realizing the words had come.

"Yeah," Bibs replied. "It's something alright."

While the others found a table, she drew closer to the outskirts, staring with disbelief. The moon was so clear she could see the texture of its surface, craters etched like stamps. Rays of angelic light reflected on the water below, where foamy ocean kisses met the shore, hardly visible from such a height. She wasn't sure how to digest the feeling that overcame her, like the heavens were opening up and offering an ungraspable universal secret—connecting her to something greater.

She returned to the others enlightened, and sat between Bibs and Westley, sinking into a chair. The cloud-like pillow absorbed her weight, unwinding her muscles in a single sigh. Only then did she take in the restaurant itself. The tables were slick and chrome—minimalist, but the cool metal was offset by glimpses of warm wood: floor, table legs, an accent wall made from walnut slabs.

"Look up," Westley whispered, and so she did. The sight was entirely unexpected: a ceiling of dangling orb lights, each a different shade of blue.

She smiled at Westley. "This place is absolutely spectacular."

Bibs leaned over and spoke from the side of his mouth. "A spectacular life, for a spectacular price."

A waiter arrived then with a tray of silver plates, "An *amuse bouche*," he said. "Courtesy of Chef Ramsay."

The bite-sized morsel of food seemed far too beautiful to eat: a small swipe of red and yellow, a stack of wafer-thin layers, dots of gelatinous white, microgreens and edible flowers placed strategically.

Across the table, Franny took a bite and moaned. "What in God's name did I just ingest? It's perfection."

The waiter grinned. "That ma'am, was a goat-cheese wafer stack, beet and spice puree, squash velouté, jelled sweet cream, and local flowers and greens."

Local. Aloe found herself evaluating the microgreens, like they might give off some sort of geographical clue—which they didn't, and then she popped the flaky stack into her mouth. Franny was right: it was sensational.

"So," Bibs said, raising his glass of sparkling water. "Shall we toast?"

"We shall," Bob replied.

They clinked glasses and Aloe was overcome with delight, like a snow globe just shaken. Her tense, overactive nerves had finally settled, thank God. But then Bob gave her a keen eye.

"Alright my dear," he said. "It's your turn in the spotlight."

Spotlight? Her calves flinched beneath the table.

"We want to know more about you, Aloe Malone. Why don't you tell us about yourself?"

Her stomach dropped. As far as personal questions went, this one in particular was her worst nightmare.

Chapter Twelve

Aloe found herself gazing up; the glowing orbs hanging from the ceiling seemed suddenly hotter, like the varied blue lights were shining focally on her, even if that was impossible. Nothing made her disconnect quite like, "Tell me about yourself." She often related to those touch-sensitive plants—the ones that coiled with contact, like the closer people came, the more she shriveled inside.

Life was safer that way: inside instead of outside.

Silence stretched through the restaurant, bordering awkward, until finally she looked at Bob, waiting for the heat to rise up her chest, and her heartbeat to quicken—the usual sensations that came with being the center of attention. But the visceral movement was less; and she wondered why that was, realizing suddenly these people were her *friends*—crazy as it was, since she'd known them less than a day. And yet, it was the truth. There was something special about Westley, Bibs, Bob, and Franny—or something special about this place, Blue Haven. Perhaps both. Either way, she found herself replying, "What do you want to know?"

"Personally," Bibs cut in. "I've been dying to discover since the moment I met you: What's your favorite color?"

Aloe laughed. "I don't have a favorite color. I'm more of a black and white kind of gal."

"Interesting," Franny replied. It came out slowly, evaluatively.

"Franny likes to read people's colors," Bob said, rolling his eyes. "It's a bunch of mumbo jumbo."

Franny shot him a playful glare. "Please, the colors people are drawn to can say a lot about them. There's plenty of psychology behind it." She fixed her gaze on Aloe. "Do you want to hear what your colors have to say about you?"

Aloe shrugged. She normally wasn't a fan of these activities: horoscopes and palm-readings and magazine personality quizzes. The *I know you, without even knowing you* claims, but in the spirit of new friendship ... "Sure," she replied. "Why not?"

Franny tilted her head to one side and paused, like she was channeling invisible spirits or divine answers. "So, you like white, which suggests you are confident and courageous at times. You seek others, wisdom, and prefer openness."

Aloe took a sip of her sparkling water, trying to stave off an eye roll. Confident and courageous? Seek others? *That* was wishful thinking.

"However," Franny continued. "You like black more, which means you savor independence. You're bold, drawn to power, strong-willed—but also sensitive. These two parts of you express themselves in tandem, often fighting for control." She paused, leaning closer. "Most days, you feel like two different people, uncertain who to be."

Aloe struggled to swallow, the fizz suddenly irritating her throat. She hemmed and hawed, pretending the description was only moderately accurate, when in truth, it caused goosebumps to flutter up her arms—the last part, specifically. She often felt like two people, one trapped inside the other. A yin and yang without balance.

She looked at Bibs, who huffed. "*Franny, Franny, Franny,*" he said. "I've told you before and I'll tell you again. That color nonsense is a load of bull testicles. A whole truck load. It's nothing more than the *Barnum Effect*—there's a psychology word for you."

"What's the Barnum Effect?" Aloe asked.

Westley answered. "Most people believe personality descriptions apply specifically to themselves, when actually, they contain information that's relevant to everyone. I related to most of what Franny just said, and my favorite color is yellow."

Franny smiled quietly. "To each their own." She draped a napkin across her lap. "I just think it's fun."

Aloe agreed, letting the uneasiness pitter away. It was actually comforting to know that a generic personality statement could be so relatable. She'd spent her whole life on an island, keeping an ocean of emotional distance with others, believing no one could possibly understand her. But maybe that wasn't true. Maybe people were more alike than she realized, and being a castaway wasn't the answer.

The server returned then with another round of elegant plates. The scent made her stomach lurch: a rich, herbaceous note.

"The next course," he began, standing tall. "Is a miniature beef Wellington. As I'm sure you know, Chef Ramsay is acclaimed for his Wellington. Today, we're featuring a morel-and-truffle duxelle, and a four-day jus."

Aloe sliced through the perfectly cooked steak and took a bite. It was immediately clear why Chef Ramsay's Wellington was world renowned.

"*What* a celebration," Bibs said.

They ate quietly for a few minutes, until Bob pushed his plate aside. "Alright," he said. "Back to Aloe. I promise I won't berate you all night. A two-minute synopsis will suffice."

She set down her fork, surprisingly less annoyed than she expected to be. *Might as well get this over with.*

"So," she said, "I was born and raised in Chicago. Not a particularly sunny upbringing. My mom liked heroin … a lot—more than she liked me, and I was shuffled around foster homes for my entire childhood. I don't have much in the way of family, just one generally irresponsible—though loving-in-her-own-way, I suppose—grandmother, and an aunt. Most recently, I was renting in the Lower West Side, working as a waitress—until I won the lottery. Now I'm here with all of you, and to be honest, I've never been happier."

She smiled, praying for a topic change, but the eyes she met all dripped with understanding. Bibs reached across the table, laying out his thick, fuzzy arm. "We get it. None of us have much in the way of family or friends. And maybe it's fate. Maybe what we lacked out there," he lifted his hand and circled it around the room. "We're destined to find in here, with each other."

Aloe batted her eyes; the tears were instant, and she looked away, blinking fast until they dissolved. She wasn't used to being around people who understood the sort of loneliness and isolation that characterized her life in every imaginable way. Usually in the company of others, she was fighting off despair, listening to beloved stories about friends and relatives. It was one of the main reasons she hated working at the diner. Overhearing other people's enriched, well-supported lives gave her a true sense of how anomalous she was. Most people had other people.

She took in a breath, filled with the unfamiliar warmth and security of feeling truly safe. "I'm really glad I'm here," she managed, still trying not to cry.

A white bowl landed before her—a perfectly timed distraction—and she admired yet another artistic endeavor: colorful baby vegetables, a striking orange broth, flaky fish with a browned sear, a single pipe of foam.

"Alright, we'll turn off the Aloe spotlight for now," Bob said. "Thanks for sharing your story." He lifted a fork, then added, "*Oh,* and welcome to the family."

She dragged her spoon through the viscous broth. *Finally*, a place she truly belonged. And it felt exactly like she hoped it would: like coming home. Not to a foster home, or a youth housing facility, or Aunt Patty's basement, or the world's shittiest apartment.

Home.

She let the warm beams of joy cast through her. And then it came—of course it did: the paranoid skeptic, starved for content and grasping at straws. No matter what, the infidel always seemed to be there, churning in the background like a well-oiled machine, adamant on ruining a nice moment.

The five of them had each other, but no one else.

That was oddly coincidental, wasn't it?

Chapter Thirteen

Day Two

"How am I doing?" the masseuse asked, rousing Aloe from a near catatonic state.

She drifted back, pleasantly attuned to the scent of lemongrass. "Great," she replied. "Never better." Her spine felt like putty—in the best possible way. Drowsiness returned and her thoughts detoured, landing on a few snippets from last night's dinner.

A decadent lava cake with oozing chocolate syrup.

A warm and unfamiliar sense of belonging.

Meeting Chef Ramsay afterwards! He'd only waved from the kitchen, but she could hardly contain her starstruck excitement.

Long strides of pressure rose up her back and an "*Ahh*," seeped out, muffled by the pillow. She'd spent the entire morning at the spa, breathing in deep gusts of eucalyptus and soaking in various places: a swirling hot tub, a cold-plunge pool, a tub full of rose petals. Her body was so relaxed she hardly acknowledged it was there, attached to her.

The masseuse buried his thumbs deep into her shoulder blades, releasing tension like an open gasket. She moaned.

This is the freaking life.

How she'd experienced any form of anxiety in this place seemed unimaginable. The moments of paranoia from yesterday, choppy like a staccato note, had all but vanished from her memory, swept away and returned to a world she was no longer a part of. It would take time, she imagined, to acclimate to this stress-free lifestyle, where razor-sharp thinking and emotional guards were unnecessary.

Afterwards—the appointment done, her body unmolded and oh so relaxed—she waltzed down the cobblestone path, heading home in a white silk robe. Her footsteps were light, airy, untroubled.

Westley approached, traveling in the opposite direction. She gave him a big wave.

"Good morning," he said, glancing at the sun. "Or should I say afternoon."

She looked up; the sky was densely blue and cheery with clouds. "Yeah, I suppose it's no longer morning, is it?"

He laughed. "I just had lunch, so no."

Lunch. Right—she'd forgotten to eat. "What do people typically do around here for lunch?"

"Whatever we want," he replied. "I just had Rebecca, my concierge, make me a few grilled cheese sandwiches. You should have seen the look on her face when I asked for a plain grilled cheese. She literally replied, *Are you sure you don't want caviar on it, or something?*" He laughed to himself. "Who eats caviar on a grilled cheese?"

Aloe pressed her lips together.

"No," he responded. "You wouldn't dare."

"I'm not saying I'd like it, but if someone offered me caviar on my grilled cheese, I'd probably take them up on it."

Westley puckered his face in playful disgust. "I'll forgive you, but I don't want to." He seemed to evaluate her for a few seconds, a grin widening.

"What?" she asked. "What is it?"

He gave her a quick wave, still grinning. "Honestly, it's nothing. Not even worth your time."

"It must be something," she replied, persisting until finally he gave in.

"Okay fine, you just seem different today, in a good way. Yesterday when we met, you were … I don't know, I can't totally put my finger on it—more apprehensive, I guess? This is going to sound ridiculously cheesy, but today you're practically … *in bloom*. Those are the best words I can find, if that makes sense."

"In bloom? Like a flower?"

"Sure, or a workable mass of wrought iron—that's also called a bloom."

She laughed. "I'll take the flower." Her face lifted toward the sun, the dewy aftermath of steamed eucalyptus still fresh on her skin. "I've spent so many years dreaming of a life like this, and now it's here, and I'm living it. I suppose I'm just … in awe."

She met Westley's soft eyes. A friendly, comfortable silence unfolded, then he gently touched her arm. "I have an appointment now. See you tonight?

She nodded. "You bet."

They'd planned dinner for six at Chaleur, a fusion restaurant with an enticing culinary cross-breeding: French technique meets creole spices.

She gave Westley a quick goodbye wave, then returned to her condo, still refreshed, but ready for a nap. Funny, how doing nothing in particular could be so tiresome. She undid her robe and let it slip to the floor, enjoying the cool charge of air across her skin.

The place was spotless—not how she left it, that's for sure. Someone must have cleaned in her absence. She entered the master bedroom, pleased to see a freshly made bed: comforter fluffed, quilt folded neatly at the end, throw pillows karate chopped like a staged home waiting to be sold. She peeled back the corner, ready to slip beneath the covers, when a notebook caught her eye. It wasn't hers—she knew that immediately. A sticky note had been placed on the front cover, with a scribble:

Found under bed.

She opened the pale gray book, perplexed, noting a handwritten name.

Eloise.

Her heart skipped a curious beat.

Who's Eloise? I don't know anyone named Eloise. She skimmed the pages—each one chock-full of cursive writing, right up until the last line—and then she set down the notebook (more of a journal, apparently) on the nightstand and crawled into bed.

She closed her eyes, ready for a sweet afternoon siesta—or not quite, apparently. The presence of this unexpected discovery roused her steady state of calm, and the creeping exhaustion taking hold suddenly vanished, replaced by a ticking curiosity. Seconds later, she found herself upright, staring at the gloomy gray cover, wondering for a second time.

Who the hell is Eloise?

Chapter Fourteen

Normally, Aloe Malone wasn't the type of person to go rifling through another's belongings, especially not something as personal as a journal. To each their own, was her personal philosophy, and she enforced this sentiment voraciously, with pay-it-forward logic.

If I leave you alone.

Maybe you'll leave me alone.

But this—a journal found on her nightstand, left by a stranger—was different, was it not? Found in *her* condo—her ... *home.* And given she was (at least, as far as she'd been informed) the only person to live in condo Number Five, the presence of foreign material authored by a woman she didn't know seemed especially suspicious—worthy of investigating, at the very least.

She sat fully and brought the journal to her lap, itching with temptation. There was nothing remarkable about it. And yet, the small, heavy book brought forth an unexplainable apprehension, like Pandora's Box. A voice inside warned prophetically: *What's open cannot be shut.* And wasn't that the truth? How many times had she ventured past ignorance, only to meet regret? Still, she traced her fingers along the blunt edges, mulling.

I shouldn't.

This was not her property, not her business. The paranoid skeptic living in her brain hardly needed new material. Why invite a series of unnecessary questions into her quiet, settled space?

Then again ...

She flung open the cover before she could think better of it. Her eyes landed on the first paragraph, reading compulsively.

I can't say I know what the fuck I'm doing here. Not here physically (well, that too I guess) but here conceptually, scratching down words in a notebook like this ridiculous activity might actually produce some-thing. Just words, that's all these are. And words can't accomplish shit— not really. They can't alter the course of history or change the past. They can't rid me of my demons or render me healed. I suppose this exercise is simply a desperate attempt to make sense of the chaos inside of me. In which case, buckle up.

Aloe's stomach clenched. Butterflies slammed against her ribcage as her eyes traveled further down the page, with more apprehension this time.

I call it chaos because that's what it is. There's a tornado raging in my chest, swirling my emotions together. Sometimes that feels like everything: like the sky and earth have collided; like the ground is unsta-ble; like doom is waiting, steps away. Other times, I feel nothing. People talk about demons like they exist in separate spaces: snarly, tentacled creatures or see-through ghosts. Satan, hiding in the shadows. Well, that's total bullshit—nothing more than stories created by normal peo-ple with nothing better to think about. Because if you want to talk about fear—real fucking fear—then there's no need to be so dramatic. True terror comes from inside.

True terror, is feeling emotions you can't control.

The page ended and Aloe paused: a natural crossroad. *Should I keep going?* A momentum rose in her chest, urging her forward. Clearly, she'd glimpsed the tip of an iceberg, its mass beneath the surface incalculable. At the same time, her hands were shaking and cheeks bloomed with heat, a sense of dread taking hold—after *one* page. Not a good sign.

She took a deep breath, knowing there was no turning back now. She turned the page with a wobbly finger.

Today was a nothing day. Zip. Zilch. Nada. It's hard to properly ex-plain what that feels like to a normal, neurochemically stable person, to properly describe a blunt, invokable world. Pure brutality, in short. To-day, I might as well have been a slug. I haven't left my bed, even though it's 4 p.m., and I have little intention to. What's the goddamn point?

The last time I showered was eight days ago. Eight. I can smell my own filth. But here's the sad, pathetic, disgusting truth: I don't care. Such is the nature of a nothing day. I'm a pile of human rot, emitting an ozone of body odor, and I don't give a shit. When it comes to feelings, my reservoir is bone dry.

Aloe snapped the journal shut.

Okay, enough.

She stared up through the skylights, at the hot sun and puffy clouds. These entries were not what she expected—not that she knew what to expect from a woman who technically shouldn't exist. Blue Haven was a rare opportunity—perhaps the rarest—to ignore the unfiltered suffering of others. To keep the outside world exactly as it were: outside. So why had she chosen to peer into a stranger's sorrow and devastation uninvited? Eloise didn't matter—shouldn't matter. And yet she did. Aloe was drawn to the woman, even if that made no sense. They'd obviously never met, and what loomed in her chest was far more than morbid curiosity.

The words left a film of disturbance over her thoughts, and she longed to clear her head. A nap would help, just an hour or so to recharge. She slipped the journal beneath her pillow and tried to forget.

But even in those early moments something told her, without a doubt, that Eloise's journal would change everything.

Nothing good would come of it.

Chapter Fifteen

The restaurant that night, Chaleur, brought forth the same level of awe and grandeur as the night before.

Except this time, Aloe was particularly grateful for the distraction.

Overall, the afternoon came and went, warm and lazy. She'd finally settled for a nap, brief but necessary, followed by a swim in the perfectly tempered ocean. Afterwards, she'd sunbathed on the porch, snacked on fresh mussels, took in the sweet scent of magnolias and the warm ocean breeze.

For the most part, she was fine, content—but not fully. The journal had undoubtedly ruffled her feathers. A subtle but sour note, like milk starting to turn.

There was a feeling in her bones, her soul, despite the loveliness all around her.

Something wasn't right.

All of this was momentarily forgotten, though, the second she stepped off the elevator.

The view once again filled her with mystery and delight, lifting her troubles away like a gust of wind might a plastic bag. The stars were endless, livening the charcoal sky with patterns she recognized: The Big Dipper, Scorpius, Lyra. Streaks of plum appeared in tight, Milky Way spirals, bordered by navy tufts, light and drifty like stretched cotton.

She gasped at the moon: large, luminous, surrounded by fuzzy fuchsia effervescence, like a halo of smudged chalk. The beauty was almost indescribable, and she had a sudden and childish urge to leap into the sky, fly among the stars, and discover the universe.

"I could stare at this forever," she said.

"Well," Bibs replied. "Depending on which side of the religious pendulum you fall, one day you just might."

Aloe wasn't religious, but had to agree. If heaven *did* exist, they were probably pretty close.

They sat at a table next to the windows. Once settled, Westley offered a toast.

"To another night in paradise!"

Glasses clinked, and Aloe took a sip of fizzy soda water. The restaurant itself was rich with texture: plush red chairs with ornate, ivory details; rich mahogany drapes separating spaces; candles everywhere, softening the mood.

Small talk flowed—a collection of daily activities. Aloe nodded here and there, but found herself drawn to the waves far below: the lulling motion, cycling in and out; water lapping at the sand before drawing back into itself.

Pushing. Pulling. Giving. Taking.

It wasn't until a hand grazed her shoulder that she faced the table.

"Aloe?" It was Bob, but everyone else was staring too. "Bibs has offered to take care of that for you, if you'd rather stare off into space."

She turned and noticed a poached prawn: pink and plump, hanging from a shot glass of creamy sauce and fresh herbs.

Bibs gave her a goofy but serious look. He wasn't joking. She had to laugh.

"Sorry, I don't mean to be distant, just a weird day. And no," she said to Bibs, lifting the shrimp from its perch. "This is all mine."

He pretended to pout as she separated the meat and the tail with her teeth. The flavor was tender and sweet with a hint of spice. The bright, creamy sauce was a perfect accompaniment. "I can see why you were trying to steal this from me."

She licked her lips and tried to harness her wandering mind. "I went to the spa earlier," she shared. "It was incredible."

After a few eager nods, she breezed through the rest of her day—omitting the part about Eloise's journal. "Actually," she said, realizing her friends probably had some insight. "We're the first people to live in these condos, right? As far as you know?"

"You bet," Bob replied. "These places are brand spanking new. And I know fresh plaster when I smell fresh plaster. Why do you ask?"

She took a sip of sparkling water to quench her pasty mouth. "Just wondering."

If I'm the first person to live in Number Five, how the hell did another woman named Eloise leave her journal there?

Half of Aloe's brain entertained this question while the other half listened to Westley talk about crossword puzzles—his recent obsession.

"I don't think I could do a single crossword without using Google," Bibs replied. "There's just no way."

"Nonsense." Westley tossed up his hand. "You're more capable than you think. That's the beauty of living in a place like this, you're forced to use your head."

More courses came, one after the other, and Aloe found herself slipping to the sidelines. She tried to focus on the smaller details happening around her, like how Bibs flushed when he talked about theater. Or how adorable Franny and Bob were, with their intermittent hand-holding and spotty kisses. Westley's rousing smile and quiet eyes.

The food was incredible, an engaging mix of spice and refinement, the flavors explosive on her tongue. She was generally enjoying the night. And yet, it was still there: a thrum of concern. How could she not dwell? That was the problem. During a lull in conversation, a passage or two from earlier would leak into the foreground and she would pause, listen.

There's a tornado raging in my chest.

A blunt, invokable world.

My reservoir is bone dry.

Every time her mind traveled in a happier direction, there was Eloise, bringing her back with magnetic force. It took real, persistent effort not to ruminate. There were so many questions to probe and dissect, peak inside of and pull apart. But now was not the time—clearly.

She gave her head a shake. Normally, she was good—skilled even—at keeping certain thoughts away from other thoughts. Her childhood, for example. Those awful memories came and went, and her ability to sweep them away like grains of dust was important—if not paramount—to moving forward. A form of resiliency, really. This journal would be no different. She would cast it far away, and get on with the night: enjoy the good food and good company. The end.

By the time dessert arrived, a shiny mango éclair, Eloise was only a small, distant speck. A secret locked in a closet. Aloe would have been proud of herself, had one lingering thought not stuck around: a stubborn question that wouldn't die, despite her efforts.

Is this woman trying to tell me something?

Chapter Sixteen

After dinner, Aloe followed the others into the lobby, now a disco-inspired club. Neon lights zipped across the walls and a rumbling bass pulsed up through her silver pumps, massaging her heels. She was drawn to the music, surprisingly full of energy.

Her feet began to pivot, shoulders bopping to the rhythm. Normally, she needed a few ounces of booze (at least) before gallivanting on some dance floor, but the mood was right—and her inhibitions around Franny, Bob, Westley and Bibs didn't seem to require a thorough drowning of alcohol anyway.

Bibs was the first to officially hit the dance floor, moonwalking like Michael Jackson. She and Westley followed, swaying and thrashing like feral creatures vexed by a full moon. Something strange had come over her: an intoxication of sorts, and she laughed at the obscenity of their actions: silly, unnatural, entirely out of control.

A few songs in, she stopped to admire Bob and Franny, dancing like a pair of fresh twenty-somethings. Franny had mounted Bob's leg and was riding full-throttle, like her knees weren't on the brink of replacement. The friction and swagger of their movements made Aloe wonder why people grew up, adjusting their personalities to fit the tight, structured expectations associated with different age groups.

I'm never growing up, she decided, wishing to stay in this moment forever, lost in a hot swirl of action.

Song after song, they danced. Time passed without awareness. Her legs moved unrecognizably, a new person taking over: some fun, gregarious, unburdened woman she liked, but didn't really know.

She'd never felt so alive, and it wasn't until later, after she returned to her condo a sopping mess, drenched with sweat, that the obscurity of it all began to settle. To think, she, Aloe Malone, had just spent hours dancing with four strangers-turned-friends in the world's most exclusive condo community. Her life had changed so swiftly she was still gobsmacked by moments of disbelief.

She looked in the mirror and had to laugh. A swamp creature stared in return: flushed cheeks, matted curls, mascara smudges like a chimney sweep. Her dress—formerly lilac and floppy—was slick to her body and eggplant with sweat. The thumping bass still rang in her ears; her limbs still tingled with movement.

She glanced at the shower, debating.

The last time I showered was eight days ago.

The words from Eloise's journal rose up unexpectedly, chasing away a moment of bliss. She'd nearly forgotten about that cursed thing, and its existence reemerged like an illness.

She slipped off her dress and entered the large walk-in, tiled on every surface, up to the ceiling. Hot, almost scalding, water came forth and she breathed in the steam. She tried to reason away the twist in her gut. Yes, she'd found a journal. And *sure*, its origins were suspicious. *But so what?* Eloise was a stranger. A total, utter stranger. None of this was technically her problem. Maybe if she told herself these sorts of statements long enough, she'd simply believe them.

She turned off the shower and stepped onto the cushy bathmat. The cool air livened her skin before exhaustion plummeted; such was the Scandinavian secret to relaxation: hot then cold then hot—she'd learned that earlier at the spa.

She tucked herself into bed, too lazy to put on pajamas. Every part of her was thoroughly tuckered: lids drowsy, shoulders concaved, calves achy from dancing. She exhaled, pressing her back into the soft mattress, beyond ready for sleep.

Minutes passed and she waited, expecting a swift knockout. But the opposite began: a slow and nervous awakening. The reserves of energy she thought were long depleted recharged, and before she knew it she was sitting upright, feeling generally on edge but wide awake.

She reached under the pillow, a compulsion returning.

No, don't do this.

Her fingernails scratched the weathered binding.

This is a bad idea. This is a really bad idea.

Despite her own advice, she'd already taken the journal in her hand—was staring at its gray cover, letting the weight of it settle in her lap, knowing she couldn't resist. She propped herself against a pillow and cracked it open, the scent of musk and despair seeping up from busy pages. Her eyes scurried over the loopy cursive.

The numbing persists. It's two in the morning, and I'm still awake.

Aloe glanced at her device and shivered. Two in the morning. What a haunting coincidence.

I should be passed out cold. That would make physiological sense, wouldn't it? Since I haven't slept in two days. But here I am, awake and tortured by my own thoughts. My legs are starting to cramp, but I can't get out of bed—a lack of motivation so profound it feels like a physical disability. Crippled by my own goddamn sadness.

She looked up from the page, aware of the night. Normally, she loved a charcoal-black sky, a bold moon and sharp breeze. But tonight, she was suddenly afraid of the dark, like a little kid.

My husband visited earlier—there's something to report. A blip in today's steady, emotional flatline. The look on his face was shattering, in every possible way. He was gutted by the sight of me. I repeat: gutted. He tried to hide his disgust—bless his soul, he tried—but it was obvious. I haven't seen myself in days, but my appearance must be terribly off-putting if my partner of fifteen years—the man who watched me push a baby from my body—is shocked by the sight of me. "Honey," he said, in such a sad, miserable way, his dense blue eyes hazy with tears. And that was it, just "Honey." I probably would have cried—if I could have. They say it's better to feel something than nothing at all. I'm still undecided.

A sound rattled and Aloe jolted. Her eyes found a branch rapping against the window. Just a branch. Still, her heartbeat thrummed: terror, yes—but beneath that, a tiny fizzle of excitement. The human compulsion for morbidity, rising up.

She turned the page, almost eager.

What next?

Chapter Seventeen
Day Three

*B*eep.

"Hi Gram," Aloe said. "Me again. Just wanted to say hi and to see how you're doing. You must be busy these days, but we'll touch base soon." She tapped her device, ending the call, then took a sip of coffee. The bitterness made her shutter. She'd asked Amir for the strongest roast available, and he'd certainly delivered.

Her temples ached with exhaustion and she massaged them with her thumbs.

She grabbed a blueberry scone and tried Aunt Patty. The answering machine beeped as she licked a zigzag of cream-cheese frosting.

"Patricia here. You know what to do."

Classic Aunt Patty—a woman of few words.

Aloe left a message and perched over the island, nibbling. She craved a familiar voice; some connection to the outside world, if only just to ground her. As much as she liked Blue Haven, there was an uncomfortable disengagement that came with living in a place like this, almost like floating in space. A quick check-in would be good for her sanity—a chance to verify the real world still existed, wherever it was.

A thought came and she tapped on her device, summoning Amir.

"Good morning, Aloe," he said for the third time in a row. "What can I do for you?"

"Hi Amir. Sorry to keep bugging you, but I have a question. Is there a significant time change between here and North America?"

"I'm sorry, you know I can't tell you that."

She sighed. It was a long shot.

"I know, I know. I just can't seem to get in touch with any of my contacts."

"My apologies. I'm sure you'll hear from them shortly."

She stared out the wall of windows: another perfect day.

"Wait," she said, realizing she had a mysterious device, not a cell phone. "How do they get in touch with *me*?"

"Apologies Aloe, I should have explained. Every message is followed by a standard, automated contact number. Calls are directed back to your device after simple screening—again, for your safety and ours."

She nodded. *Makes sense. No room for leaky channels.*

"Okay, thanks Amir."

She disconnected and drank the rest of her coffee, trying to blink away the puffy swell of skin resting atop her eyelids.

Eloise's journal had kept her awake until three in the morning, and afterwards she'd slept poorly and fitfully, her mind invaded by the woman's unsettling words.

It didn't help that Eloise had disclosed enough personal details to evoke a clear image of her character. She was white, thin, pale, forty-five, and had graying hair that remained anonymous thanks to frequent blonde highlights. She also wore a pair of large-rimmed glasses that slipped down her nose on occasion. That was the extent of her literal clues, but Aloe's imagination had filled in the gaps. She could picture Eloise with effortless clarity: her thin-bridged nose and jagged, arched eyebrows; harsh cheekbones and skeletal fingers. Her movements were slow and stale—save her gaze, driven by fast, sporadic eyes, full of paranoia.

"Enough," Aloe said out loud, shaking Eloise from her thoughts.

She changed into a bathing suit and ventured outside, soon plopping onto a lounger. The weather was beautiful, per usual. Hot but not humid, the air bright with saltwater.

She closed her eyes and let the sunshine fill her pores. The warmth felt good on her skin. After only a few seconds, the events of last night—page after page, heart fluttering silence, eyes dry from lack of blinking—seemed to fade beneath the heat. Vitamin D therapy.

The lull of waves came and went, *in and out and in and out*. Time passed—she wasn't keeping track; like a lizard on a hot stone, just existing.

After a while, she sat and took in the beachfront: white, unimaginable sand; clouds drifting through the bottom half of the sky, like an incomplete portrait; the water unnaturally azure, bristled with silver sun.

The smell of hibiscus sweetened the air and she drew a deep breath, then another.

Two doors down, Bob and Franny stepped out.

"Off to brunch!" Franny hollered, sending a big wave.

Aloe waved back. "Pretending to tan!"

Franny laughed.

As they disappeared down the cobblestone path, she leaned back, at ease.

Her lids began to close, but then a snippet of movement caught her eye. There was a figure in the distance. A man, about fifty feet away.

The muscles in her torso jerked, and her eyes hyper focused. He was middle-aged, tall, standing completely still. Beige shorts. White cotton shirt. Face as stiff as a bulldog.

Most notably.

He was staring directly at her.

She quickly looked away, heart flinching. *That was weird.* After a few seconds of nervous hesitation, she glanced back. There he was, just staring, unmoved. She turned once more, shielding an awkward moment with her shoulder. Panic revved in her chest, and she considered calling Amir for assistance.

She raised her wrist, prepared.

Then again, *assistance with what?*

Blue Haven was a large, luxury condo development anticipating new residents, and the place was swarming with staff. The fact she'd never seen this man before meant nothing. He could be lucky Number Six—her direct neighbor, just arriving—or a new hire.

She looked at the condo next door—lights off, completely dark—and turned toward the ocean, keeping tabs on the man in her periphery without staring directly at him. She could sense his movement from the corner of her eye, coming closer. And closer. And closer.

Shit, shit, shit.

Just as she drew the device to her lips, fingers trembling, cool beads of sweat forming along her hairline, the man turned down the cobblestone path and disappeared.

Just like that. *Gone.*

Reassuring breaths filled her lungs. Her heartbeat steadied and spine flattened against the chair. For some reason, the moment seemed like a close call, and yet there was nothing close about it—not really.

Lately, her shaky nerves and racing mind were like disobedient children, throwing tantrums over nothing. A stranger's notebook. A man she didn't recognize. These were hardly reasons to get worked up!

She tapped on her device and Amir answered. "Good afternoon, Aloe. What can I do for you?"

"Just mulling over lunch options," she replied, trying to move on. "I'm feeling something decadent. Any ideas?"

"Oh, I have plenty of ideas. Do you like lobster?"

"I *love* lobster." She twirled a strand of hair around her finger, suddenly wishing she had a floppy, large-brimmed hat, the sort uppity women wore on vacation, though she didn't care so much about that. She just liked the idea of walking shade. "Also—since I have you—how does a person … shop around here?"

"Easy, just visit Le Boutique. It's in the Hexagon. The staff there will be happy to assist."

"Thanks," she replied, deciding that might be a nice afternoon activity, after lunch.

"So," Amir said. "How does this sound: lobster thermidor with shaved white truffle. And—" his voice went quiet, like he was sharing a secret. "I'll have Chef go heavy on the truffle. It's rare Summer White."

"You're the absolute best," she replied, her mouth practically watering. She'd never had white truffle before, only dreamed of it.

"Anything else, Aloe?"

She considered asking about the man, but refrained on account of sounding foolish. Besides, what was there to ask?

"Nope, that should do it," she replied. "Thanks Amir."

She disconnected and pulled her eyes shut.

Honestly Aloe. This is paradise, she scolded. *Let it be paradise.*

Chapter Eighteen

The lobby was vacant—per usual.

The *click click click* of Aloe's kitten heels echoed in the vast space as she grabbed a glass of cucumber water, admiring the lovely, natural light amply flowing through the windows. Memories from last night surfaced: a hot mess of movement and music. She pictured Bibs spinning his hands at a fake DJ table, his red-hot cheeks bookending a massive smile; Franny and Bob grinding in the background like horny teenagers; Westley circling like a vulture with solid stepwork.

She smiled to herself, then scanned the Directory in search of Le Boutique. The number of amenities in Blue Haven continued to shock and awe—everything a person could possibly need, housed in one sky-high tower. She moved her finger down the stone, the letters rough against her fingertips, until she found what she was looking for. *Le Boutique. Floor 88.*

She turned toward the elevator then whipped back around, eyes landing on the Residents section. Her name was still last on the list.

Aloe Malone, Number Five.

There wasn't a Number Six.

Her heart skipped a beat. *Oh, stop it!* The property next door was quiet as a crypt; she suspected as much. The man from earlier—whoever he was—was not her new neighbor.

She clicked to the elevator, shifting focus. *Hats, hats, hats.* She'd made up her mind when it came to design: big, bold, and floppy. Color choice was still undecided. Neutral or bright? Neutral was more her style—she preferred blending in over standing out—but maybe a splash of color wouldn't hurt, especially in the tropics.

She entered the elevator and pressed number eighty-eight. Up she soared, her stomach landing in her chest until the motion eased and the elevator doors pinged open.

Le Boutique awaited, and she gasped, instantly taken by rows of marble tables with gold embossment. Something gleamed in every direction: slick chrome, large mirrors, shimmering jewelry. She took a cautious step forward, feeling out of place. All her life, she'd shopped second-hand. Even as a kid, everything she owned or received was old and tattered, some smelly hand-me-down from an unknown source. Le Boutique was certainly a dramatic upgrade from Oli's Closet, the grubby consignment store around the block. How a person was supposed to carry themselves in a place like this was pure mystery.

She lifted her chin and widened her stride, wandering past monstrous diamonds in glass displays, purses and wallets positioned on ivory tables, mannequins dressed in high-end fashions, silk scarves hanging on 24-karat pegs. The space was lavish in every sense of the word, like a Nordstrom for the *filthy* rich.

She drifted further through the space, running her fingers over chiffon blouses and floor-length gowns. Everything was shiny and new and beautiful and foreign.

"Hi!" a voice chirped.

Aloe turned to discover a tall brunette with a model-esque build and gorgeous features: stormy eyes and long lashes, thick lips, cheekbones swept with dark bronze. She was wearing the same outfit as the rest of the staff members: a drafty white pantsuit, her face drenched with cheer. "I'm Rayla! Welcome to Le Boutique. Can I help you find anything?"

"Wow, you're beautiful," Aloe blurted, then quickly added, "Yes, actually. I'm looking for a hat, one of those wide-brimmed ones?"

Rayla sucked in her chiseled cheeks as her eyes moved up and down Aloe's figure. "Yes, I think you'd look perfect in Nina Ricci." She left for a moment and returned with a floppy blush-colored number.

"Here," she said, ushering Aloe toward an extravagant gold-rimmed mirror. The hat came down carefully, like a UFO, landing on her head with a slight tilt. Aloe couldn't help but admire her reflection. She'd never worn blush before, suspecting the color would wash out her pale, pinkish skin, but it surprisingly complimented her complexion and brought out the blue in her eyes.

"Do you love it?" Rayla asked. "Because I love it."

Aloe nodded. "I do love it, actually. I'm not normally a blush girl, but it's perfect."

"That's why I'm here." Rayla smiled. "Your personal stylist." She had a cute, lopsided smile—perhaps the only thing about her that wasn't perfect. "Now, how are you for handbags? Might I interest you in our Hermes collection?"

Hermes collection? Aloe had no idea what that meant, but a hermit crab came to mind. *Purses in some sort of shell?* "I could use a handbag," she replied. "I don't have one right now."

"Well then, let's hook you up! What sort of brands were you into before Blue Haven?"

Aloe paused, recalling her old purse: a brown, medium-sized bag, well-worn to the point of dissolving, with one fraying strap. She tried to picture the label, but nothing came to mind.

"*Umm,*" she began, and Rayla smiled sympathetically. She took Aloe's hand, tugging gently. "Doesn't matter. Come, come. You *have* to see this."

Moments later, they were standing in front of a glass display cabinet, and Rayla was lifting out a white textured handbag with notable care, as though it were an atomic bomb.

"This is my favorite of the new Hermes collection," she said. "It's an exclusive white Himalayan Birkin, made from the rare Niloticus crocodile."

She draped the strap over Aloe's shoulder, and the purse fell to her side, unassisted. Aloe froze, afraid she might somehow ruin it.

Rayla leaned in. "Want to know what it retails for?" Rayla whispered the price before Aloe could answer. She nearly choked. Had she heard that correctly?

"*Two-hundred grand?*" she repeated, imagining what that amount could have done for her before Blue Haven—for millions just like her. Or behold: a purse. "That's idiotically expensive," she said.

Rayla smiled. "Right? I agree. Lucky for you, it's free—one of the perks of living in Blue Haven. We want our residents to have the best of everything."

Aloe looked again at her reflection: a ridiculously privileged white girl in a floppy-brimmed brunch hat wearing a handbag that cost more than some people's house. She wasn't sure how she felt about that, or how she ought to feel.

"You'll take it, I assume?" Rayla asked.

"Sure, I mean—*yes*, I guess I'll take this gorgeous, insanely expensive handbag if you're giving it to me."

"Perfect, mind if I pass along a few more goodies?"

Aloe shrugged. *When in Rome ...*

A measuring tape suddenly coiled around her as Rayla focused on her body with laser-like intensity. She moved quickly and precisely, making little clicks with her tongue like some sort of fashion surgeon. After a whirlwind of movement, she retracted.

"I'll prepare some outfits. No need to try anything on—part of the convenience. If you're unhappy, I'm here every day to accept returns. Follow me, alright?"

"*Umm*, okay," Aloe replied. An unorthodox approach to shopping, but she couldn't dismiss it. Who actually *liked* trying on clothes?

Rayla stopped at a counter, then ducked into the back, "*Hold tight!*"

Aloe ran her hands over the crocodile bag, tracing the lumps with her fingertips. Her eyes roamed the space, finding mirror after mirror, each unique and ornate, fit for a palace—or Le Boutique, apparently. She moved toward the closest one, an oval bordered by flying gold cherubs.

She wasn't paying much attention to her reflection, focused instead on the cute and peculiar details—a series of nude babies with knobby, golden wings; thorny roses weaving throughout—when all at once, there he was, standing directly behind her.

The man from earlier.

Chapter Nineteen

A loe paused, taken at first by disbelief. The man was only feet away, standing firmly with his bulbous shoulder blades and salty blonde hair, something about his posture so familiar.

Only his profile was visible: a swell of nose and sharp cut of jaw, his attention averted elsewhere. Scalding blood surged through her, and she tried to control her quickening heartbeat—until suddenly he shifted focus and their eyes locked, quick as a gun draw. Her entire body shuddered, shaken by his icy blue stare, the tension between them enough to strangulate a person.

After a split second that seemed eternal, she turned away, heat rushing to her cheeks. Her lungs clotted with air and she summoned the courage to look again, if nothing more than to keep tabs on his whereabouts. Except he was gone; the space was empty.

She searched the mirror's reflection, too terrified to turn around and see him in person. *What if he's right behind me?*

Heavy warm breaths, seeping up her neck.

Those piercing blue eyes, fixating on her skull, waiting.

Just as she imagined his touch, the weight of his hand on her shoulder, he came into view: far left corner, casually eying a mannequin—evaluating, like a casual shopper might. But he wasn't a shopper, couldn't be, because he didn't live here. He wasn't Number Six.

She tried to glance around the man's feathery blonde hair, but he shifted further, straightening the mannequin's bowtie and smoothing its hem.

Wait, she paused, thoughts grinding to a halt. *Does he work here? At the Boutique?*

His hands moved swiftly and with skill, seemingly unaware of her bewilderment. Her rational brain began to peak through the chaos of adrenaline, piping up. *Seriously, this guy is probably just a harmless employee.* She noted his white linen shirt, loose and flowy. Not exactly like Amir's, but close. And the way his hands fiddled with the mannequin's jacket. Why else would he be toying with the merchandise?

Realistically, she had no *actual* reason to fear this man. And yet, the sight of him made her squirm. He rattled her in ways she couldn't explain, for reasons she couldn't articulate.

"Aloe?"

It was Rayla. She turned back to the counter.

"Here." A shimmery coral bag awaited. "I picked out a few outfits for you. Something casual, and then a nice dress for dinner. It's all Dolce."

"Thanks," she replied, distracted.

Rayla smiled. "Like I said, if there are any issues, just come back. I'm here every day."

"Great." Aloe nodded, still preoccupied with the man in her periphery—the normal guy who was probably a staff member. And there she was, blowing everything out of proportion. Maybe she should just talk to him already. A simple question or two on the way out.

Hi, I saw you on the beach earlier. Do you work here, at Le Boutique?

She imagined the man's response: a reassuring head nod, mouth curving into a smile, eyes less piercing and much friendlier. "Yeah, I do."

And that would be the end of it. Life would resume. Another day in paradise.

"Anything else?" Rayla asked.

"Nope." She snapped back to reality and turned away, ready to ride her plan like a gust of wind.

Except the man was gone.

She moved cautiously toward the elevator, eyes darting, tense and cat-like. Hopefully, she could catch him in the lobby. But when she arrived, seconds later, there was nothing to see. The space was vacant, as always.

It was an odd sense of disappointment, a craving for relief. She wanted—needed—to know that her racing heartbeat was nothing more than paranoia. Instead, it raced on, and she was left to quell her silly, irrational thinking with nothing but willpower. And maybe—in the safe, sunny light of day—that wasn't so difficult, but what about later? What sort of mental fate awaited her when the sun had set, and the journal was hard in her grasp, and the hair on the back of her neck stood tall with fear?

She turned on a whim and stepped back into the elevator. One quick rise, and she was back on the eighty-eighth floor. The sharp smell of retail wafted as she hustled through Le Boutique, searching for Rayla.

The plethora of mirrors was suddenly jolting. Her reflection moved in every direction: a startling series of false alarms. She weaved around mannequins and tables and glass displays, an urgency rising in her chest for reasons that seemed unwarranted but were real nonetheless.

Rayla was just here. Where did she go?

Her heartbeat intensified—hard, uncomfortable—as she neared the empty back counter. "Rayla?" she called out, struck with a dreadful gust of intuition, a voice from within she couldn't silence.

Rayla is in danger.

The man took her.

The certainty of these thoughts surprised her, gutful and knowing, like a hunch. "Rayla?" she called out again, louder. The walls wavered, closing in. *Where are they? Where did he take her?*

Just as she eyed the room behind the counter, ready to burst through the door—the image of them already unfolding: the unidentified man, caught in a devious act; and Rayla: limp, sprawled, wide eyed—Rayla turned the corner with a surprised smile.

"Hi again! Sorry, I was just stocking inventory. Is everything alright?"

Aloe gripped a display cabinet. Reality wavered as she stared at Rayla, perfectly alive and well, despite a flair of concern flashing across her dark blue eyes—for Aloe's wellbeing.

She'd seen this look before: a form of pity that bordered alarm, and it made her uncomfortable.

"I'm okay," she managed, realizing she was okay—everything was okay—despite the climate of her thoughts, clearly tainted with anxiety. For a moment, she focused on the grounding sensations of her body: the tingles in her fingertips, the weight of her feet against the floor, the gusts of air diffusing through her lungs.

A flush of calm arrived, tenting through her chest like an umbrella, and she almost laughed at the absurdity of it all—so much terror, *based on absolutely nothing*. A boogeyman, hiding in the closet. *What the hell is wrong with you lately?*

"Is there something I can do for you?" Rayla asked.

"Yes," she replied, standing straighter, more composed. "I was just wondering how many people work here, at Le Boutique."

Rayla lifted an eyebrow, probably curious why such a simple question had her running back breathless.

"It's just me," Rayla said.

"Just you?" she confirmed, fighting a full-body chill. "Are you sure?"

Rayla laughed. "Yeah, unless my coworker is invisible."

Chapter Twenty

"You sang at the *Sydney Opera House*?" Westley asked Bibs. "Isn't that the largest in the world?"

Bibs gave a bashful smile. "Yeah, it's a monster, for sure. Acoustics like no other. Actually, I digress, the Royal Opera House is quite nice. I sang there for the Queen just before I retired."

"That's wild," Westley replied, plunging a chip into a pot of cheesy artichoke dip.

Bob leaned across the table. "I had no idea you were such a big shot. Remind me to get your autograph."

"What can I say, old friend. My *helden* was in high demand."

"Helden?" Bob asked. "What the hell is that?"

"It's a German word. Refers to a powerful voice capable of singing very difficult roles. Like this."

Bibs stood and stretched his hand toward the sky. The sounds that came next were so loud and deeply resonant that Aloe's arm hair stood on end. The man could sing—incredibly—yet imagining Bibs dressed in some formal, frilly suit on a world-renowned stage made her chuckle. He was more of a tuxedo T-shirt kind of guy.

The performance drew a standing ovation. They were outside, just a few feet from Aloe's condo. Tonight's dinner was something different: the five of them dining beachfront. Instead of another fancy, Michelin-star restaurant in the Hexagon, they opted for casual pub food—the best damn pub food Aloe had ever tasted, mind you: crispy, salty chicken wings with sticky honey; oozing mozzarella sticks with tangy marinara sauce. And now: the creamiest, most decadent artichoke dip.

She grabbed a chip and scooped up a healthy serving of greasy goodness, more dip than chip.

"This is really nice," Franny said. "I like the change of pace."

Aloe agreed. The staff had created a lovely oceanfront ambiance. Thin white linens hung from a pergola, creating an indoor-outdoor feel, and they were surrounded by glowing tiki torches, soft and hot in the dark. There was a casual, vacationy vibe in the air—much more relaxed and low-key than the Hexagon.

She pressed her feet into the cool sand and stared at the ocean. The water was mostly still, save a few shy waves. She took in long gusts of damp air—this is exactly what she needed: a humble dinner with friends. All afternoon her nerves had been tight and primed, just waiting for a fresh coat of terror. And yet, nothing had happened. No steel-eyed mystery man, or suspicious events to send her thoughts racing in all directions. She'd avoided the journal entirely, opting instead for a quiet lounge in the sun. Still, her heart raced all the same, anticipating something she couldn't place, a foreboding sensation with no real origin.

She lifted her soda and took it to the water's edge, only feet away.

"Going for a dip?" Bob hollered.

She slipped her toe into the warm ocean. "I'm not exactly dressed for it," she called back.

"That didn't stop Franny back in seventy-three. Remember honey, when we went swimming in the Pacific after that Gala? You peeled off your dress faster than a—"

Franny thwacked him on the shoulder and everyone laughed.

Aloe let the water reach her ankles, wanting to go further but wary of her outfit choice: a linen pant suit from Rayla—which happened to be pure white and somewhat transparent. She imagined the moment instead. The wet sand unmolding with each footstep. A gentle current, nudging her thighs. The movement of her hands beneath the water, creating long strides of motion.

Above, the bright moon shone brilliantly, casting hazy streams of light across the water. She took in the stars, a gust of wonder rising in her chest. The beauty of it all was remarkable.

And then, out of nowhere, came a jolt.

Her spine tensed and she spun around, overcome by a fleeting sensation of being watched. Her eyes darted—left, right, up, down—searching for something she couldn't identify. There was nothing to see: her friends were chatting and laughing in the night; a backdrop of still condos; the Hexagon, casting soft, golden light into the dark like a giant lamp.

She wiped her clammy palms against the sheer white material as the heat drained from her face, leaving it cold. Her hands began to tingle. She gasped. Again. The air was suddenly sparse. A volcanic wave of dread rose through her chest, erupting uncontrolled.

Breathe.

Just breathe.

Come on, breathe.

But she couldn't. The air was thin and unsatisfying, like sipping through a straw. She clutched her chest. *Am I having a heart attack?*

It was Franny who caught her eye, and what she saw—what she must have seen—flattened her smile to a straight line.

"Aloe," she called. "Are you okay?"

"No," she said—or tried to say. All that came out was a *huff*, exasperated. The glass in her hand dropped, hitting the water with a splash.

Rapid breaths passed through her lungs, but there was no oxygen. None. The world began to spin and her vision disfigured, shifting into multiples like a fun-house mirror. As her knees weakened, threatening to give way, Westley arrived. The others were close behind, coming toward her as a choppy kaleidoscope of people. She tried to focus, but was losing all control.

"I think I'm going to pass out," she whispered.

Westley took hold of her arms and she started to move, weakly, each step an impossible feat. A hand supported her back—Bibs or Bob—and Franny spoke from somewhere; her calm, motherly voice floated through the air. "It's alright, darling. It's going to be okay."

The second she neared a chair, her body concaved, lungs heaving. This was the end—it had to be. She was going to die on a wooden Adirondack in paradise, a life barely lived. And of all the things to think about it, she thought of Eloise.

Just as the group discussed emergency services, their voices faint and loopy—*Quick, call somebody. She needs a doctor*—the world eased back into focus. Blood returned to her face, circling her body with warmth. Her breath softened, slowed, and the strangeness of what she'd experienced moved to the forefront.

After a few dazed seconds, she sat upright. "I'm okay," she said, stunned. "I'm suddenly starting to feel better."

"Oh, thank God," Franny replied, dotting her forehead with a dry napkin. "Here," she said, passing over a nacho. "Eat. Do you have any problems with blood sugar?"

Aloe shook her head and accepted the chip; it crunched between her teeth, dry and unpleasant. "No, I'm perfectly healthy," she replied. "As far as I know."

A hand gripped her shoulder; Westley crouched beside her. "Aloe," he said softly. "Have you ever had a panic attack?"

A panic attack? She took a moment to think. Nothing came to mind. Surely, she'd remember something like that, even if the episode felt vaguely familiar, now that it was over.

"No," she replied, then added, "I don't think anyway."

"I ask, because I used to get them often. Actually," Westley paused, like he wasn't sure whether he wanted to share what came next. "I had a panic attack on my first day in Blue Haven. I was very … overwhelmed. New experiences do that to me. Anyway, there are therapists and shrinks on staff in the Hexagon. They can help."

Aloe bobbed her head, unsure. Maybe she'd had a panic attack— it seemed to make sense, based on her symptoms and quick recovery—but triggered by what, a moonscape?

She'd endured a lot over the past twenty-five-years: a drug-addicted mother, long dead and entirely absent, but still a stain on her existence like an impurity she couldn't wash away; the sort of childhood that ruined people—*had* ruined her, for years, typified by overcrowded institutions and touchy "uncles," even well-meaning families whose love for their own children was so much greater, by proxy, that simply existing became its own form of torture. All of this to assume a life so small and quiet she was hardly alive at all: a flower stripped of its roots, left to wilt.

And yet, this flower was now in bloom. She'd survived. She'd overcome adversity. Not perfectly, of course, but she was *here*, on the precipice of something better—the best yet. So why would her healing brain suffer a mental breakdown in the middle of paradise, when everything in her life was finally going right?

"Thanks Westley," she replied. "I'll look into those services tomorrow. I'm really sorry for all this. We were having such a nice night."

"To hell with a nice night," Bibs said. "We're just glad you're okay."

"Yes, I'm okay," she replied. At least it seemed so.

Her hand reached loosely for another chip, but the weight of her own arm was tremendous. Exhaustion came like a forcefield. Recent events—panic induced or otherwise—had clearly taken a toll. She hung on for a few minutes longer before accepting defeat.

"I'm sorry everyone," she said. "I'm wiped. I think I need to call it a night."

"Of course," Bob replied. "Go, hit the sheets. Please let us know if you need anything."

The saggy, sympathetic stares she met in return were somewhat comforting. Even though she hated pity, it was nice to know she had friends who legitimately cared.

She struggled to move her chair against the unforgiving sand— Westley assisted. As she returned to the safety of her own condo, sleep had never been so appealing. She sunk into bed, craving reprieve— from everything: the fatigue feasting on her muscles; thoughts dashing through her mind like rogue arrows; the mysterious, steely eyed man who left her perturbed; the embarrassment of tonight, and the toll of vulnerability that came with it.

Moonlight oozed through the windows, gentle and soft. She closed her eyes, hoping the abyss would come quickly.

But it didn't. Astonishingly, it did not. After a while, her lids flashed open and she searched the ceiling for imperfections, like counting sheep. There were so many unsightly spots in her old apartment: rust-colored watermarks bleeding from the corners; unidentifiable smudges of black, like soot; general yellowing from decades of indoor smoking. Here, though, inside of her immaculate new home, there was nothing—not a speck of interest to divert her attention.

Minutes passed.

Seriously! Go to sleep! Her physical body ached for rest, but her mind refused to cooperate.

THE JOURNAL.

It arrived in her thoughts, big and bold as a headline, and she cringed. A terrible idea, of course—indisputably terrible. Still, her hand reached beneath the pillow, powerless, greeting a hard edge. Her stomach curdled with dread and curiosity.

Why am I doing this to myself?

She didn't know—couldn't know.

Her eyes landed on the page, and she prayed for answers.

Chapter Twenty-One
Day Four

"So, tell me why you're here?"

Aloe gripped the polyester chair, a striking shade of emerald. *Because I've almost finished reading the profoundly disturbing journal of a deeply depressed woman who shouldn't exist, and I'm possibly being stalked by a man who also shouldn't exist.*

"I had a panic attack," she said, and then she sucked on the inside of her cheek. "I think."

The woman across from her—Doctor Leslie Marks, according to the door—paused for an inappropriate (though probably intentional) amount of time before responding. "I'm so sorry. Those can be terrifying."

Another pause.

Aloe hoped Doctor Marks was evaluating her words instead of her appearance. She probably should have showered, or at least combed through her tangled waves. But she'd rushed over, in part, with concerns for her safety, still wearing the same outfit from last night: a thin, white pantsuit, now disfigured with wrinkles.

A choke formed in her throat as she remembered the event from less than an hour ago.

The man had come.

She'd woken in a haze, eyelids still heavy and caked with sleep. Against her better judgment, she'd read the journal—just a few entries, but enough to fuel the fire of insomnia. It was late morning; she could tell by the sun, high and shining ruthlessly through the skylights—a testament to how tired she was, sleeping in a spotlight.

The man's abrupt appearance caused a staggered reaction: a moment of disbelief, and then a bolt of shock that lifted her from bed. He was standing on the other side of the window, feet·away, a mere pane of glass between them and nothing more. Before she had time to respond, he dashed, caught in the act.

She frenzied around the room, closing the roman shades and covering the skylights until darkness enveloped. Her breath was staggered, panicked. She stood for a moment, paralyzed with violation, wanting to hide and huddle. This man—whoever he was—had been watching her during an intimate moment: while she lay helpless and asleep.

"Can you tell me about the events leading up to your panic attack?" Doctor Marks asked. Aloe nodded, digressing to the night before: the calm waves and glassy ocean, moonlight slick and silver.

"Well, we were having dinner on the beach and I was standing in the water, hardly past my toes. I remember feeling calm, at ease, and then … the exact opposite."

Doctor Marks shifted her hands and crossed her legs. "Sometimes panic strikes when we let down our guard. Have you experienced any newfound stressors since coming to Blue Haven? The transition can be an adjustment for some."

Aloe carefully considered how much she was prepared to disclose. Definitely not the journal—at least not yet, before she'd reached the end. The mysterious—and now, downright obtrusive—man, was a different matter entirely. She didn't have much in the way of rapport with Doctor Marks, but as a woman, she'd surely empathize.

"There's this man," she began.

"*Oh*?" Doctor Marks shuffled. "A man *here*? At Blue Haven?"

"Yes, I don't know who he is, but I've seen him a few times now, including this morning. He was standing at my window, staring."

As the words came out of her mouth, she realized they sounded unsubstantial. Doctor Marks blinked, waiting for the punchline—except there wasn't one.

"Did this man say anything hurtful to you? Do anything offensive?"

She shook her head.

"So, it's the sight of this man that bothers you, is that correct?" Doctor Marks paraphrased.

Oh God, that sounded incredibly pathetic.

"I'm …" she paused, trying not to fumble her way through this. "I guess I'm bothered because I think he's trying to intimidate me. He keeps … watching me, and I have no idea who he is. He's not a resident here—at least not one listed on the Directory."

"Perhaps he is a staff member?" Doctor Marks offered. "Blue Haven has many employees."

"Yes, but …" she trailed off, unsure how to properly articulate the sense of unease she felt in his presence.

"Aloe," Doctor Marks said, saying her name with such assurance. "I want to remind you that Blue Haven is an incredibly secure facility. Everything is monitored—for your safety. I truly hope that comforts you in some capacity."

"Right," she replied, somewhat comforted. Whoever this man was, he hadn't wandered into the world's most exclusive condo development uninvited. "He just bothers me," she said bluntly. "I don't know why, but he does."

Doctor Marks flattened her lips, nodding. "I see." A long moment came and passed before she continued. "I'd like to switch gears, if that's okay. Can you tell me about your father?"

Aloe suppressed an eye roll. Seriously? She'd been to therapy before, and knew exactly where this was going. *Daddy issues*. Everything revolved around daddy issues. Frustration broiled. Her problem wasn't *men*, shapeshifted by an absent father-figure. It was *this* man, singular.

"I don't know who my father is," she replied. "My mom left after I was born. She was into drugs. Long story short, I survived, and my childhood problems are behind me."

The look on Doctor Mark's face made Aloe cringe with regret. She was trying to divert their discussion away from the past, but instead she'd done the opposite, pointing Doctor Marks to a goddamn block fire of issues, raging sky high. A psychiatrist's gold mine.

"Do you remember your mother?"

"No, she abandoned me. Look, this isn't why I'm—"

"If I may," Doctor Marks held out her hand. "I know you don't believe your fear of this man has anything to do with your upbringing—and perhaps it doesn't—but it's my job to help you explore answers, and I wouldn't be a thorough therapist, or a competent one, if I ignored what you just told me."

Aloe sighed, she couldn't fault the woman; she'd handed her a motherload of content, neatly packaged in one breath. But this was a waste of time—even if she had time to waste.

"I'm not sure I'm ready for this," she said, causing Doctor Marks to frown.

"I'm sorry to hear that, Aloe, but I understand. Therapy is work, and readiness is critical. Before I can help you, you must *want* help. You know where to find me."

Aloe nodded. "For sure, thank you."

She stood and took one last look around. The walls were a soothing, coastal gray, and like everything else in Blue Haven, the room was perfectly crafted: velvety furniture at precise angles, calming photographs, ample Kleenexes.

She gave Doctor Marks a parting wave, fairly confident she'd never see this woman again. And then she left.

Chapter Twenty-Two

"Here you are, Aloe" Amir said, passing over a virgin pina colada.

She took a sip: sweet and intensely tropical. The only thing missing was a blast of rum.

"Delish," she replied. "Thank you."

"My pleasure."

Amir left and she stared at the ocean. The windows to her condo were wide open, welcoming the late afternoon breeze in long, warm strides. She set her drink on the glass coffee table, reflecting on the brief and largely unsuccessful session with Doctor Leslie Marks.

It was her own fault, really. When it came to rousing concern, she should have described the mysterious man in more compelling detail: his chilly, almost abandoned blue eyes; this disengagement about him, like he wasn't a real person. How he wasn't just watching her, but watching her *sleep*. A steely eyed creeper, is what he was. Her stomach curdled at the thought of him ogling parts she couldn't control: the lazy sprawl of her body, a twisted neckline exposing cleavage, a trickle of drool collecting on her pillow.

She glanced around the living room, further bothered by something Doctor Marks had mentioned—a statement made in passing about the facility itself. She'd said it to ease Aloe's paranoia, but now, after letting the words settle, she felt anything but eased.

"I want to remind you, Aloe, that Blue Haven is an incredibly secure facility. Everything is monitored—for your safety."

She shuddered, feeling suddenly claustrophobic.

Everything is monitored.

What did Doctor Marks mean by everything? Surely, they weren't peering inside of people's homes, were they? And who were *they*? The only staff she'd met at Blue Haven were common employees, not executives. Come to think of it, she'd never heard from anyone "in charge" at all. Was there some elusive panel of overseers, keeping tabs on each resident? A president or CEO?

She reined in focus and reached beneath the sofa, finding Eloise's journal. The end was near. Maybe ten pages left, at most, and she was eager to finish—eager to find relief. Her mounting anxiety began with the discovery of this journal. Employing similar logic, maybe if she finished the cursed thing, it would all be over with.

She had daylight on her side this time. No more 2 a.m. compulsion reads—she promised. That was half the problem, wasn't it? Reading scary stories in the middle of the night. Even children knew better.

Her fingers flipped to the newest entry. Already, her heart was starting to rumble: an engine, just warming up. *You're fine*, she coaxed, pulling positive energy from the brilliant blue sky, the salty ocean. *This will all be over soon.*

Yet, as she began to read, that hardly seemed true.

Fifty pages in, and I'm still not ready to talk about it—about him. Maybe I never will be. Maybe he'll haunt me forever, scraping me hollow like a spaghetti squash, leaving me nothing more than an empty cavity.

I still see his eyes, clear as day: freakishly teal and arresting. The sort of eyes that make a person stop and stare.

Your son has gorgeous eyes. How many times have I heard that?

In other news, I got bedsheets today: Egyptian cotton with a high thread count, one thousand, or something ridiculous. Kitten soft, with an almost melted texture, like chocolate. They're perfect, naturally— like everything else here. Designed to make me happy as pie.

I bring up the bedsheets, because they were a point of focus in my session today with Dr. Marks.

Aloe paused. *Doctor Marks?* The same Doctor Leslie Marks she'd seen earlier? Marks was a common last name, but the coincidence seemed unlikely. Her eyes fell back to the page.

Truthfully, I don't give a shit about the thread count of these sheets, because I envisioned them serving a different purpose, besides keeping me sparsely warm at night. These sheets have the proper square footage for length. They can withstand a tight twist—a solid thrash. It's import-ant to ask the right questions.

Will it slip off my neck? No.

Can I tie it in knots? Yes.

Does it have the strength to withhold a last-minute flail of regret? Importantly, yes.

Aloe reread the passage, letting the words sink in. The conclu-sion snapped together. *Jesus, Eloise wanted to hang herself?* There was no denying the woman was severely depressed—that had been clear throughout her writing—but suicidality was new.

She gazed back through her condo, eying the corner of her own bed, visible from the living room. Sheets spilled over the side; her stomach dove. Were those the same morbid bedsheets, simply washed and recycled like at a hotel? A strange agnosia arrived as she imagined Eloise in this space. *Her* space—or maybe not, if Eloise was here first. Maybe, she was in Eloise's space.

She returned to the journal. There were two final sentences before the page ended.

I don't feel safe here. I don't feel safe anywhere.

She chugged some pina colada, hoping to stifle the dread splash-ing up her throat as bile. *Why didn't Eloise feel safe here? And where's here, exactly?* Aloe had previously consulted the possibility that the journal was from elsewhere, perhaps brought to Blue Haven as a re-minder of Eloise's troubled past, but the more she read, the more she became convinced that this notebook—these words—were written right here, in her condo, especially after mention of Doctor Marks.

The *pat pat pat* of footsteps approached from behind and Aloe whipped around to greet a small, smiling woman standing by the doorway—another staff member.

"Sorry, I scare you," the woman said in somewhat broken English.

Aloe sucked in a breath. Her startle reflex was downright annoy-ing lately. "It's okay. No worries."

The woman pointed to a mop bucket and nodded. "Clean?"

"Yes, please. Thanks." She stood with the intention of heading outside, then turned back toward the woman. "What's your name?"

"Ronda."

"Do you typically clean my house?"

The woman nodded. "Yes, I clean."

"So, you found this?" Aloe held up the notebook and Ronda paused.

"Yes."

"Do you mind showing me where?"

Ronda stared back, perplexed, before ultimately nodding. She summoned Aloe to the bedroom, where she lifted up the mattress and pointed beneath, to the box spring. "Here."

Aloe's lips came together, parched. The tight, unassuming space was a perfect hiding spot. *But why was it hidden?* The journal's contents were unarguably personal, but if Eloise lived here (presumably alone, since she referenced her husband only visiting) why did she feel compelled to hide her journal so thoroughly?

Who was she hiding it *from*?

There was something so unsavory about it all.

"I have a confession," Aloe said, unconvinced she should be confessing anything at this point. Still, she was desperate for answers. "This journal isn't mine, but I don't know why it was under my bed. Was there someone else living here before me?"

Ronda tilted her head like a parrot, a clear indication she didn't understand.

Aloe pointed to the journal's gray cover, aware she needed to slow down and simplify.

"This isn't mine. Did another woman live here?"

After a few moments of obvious incomprehension, Aloe added, "Eloise."

She studied Ronda carefully, swearing a pulse of recognition flashed across her eyes, though she ultimately shook her head.

"Sorry Miss," Ronda replied, seeming genuinely apologetic.

"It's okay." A long shot, really, though she couldn't shake the feeling that this woman knew more than she was letting on—or was *allowed* to let on, hence the remorse?

Aloe made her way back to the living room. Her temples throbbed. *Paranoia?* Maybe. Her nerves were undeniably tight with anticipation, ready to take hold of anything and ring it dry like a wet cloth: a subtle glance, a quiet gesture, the presence of a man who, for all intents and purposes, had done nothing but *look* at her.

Her hand clasped the cool pina colada and she wandered out into the sun, still wearing the flowy white pantsuit from Rayla—a full day old, its wrinkles now gouged and sporadic.

It was nearly dinner. The others were heading to Bravado, a Brazilian steakhouse. She'd passed Westley on the way back from therapy (or hardly therapy) and conceded her regrets, citing a headache—which wasn't a total lie. Her head was currently throbbing, even if it wasn't earlier.

Her new friends were lovely people, but sometimes a person needed to be alone, didn't they? And besides, the last thing she wanted was another dinnertime panic attack, served up and on display, some awkward accompaniment to an arm-sized porterhouse.

Instead, she'd have a nice, relaxing night in, finish the journal, and have Amir bring over something light and fresh—a salad maybe. The line-up felt tight, solid, sensible.

She would channel her efforts into getting a grip.

And by tomorrow, she'd be good as new.

Chapter Twenty-Three

The sky was dark, and Aloe stared at the somber gray cover. *Damn it.*

Reading at night was a bad idea—and she promised she wouldn't. But technically, she'd been rereading, and that was different, was it not? The impact would surely be lessened, blunted.

She'd finished the last page just after dinner, but finished was hardly the word to describe what awaited her at the end: half a sentence, snipped in the middle like a lock of hair.

She'd hoped for closure but found the opposite: another layer of confusion. Now, at nearly midnight, those final pages haunted her. Perhaps, if she gave them a quick once-over, she'd find a clue or overlooked detail, enough substance to procure a solid "the end"—and a good night's sleep.

She stood from her bed and wandered into the living room. Her finger flicked on all of the lights, every last one, and she squinted into the brightness. How scared could a person get in a room so lit? The problem was less the journal than it was the night—or that's what she told herself.

She reached for a fluffy throw and draped it over her legs. Comfy. Cozy. *I feel normal. This is normal.* Just a gal reading a story, trying to get to the bottom of something—in a lighthearted way. A casual moment of sleuthing.

She flipped to the back of the journal, ignoring the dip in her stomach, as forceful and nauseating as descending down a roller coaster.

I woke up this morning and everything was different. There was air in my lungs and blood in my veins and a surge of real, thrumming gusto. Today, for the first time in ages, I felt legitimately human.

I hardly looked human—I'll admit that. My reflection was a punch in the lungs: roots ambushed by gray, skin parched, lips flaking and chapped, everything about me haggled. A worn sweater, starting to smell.

But then I took a shower. A shower! I've never scrubbed so hard in my life, grinding the loofah against my skin like a board being sandpapered. Afterwards, I ran my fingers along my smooth leg, and flinched in response to my own touch! Impressive stuff. Not a numb, catatonic shell. Not today!

That said, I have to get the fuck out of here. This place is doing something to me. I can see that now, through a rare glimpse of clarity. My partner will contest—of course he will. He wants me here, trapped and contained in this perfect prison—perfect insofar that it's whittling me raw. He's the one who sent me here, after all. Stash away the wife. Keep her quiet and contained. Nice and drugged. Give her a decent view and a bit of fresh air. She'll be fine!

Ridiculous, of course. I won't be fine. A place like this isn't real life. A place like this is...

And that was it.

As before, Aloe flipped through the last few pages, looking for more words, or evidence of a rip or tear. But there was nothing.

She leaned back and closed her eyes, thoughts running rampant. It was starting to seem as though Eloise was forced into Blue Haven, allegedly, by her husband for reasons that were unclear. Sure, the woman was obviously contending with mental-health challenges, but what if those weren't organic, as Aloe had assumed, but a systemic response to being locked away against her will?

This place is doing something to me. I see that now.

Her mind pulled at other clues. Eloise was seeing Doctor Marks (the same woman she'd met earlier for therapy), and she had a son—though she'd only referenced him once, and somewhat coldly, enough to suggest their relationship was probably strained.

Aloe stared through the expansive windows, watching the waves gently break against the shore. The moon was large and silver and porous, like skin.

It started first in her palms, a familiar hot-cold sensation that broadened up her arms, followed by weakness. She knew all at once what was coming: the fast, hot rush of terror.

Another panic attack.

She tapped frantically on her device, calling Amir, breaths growing rapid, fighting against the tide.

"Hi Aloe, what can I do for you this evening?"

"Amir," she said, voice shaky. "Can you bring me a tea?"

She wondered if he could sense the desperation in her voice, the strong undertone of, *I feel like I'm going to die. Please come, I don't want to be alone.*

"Absolutely, I'll be there right away."

"Thanks," she managed.

A breath of air came, another—and then an avalanche of fear swallowed her whole.

Her experience with these attacks was limited, but there was no use fighting back, it only made things worse. Moments passed, merciless, but as the door opened and Amir stepped in, the intensity of it all began to fade.

His dark eyes widened with concern; it was clear he'd successfully read between the lines. The tea in his hands curled with steam and she could already smell the sweet, subtle scent of chamomile.

Now that Amir was here, her dread seemed to scatter like a burglar caught in the act, and she felt almost silly for getting so worked up.

"Here," he said, rushing over. "I brought you this."

She took the mug and huffed in a plume of hot steam. "Thanks Amir."

A few sips later, she felt better, calmer.

Amir's eyes wavered over her body and he winced with sympathy. She was still wearing the wrinkled Dolce pantsuit, now soiled with a stain from dinner. She'd forgotten about that.

"Aloe," he said, dragging it out. "I have to ask. Are you alright?"

"Yes, I'm fine." It came out instinctively, like a reflex.

He drew a breath, clearly unconvinced. "I know I'm just your concierge, but if something's wrong, if you need someone to talk to, I want you to know I'm here."

His voice was cushy, soothing, and he appeared truly burdened by her obvious distress. She *did* need someone to talk to, frankly. Why not Amir?

"Alright," she began, smoothing her hands over the cushion. She tried to look him in the eye, but couldn't. These sorts of conversations were definitely not her strong suit. "I've been struggling with anxiety lately, and this is very new to me. I've never had anxiety like this before."

"I'm sorry to hear that, Aloe." He sat down beside her. "But please know you're not alone. This place is a lot to take in, and the adjustment can be challenging for some. Have you looked into any of the mental-health services we offer in the Hexagon?"

"Sort of." She took another sip of tea. "I went to see Doctor Marks today. The session wasn't what I was hoping for—at least not right now." She brought her eyes to his. "Can you tell me what you meant by *the adjustment can be challenging for some?*"

"Of course. Blue Haven is a very … *different* lifestyle, and that can be difficult. We're a closed-off community. No social media, no television, no Googling." He chuckled, amused by the word googling. "Returning to the basics can make people uncomfortable. Fidgety, anxious, paranoid."

Aloe found herself nodding along. There was probably some truth to this.

"—But," Amir continued. "These feelings lessen with time, and ultimately, research has shown that most people who disengage from technology, social media, toxic culture, etcetera, are happier because of it. It's a much simpler lifestyle."

Aloe stopped nodding, thinking suddenly of Eloise. She was the opposite of happy. Then again, Amir had said most people, as in: *most people are happier*. With every rule came exceptions.

"Does that help?" Amir asked. The grin on his face lifted. He seemed genuinely inspired by Blue Haven's vision.

She strained a smile. "Yes, it does. Thank you."

He leaned forward, ready to leave. "Wait," Aloe said, before he could stand. "Has anyone ever … left this place?"

"*Left Blue Haven?*" He seemed taken back. "What do you mean?"

"I mean *left*, because they didn't like it here."

He shook his head. "No. So far so good. We continue to receive a wealth of positive feedback from our small but growing number of residents, and we're happy to accommodate any additional requests and demands."

Aloe searched his face for a flicker of deception or a single break in eye contact, but there was nothing. She decided to press further. "So, I'm the first person to live in this condo? No one else lived here before me?" Her tone was accusatory; she couldn't help it.

His eyebrows zigzagged with confusion. "Yes, you're the only person who's lived in this condo, Aloe. I promise."

"Okay," she replied, her voice quiet. She was skilled at reading people, but Amir read like an open book. Not a speck of deceit. He was either true to his word, or an incredibly accomplished actor.

"Are you sure you're okay, Aloe? These are very unusual questions."

She nestled her hand between the cushions, where she'd wedged the journal. Her fingernail flicked over the pages. *Should I tell him?* For a terse moment, she considered it, but something wasn't right. Though Amir seemed genuine, a woman named Eloise was here, and now she wasn't.

"Sorry," she replied. "I'm fine, just not myself lately. I really appreciate the tea—and the chat. It's nice to know I have someone to talk to."

Amir's hand landed over hers. "Give it time, Aloe. You've only been here four days."

Four days? Was that all? She'd arrived a bright-eyed, bushy-tailed tourist, hungry for life in Blue Haven, ready to start fresh. And now look at her? Wearing a days-old pantsuit stained with salad dressing, a damp and salty smell leaking from her pores, her sanity snapping in and out like a flip-flop.

Amir stood and tapped his wrist. "Please let me know if you need anything. I'm just a tap away."

Chapter Twenty-Four
Day Five

It was the heat that woke her, and she was left with a foggy impression of a man and a boy—a dream she couldn't embrace. And then her lungs drew a gasp of fervid, stuffy air that raised her from the couch reflexively. Her hair was tangled and damp, thanks to a scorching beam of sunlight blazing through the windows unrestrained.

She looked at her device: 1:00 p.m. *Jesus*.

Outside, along the beachfront, a body moved slowly and strangely, either performing Tai Chi or yoga. She instantly recognized the figure as Bibs. His clumsy shapeshifting with periodic hand thrusts (*Was he singing?* Probably), made her want to laugh, but she lacked the energy.

It had been another late night.

After Amir left, she'd stood by the front windows wrapped in a throw, worried. It was drafty, cold, and her heartbeat came to the forefront, making itself known. Not faster, but harder: a jackhammer in her chest that knocked against her ribcage. She scanned the beachfront, looking for signs of life, but there was only sand and water and stillness.

She couldn't see the steely eyed creeper, but she could sense him—she swore she could sense him, like her brain knew when he was near and responded in kind: stirred and rustled like leaves on the pavement, spiraling with fear.

She stayed like that for a long while, guard-dog stiff, cells on high alert. Her body begged for sleep, but her mind wouldn't allow it. *He's out there*, she told her weakening muscles, clenching with fatigue. *I know he's out there.*

As night finally lifted, her hammerhead heartbeat eased just enough to appreciate the sky. The colors were glorious: hot pink and sneaker orange and lemon-lime green, all reaching up from the horizon like Northern lights. Palm trees came to life. No longer skeletons swaying ghoulishly in the dark, but lush, sprawling, friendly things. The water rippled with color, sucking up the sky. Before she dozed off, a spreading sense of tranquility washed up from her toes: peace—or incapacitating exhaustion.

Now though, her body ached with soreness. She'd stood for hours last night. Waiting. Watching. All for nothing—not a single goddamn thing. And maybe there was nothing to see. She'd sensed the man's presence, but had no real evidence, just a hunch. Even if he was out there waiting in the night, so what? She was safely harbored in a surveilled condo, further protected by state-of-the-art security—and she was wearing a device that afforded her twenty-four hour assistance. *How much safer could a person get?*

Give it time, Amir had said.

She let the words settle in her gut.

Give it time.

She tapped the device and directed a call to Gram ... then Aunt Patty ... then Tess. No answers—yet again. She didn't bother leaving any messages, because what was the point? Her fingers drummed against the quartz countertop, the condo walls enclosing. Every time she started to feel slightly settled, paranoia rapped against her chest.

A few missed calls were excusable, but *all* of them, always?

She swallowed her temper. *Honestly.* She'd paid good money to live here—really good money—and somehow, she'd become little more than a human tornado of emotions in a two-and-a-half-day-old pantsuit. It was mildly infuriating.

She marched to the en suite and shed the pantsuit, sections clinging to her body like a second skin. Her own foulness hung dense in the air, though she ignored the smell, too ashamed to admit it belonged to her.

She entered the shower and turned on the water: warm and welcoming.

Don't think about Eloise.

But of course, she was already thinking about Eloise. The woman had ambushed her thoughts, her sense of wellbeing, and as much as she wanted to go back in time and roast the cursed journal over a tiki torch, it was too late. Now, she owed it to Eloise to find out what happened, even if the woman was a stranger.

Well ... not a stranger, exactly. One can't compulsively read the deepest inner workings of another human being's thoughts and call them a stranger. Eloise was a living, breathing character, far more than a collection of words, and Aloe could envision her perfectly: ash blonde hair and slotted eyes; fine wrinkles and thin lips; large plastic glasses—something chunky; left-handed, based on the slant of her cursive; an early riser—up with the sun; kind, but firm; often misjudged. Odd as it were, Aloe knew more about Eloise than anyone else in her life, and whether she liked it or not, they were tethered together, tight as a French braid.

As she lathered her body with soap, a thought came forward, followed by a rush of excitement.

No one had ever left Blue Haven, according to Amir.

What if he was telling the truth?

Just because Eloise wasn't currently living in condo Number Five didn't mean she wasn't still here, somewhere. There were a thousand places for a person to be, including the world's tallest building, and while Aloe had assumed Eloise's journal was written from inside her own condo, what if it wasn't? What if it was written somewhere else on the premises? What if—her heart began racing with possibilities—the house cleaner actually *brought* Eloise's journal to her personally, hoping she could help in some way.

Maybe the journal wasn't a curse, but a calling.

It came like a revelation and her chest broadened with hope. She twisted the valve shut and leapt out of the shower, tossing a towel over her shoulder. Her sopping wet feet left slick footprints across the wood as she rushed into her closet and pulled on a cotton dress, half wet.

Eloise is still here.

She knew it, plain and sturdy, as indisputable as any other truth she'd come to know.

The sky is blue.

The grass is green.

Eloise is still in Blue Haven!

She lifted the floppy-brimmed hat from its peg and dropped it on her head. It was hardly a selling feature at the time, but a hat so large and concealing was perfect for two things: shade, and spying. She grabbed a pair of oversized sunglasses, big and bug-eyed, then took the side door.

The sun was bright, blinding, and she walked quickly along the cobblestone path with the brim of her hat slanted down. The scalding stones singed her feet. "Shit," she cursed, forgetting a pair of flip-flops. Still, she pressed forward, her soles soon leathering to the heat. The path swerved around vacant condos that flanked her own—*Number Six, Number Seven, Number Eight*. She passed them slowly, staring into their interiors, each a sprawling sightline of vacancy. These empty shells seemed innocent enough. Rooms waiting for inhabitants. No Eloise.

At condo Number Twenty, the cobblestone path looped back around, returning to the Hexagon—the "flower design," Amir boasted on Day One.

Instead of following the path, she stepped onto the sand, finding the ocean moments later.

She carried on along the water, periodically glancing back down the beach as her nerves percolated with anticipation, like she was breaking a rule. *Strolling down the beach.* Hardly a crime, even though it felt like one.

The beach was unrestrained in both directions: a crescent moon of bone-white sand, hugging a body of blue. The sporadic palms speckled here and there eventually came together into denser forests, while the sweep of sand prevailed, like a person could walk forever along the ocean—or at least many, many miles.

Aloe imagined herself walking those miles until Blue Haven was only a dot behind her and she was thoroughly alone: a castaway stranded in paradise. Maybe—and this was a long shot, but so was winning the lottery, one in fourteen million, actually—Eloise had traveled a similar path and was living off-the-grid nearby. It was unusual, and somewhat unexplainable, but Aloe swore she could feel the spirit of this woman guiding her, and for a moment Eloise seemed less like someone she'd never met, and more like a guardian angel leading her out of this place, the dangers of which she couldn't articulate but was certain existed.

"Eloise," she whispered. "Where are—"

But before she could say *"you,"* she was punched in the face by a fist of thin air. The force was swift and unexpected, and she leapt back clutching her cheek, searching frantically for whatever made contact.

Except there was nothing—nothing at all.

As the hot, searing pain lessened to a dull ache, she reached out her hand, one finger leading. The tip of her fingernail tapped against a surface.

"What the ..." she whispered, as her palm swiped down a slick, cool structure, perfectly transparent, like a sky-high window. She paused, and then touched it again with disbelief, verifying.

Her eyes dashed along the coast, finding the horizon. She lifted her dress and followed the partition into the water, past her ankles, knees, and thighs, at which point she stopped, not willing to go any further—at least not yet.

For a moment she stood in shock and awe, not quite believing what she'd stumbled upon.

A giant, invisible wall.

Slicing straight through paradise.

She returned to the beach, shaken. Her quest for Eloise had shapeshifted dramatically. She stared at the crystal-clear partition, invisible to the naked eye. The existence of this wall made her stomach hard and tight. *This isn't supposed to be here.* And yet it was, hiding in broad daylight. *Where does it start?*

She dragged her fingers along the surface, slowly at first but gaining momentum as her feet whipped through the sand, following the periphery. She kept watch, constantly searching for figures in the distance. No one had mentioned the existence of this structure, which seemed incriminating—enough to keep her on high alert.

She circled the compound, greeting unexplored terrain. Condos prevailed, all vacant, seemingly, and identical to her own. The ocean view on *this* side of Blue Haven was much different than her vantage: a distant swipe of water miles away, separated by rock formations and clusters of monstrous, mature palms, which she could see but not reach, thanks to the invisible wall.

The scene was striking, a different feel to it. Dense and mighty, like the amazon. She soaked in the gray shade, happy for a few moments of cool relief, and then all too soon the sun was back and she emerged on the other side, the ocean at her feet. She found herself staring into the same bleak beyond, wondering if the wall ended or looped back around, knifing through the water to create some giant, invisible globe.

Her stomach tightened as she pressed her face to the structure, staring beyond like a mouse in a vivarium.

Trapped.

Suddenly, a sound came—*Bzzzz*—followed by a full-body tremor. She leapt.

What the hell was that?

Chapter Twenty-Five

It took a moment for the shock value to diminish—for Aloe to realize the rumbling sensation was coming from her wrist. It was only her device, vibrating.

She tapped on the screen and Amir's voice rose up.

"Hi Aloe. How are you doing today?"

"Great," she lied. "And you?"

"I'm well. Thanks for asking."

There was a long, uncomfortable pause, and she considered ending the call before it even started. *Sorry Amir, I'm a little busy at the moment, do you mind—*

"I see you're at the wall."

Her chest flinched and she looked around, expecting to see Amir in the periphery.

"What do you mean *you see I'm at the wall?* Where are you?"

"I'm in the Hexagon. A member of our security team informed me."

Security team? She'd never seen any security presence, but maybe they operated from elsewhere, or were particularly sleuthy. Her thoughts halted. *The steely eyed creeper.* Was he part of that security team?

"Aloe?"

"Sorry," she replied. "It's been a day so far."

"No worries. Is there something I can help you with?"

"Actually yes." Her voice was prickly, but she didn't care. People became irritated when deceived. *Fact.* "You can start by explaining what this wall is all about."

"I'm sorry Aloe, you seem upset."

Her breath was hot and heavy against her wrist. "Shocked, is a better adjective."

"My apologies. The wall exists to protect Blue Haven and its residents."

"*Protect?*" she repeated, still reeling with the claustrophobic feeling of being contained.

"Aloe," he replied calmly. "Blue Haven is an experience—one our residents pay good money for, yourself included. We offer luxury, indulgence, and relaxation—but above all, we offer a level of unparalleled privacy. Do you know what would happen without some kind of protection?" He paused briefly, rhetorically. "Paparazzi. Pictures. Instagram stories. People weaseling inside of Blue Haven, making it accessible to everyone. *Imagine?* Influencers lounging on the beach, food critics sharing the experience of Chef Ramsay's Wellington—everything that's poisoned our society, leaking through. We tried to make the wall unimposing, but it's necessary. We're not the old world, Aloe. We're the new world."

She opened her mouth and paused, the fiery momentum subsiding. It was hard to be mad at Amir. His voice was so soft and resolute—and his answers always seemed to make sense. She hadn't thought about the implications of an open, borderless space, and how that might jeopardize her safety and wellbeing.

Of course Blue Haven required substantial security and protection to ensure its residents were afforded the level of privacy they paid for. She appreciated that protection personally. And what would she rather have in place of a sleek, transparent partition? A clunky, concrete divide? Barbed wire tangled overhead? Security marching along the outskirts? Uninvited guests venturing inside?

"Do you understand now?" Amir asked.

She fanned out her dress; the sweat on her torso was causing it to stick. The sun's reflection was hot and stifling against the water, and she suddenly felt incredibly foolish for her conspiratory thinking.

"Yes," she replied. "I wasn't expecting a wall, but it does make sense. Thanks for explaining."

The call ended and she returned to the cobblestone path, trying to regain focus. This afternoon's conquest wasn't about the wall; it was about Eloise. Amir's response was satisfying enough—per usual—

and nearly overshadowed the small but sharp voice pushing through her subconscious.

What's more important, keeping people out, or keeping people in?

"Stop it!" she yelled, then she shook her head, embarrassed.

Great, now I'm talking to myself.

Focus. Focus. Focus.

Eloise. Eloise. Eloise.

She marched back toward the Hexagon, following the loops and swirls. Under different circumstances, she probably would have enjoyed the route. There was always something to appreciate: dew-speckled vegetation bordering the walkway with curious shapes and varieties; colors like she'd never seen in the natural world: neon lime, indigo, rainbow-bright fuchsia; sprawling archways with flowery vines; sand carefully raked into captivating designs; shaded tiki huts with freshly cracked coconuts and ripe papayas. But she wasn't in the mood for awe or appreciation. Not today. Her eyes scattered across the grounds, searching for evidence, feet moving quickly, dress bopping.

Staff circled like vultures, offering canapés on wide, glass trays shaped like seashells or palm leaves. Aloe skirted around them, a ghost in bug-eyed sunglasses, further concealed by a flop of interwoven straw.

As she passed the foray of condos leading around the backside—the cliffside view—she peered inside, pressing her nose against each pane of glass. *Eloise?* Her heart leapt at the prospect of witnessing a dash or scurry, anything out of place. She waited, ears ready to receive a muffled cry or weak call for help, but there was nothing. Just a series of living rooms much like her own: wide and perfectly exposed sightlines. Homes awaiting their owners.

Sunshine and happiness and expansion.

Nothing more.

When she finally reached the Hexagon, she stopped and drew a full breath—always the Hexagon; each pathway folding back onto itself. The dark-tinted windows reflected a palpable warmth and her cheeks flushed. She smoothed her hands across her dress, dispersing the sweat, as her neck swanned upward.

So many floors to inspect. Eloise could be anywhere.

This might take longer than a few hours.

She entered the building and greeted an empty lobby—of course: a big show with no audience. Her focus narrowed on a tray of citrus-spiked water. Her throat yearned for anything liquid, and she chugged one glass, then another, disliking the acidity but hardly caring.

The Directory was up ahead, wide and prominent as a commandment, and she marched toward it, a sense of urgency returning. The tiles were cold on her bare feet, causing goosebumps to flutter up her arms. She scanned the various floors—*How should I do this? Top to bottom? Bottom to Top?*—her concentration so narrow the figure practically beamed down beside her.

"Aloe?"

She jolted. "Jesus Christ!" The familiar face settled. "Amir, you scared the shit out of me."

"I'm sorry." He touched her arm and frowned with such warmth she was instantly soothed. "I was just passing through and saw you standing here. Thought I'd say hi. What brings you to the Hexagon?"

"Well." She bit her lip. "I guess I just wanted to explore this giant, mysterious place."

His left eyebrow furrowed. "You know most of our vendors are currently closed, right?"

"*Closed?*" Her head pulled back in surprise. She glanced at her device: 2:41 p.m. That was a normal operating hour, wasn't it? Unless. Is it Sunday? A rush circled her head, leaving behind a cloudy film of confusion. She had no idea what the date was.

"Aloe." Amir offered a subtle smirk. "There are hundreds of services listed on this Directory, and we currently have five residents. If we kept everything open indefinitely, we'd be standing around twiddling our thumbs."

"So ..." Her eyes narrowed. "This is all just a ... *facade?*"

"Facade? Of course not! Every resident is welcome—entitled—to every service in this facility. For some, we simply need a little head's up. Our most popular options are always available: the spas, for example. Le Boutique. Any health-related services, those are accessible twenty-four seven. We open one restaurant during lunch, even though most of our residents prefer a more casual, light plate at home."

He paused to smile, teeth gleaming. "That said, if you want to try—" he shifted his eyes momentarily to the Directory. "Bermuda

Seafood, for example, right here right now, we're happy to accommodate. Just let me know and we'll have it fully staffed and ready in less than twenty minutes."

"We'll take it!" a voice boomed. It was Bibs, practically bursting through the front doors; he was wearing a pair of orange Crocs that squished with each step. "Aloe—there you are … I think." He took a moment to nudge down her sunglasses, and then beamed. "Yep. Aloe Malone. Identity confirmed."

She had to laugh.

"I've been tasked with giving you these." He offered up a hefty bouquet of flowers.

"You got me flowers?" A choke formed in her throat.

"Indeed, from the whole crew. Just a little something to brighten your day after the other night."

"You didn't have to …" she trailed off.

"Of course we did! Friends do nice things for each other, and you certainly deserve a nice thing."

Her chest ripped with guilt. To think, she'd spent the morning being more infatuated with a woman she'd never met than her thoughtful, flesh-and-blood friends—all of whom she'd been trying to avoid. She stared again at the brilliant tropical flowers. *I don't deserve these.*

"Thank you," she said. "Truly, they're beautiful."

Bibs smiled with half his mouth. "Have you had lunch yet?"

She shook her head. "No, I haven't." *Or breakfast, actually. And come to think of it, I didn't have much in the way of dinner last night …*

"Well then." Bibs turned to Amir. "How about Bermuda Seafood in twenty?"

Chapter Twenty-Six

Ten minutes into lunch with Bibs, Aloe finally noticed his T-shirt: a deep-set V-neck, soft peach in color, and sharply juxtaposed with the words, "GANGSTA'S PARADISE," in hard, bold cursive.

"I like your shirt," she said, surprised it'd taken her so long to notice—a true testament to her current level of brain functioning.

"Why thank you," he replied. "I may be the only modern tenor capable of achieving proper diminuendo at the finale of *Celeste Aida*, but that doesn't mean I can't celebrate Coolio's *Gangsta's Paradise*."

She laughed. "Good for you. *Gangsta's Paradise* deserves to be celebrated."

Amir returned with her lovely bouquet, now soaking in a glass vase. She still couldn't believe how thoughtful her friends had been, gifting her something so beautiful. The bright flowers complimented a nearby installation of metal fish, swimming across the walls and onto the ceiling. An engaging display, each hue a kaleidoscope of patterns. She liked the decor here—not that decor was necessary. They were on the one hundredth floor, and the view of the ocean was decor itself, like something from a postcard.

She snapped a mental photograph, admiring the surreal quality of it all. Varying floor depths gave shape and contrast to the blue water, offering every variation from teal to navy. Dark, splotchy patches emerged like a patchwork quilt, surrounded by frothy egg-white collars of waves. The sky was a softer blue, dreamy, with vagrant clouds pulling apart as they drifted.

It all evoked a sense of peace, and she fought strongly against it.

Eloise.

Must. Find. Eloise.

"Alright kid," Bibs said. "Tell me what's going on."

"What do you mean?"

"Something's off with you."

She looked away, feigning a shrug. He was right of course, but she wasn't accustomed to being called out so candidly. Most people didn't confront the emotional burdens of others, because they were exactly that: *burdens.*

"Aloe, please." His voice was tender, and it made her want to cry.

"I'm just …" She struggled to find the words. "I'm not myself lately, I guess."

Bibs took a sip of dark cola. "Have you ever heard a baritone crescendo in a live opera theater with reasonable acoustics?"

She shook her head. She'd never listened to opera. Period.

"Let me articulate the experience. The sound starts off as this small, contained note—a whisper almost. Your ear perks. *Hello there, little sound. Let me hear you.* And then it grows, pleasantly at first but quickly evolving, pulling in air—*your air*—feeding from you like a leach until a full, encompassing beast arrives. It's all very exciting but also terrifying, how quickly it takes over your senses, consuming every part of you. For a few seconds, you aren't yourself. You're just the sound. And then it stops."

He paused, clearly waiting for the metaphor to sink in. Maybe it was her general brain fog, or the fact she hadn't eaten in nearly twenty-four hours, but she lacked the mental capacity to read between the lines.

"In other words," Bibs said, thankfully spelling it out for her, "Something small, can become something large, very quickly." His hand landed over hers and she was surprised by its softness, expecting his palm to be gritty and coarse. "Let's chat. Talk to me."

"Okay," she said, before she could think better of it. "So … God, I don't even know where to start. I guess—" she glanced around, suddenly wary of imposing eyes— "I think something strange is happening here."

"*Here?* At Bermuda Seafood?"

"No, here at Blue Haven."

He leaned in, eyes glowing with interest. "What do you mean something strange?"

Her mind instantly landed on Eloise, but she decided to temper the subject. "Since you've been here, at Blue Haven, have you talked to anyone from … the outside world?" *Dear Lord*, as if she'd just said "outside world" like they were living on another planet. Still, it was starting to feel that way.

Bibs ripped a piece of fresh pumpernickel and smeared it across a plate of oil and balsamic. "I haven't, no. The outside world has little to offer me these days. Parents are dead. My brother and I were never close. A few ex-girlfriends here and there, but nothing worth keeping in touch over. Friends?" He winked. "Who needs 'em."

He tore off another piece of bread, pausing to swallow the first, then added, "This was a fresh start for me."

"I see," Aloe replied. "What about the others? Westley, Bob, Franny? Have they mentioned anything to you about their phone calls going unanswered?"

Bibs glanced at the ceiling. "Actually yeah, Westley said he was trying to contact his buddy but couldn't get a hold of him."

Aloe found herself sliding closer, drawn to the possibility of something greater at play.

"But," Bibs added, "he also called the guy a drifter. One of those flaky, world traveler sorts. Granola, I guess. Likes being off the grid."

"What about Bob and Franny?"

"I don't think Bob and Franny have anyone in their lives besides Bob and Franny."

She took a sip of sparkling water, keeping her voice quiet. "Don't you think it's weird that we all seem to lack close ties? Almost like we were ..." she wanted to say chosen, but that sounded ridiculous, even to her paranoid mind. She shook her head. "I don't know what I'm trying to say."

"I'm picking up what you're putting down," Bibs said. "But—to play devil's advocate—perhaps it's the case that a place like Blue Haven attracts a certain type of vagrant. I mean, if you had a husband and kids, a stash of friends, would you be here?"

Her chest sunk; Bibs was right. Blue Haven filled a niche market for people who were rich, and also lonely. Most people wouldn't stand for Blue Haven's strict policies—probably why there were so few residents.

"Okay," she said, deciding to go for it. "I found a journal."

"*A journal?*" Bibs swallowed thickly. "Interesting, do tell."

Just as she opened her mouth, Amir arrived with their plates. *Perfect timing.* They'd both ordered the seared barramundi with lemon risotto, and even though she was annoyed by the food's arrival, her stomach was practically begging at this point. She flaked the fish apart and shoveled in a few bites.

"So, the journal," she said, her mouth half-full. "My housecleaner allegedly found it under my bed, wedged between the mattress and box spring. According to the inside cover it belonged to a woman named Eloise who seemingly lived here—even though she definitely didn't want to."

Bib's squeezed a slice of lemon over his fillet. "Eloise ... that name sounds familiar. Might have been the lady who left."

Aloe almost choked on her half-chewed bite. "*Pardon?* What do you mean *left?* Like ... left Blue Haven?"

"Yeah," he replied, taking in a spoonful of risotto. "We only chatted a few times. She mentioned her name at one point, but I'm terrible with names. She was a middle-aged gal. A bit on the melancholy side."

Aloe gripped the table, her pulse beating through her fingertips. A new floodgate of questions opened. *Finally*, she was getting somewhere. "So, the woman you're referring to is definitely gone? When did she leave?"

Bibs shrugged. "Oh, a while ago—a year even. We were the first two people here, actually, but she was in and out in less than a week. Honestly, I hardly saw her. She seemed like a bit of a loner, preferred keeping to herself."

Aloe pushed her plate aside, leaning in further to keep her voice hushed. "How do you know she's gone?"

"Easy," he said. "She was in Number One, and now it's empty."

Condo Number One! She knew there was something odd about Number One. Her thoughts spun.

"Do you know why she left?"

"Missed the outside world, apparently. Wasn't ready for such a big change—or that's what her concierge told me. Made sense to me. A place like this isn't for everyone, and to be frank, she didn't seem overly happy here."

"Right." Aloe swirled her water, trying to bring the pieces together. The husband. In her journal, Eloise referenced a man coming to check on her, which meant he was here too, inside of Blue Haven—or was at some point. Unless. Goosebumps rushed up from her toes, reaching her cheeks as a cool flush. The steely eyed creeper: could that be Eloise's husband, still on the premises somehow?

She brought her trembling fingers below the table, trying to hide her shakiness. "Did you ever see this woman with another man—her husband?"

Bibs immediately shook his head. "No, she was here alone—single, she said, and never married. Was some big shot lawyer from New York before all of this."

A tense pressure formed along the base of Aloe's head, between her ears. "Nothing makes any sense," she whispered, pressing her thumbs into her temples. Thoughts were becoming painful.

"*Hey.*" Bibs squeezed her arm. "We'll figure this out, alright? The others and I were thinking of doing a patio dinner tonight—at your place, actually, if you're up for it. Nice and close, casual, comfortable. Why don't you show me the journal later and I can read through it? I'll help you get to the bottom of this, I promise."

Her head bobbed in response. "I would really appreciate that." So many questions lingered: *Was the woman Bibs described truly Eloise? If so, what about the husband? Was she lying about never being married? And how was the steely eyed creeper connected—if at all?* At this point, she was sick of mulling. She took in a spoonful of buttery risotto, issuing a temporary layoff to all brain cells. It was nice, though, that Bibs wanted to help. She needed someone in her corner.

"Do you feel better?" Bibs asked.

She projected a smile. "I do, actually. It's hard for me to open up sometimes."

He let out a big, hearty laugh. "Welcome to the club, sister. That's a human thing."

Amir approached then, carrying a pitcher. Her smile vanished and she looked down, pretending to craft the perfect bite as he filled their drinks.

"Anything else I can get for you?" he asked.

"I'm okay," Bibs said. "Tasty stuff."

"Same," Aloe replied, looking away. Her grip tightened, the fork sharp in her grasp. Up until ten minutes ago, she'd seen Amir as an ally. Now, she knew better than to trust his beaming smile and sappy voice, dripping with fake concern.

A woman—Eloise or otherwise—had left Blue Haven.

Which meant Amir had officially lied.

Chapter Twenty-Seven

"*Ugggh*," Bibs groaned, his arm shaped like a tilted "L" and hand wrapped around Bob's. "You're stronger than you look old man."

"Ha!" The grimace on Bob's tight, red face relaxed for a split second.

The two had been arm wrestling for several minutes while Aloe and the others watched in amusement.

"Remember," Westley said from the sidelines. "I take the winner." He flexed a bicep, easily the size of Aloe's head, and Franny pinched her flamingo-pink lips together like a closing envelope. "*Please*, you've got nothing on my darling husband, right hun?" She latched onto Bob's other arm.

"No distractions," he said between his teeth.

She reeled back. "See? True dedication, right there."

Aloe took a sip of sweet iced tea. "You guys are boring me now." She said it with a smile, facing the sky instead. Another gorgeous night: blackness and stars and smudgy clouds like thumbprints in the sky. The air was whole, fulsome, almost cool enough for sleeves but not quite.

They'd just finished a late dinner of lobster mac and cheese—Aloe's choice. Technically, she'd said Kraft Dinner (no lobster imposed), imagining the blue-boxed variety with elbow macaroni and powdered cheddar that came in radioactive orange. She missed that two-dollar box of sheer convenience; eating it straight from the pot, some bites still gritty with powder.

Not to say the rendition with tender flakes of lobster and ample Gruyere wasn't good—sensational, even—it just wasn't KD. Some things were like that: perfectly imperfect.

A fist slammed against the table and Aloe jolted.

"Champion!" Bibs stood and tossed his hands in the air. The movement raised his too-short T-shirt over his belly to expose a sag of hairy skin.

"*Ahh*, I let cha have it," Bob replied.

Franny planted a kiss on his cheek, leaving a flower-petal stain of pink. "Jokes on you Bibs," she said, lifting a brow. "Bob just fed you to the wolves." She pointed to Westley and he howled, flashing his gargantuan muscles. A thick vein orbited his arms, almost pulsing in the moonlight. Aloe laughed along with the rest of them, taking a sip of coffee. It was her third cup of the night, each more necessary than the last. Since lunch with Bibs, she'd been stuck in a hypnotic lull of exhaustion, everything falling flat and two-dimensional.

She had a lot to think about, but couldn't muster the energy. Her brain was simply sputtering in idle, refusing to move forward and begging for rest. She'd tried unsuccessfully to nap before dinner, but laid awake instead, brooding and perplexed. *How are you not asleep?*

"Are you okay?" Westley whispered, off to the side.

She chugged the rest of her coffee, praying for a jolt of energy—enough to get her through the night. Dessert was coming, only one course left. Afterwards, she'd slip inside, excuse herself—let the others carry on without her, no need to damper an otherwise great evening.

"I'm fine," she replied, pushing out a weak smile.

"Are you sure? You look a little under the weather."

"I'm not sick or anything, just exhausted. I haven't been sleeping well lately and it's getting the better of me. I'll be okay though."

He rested a hand on her shoulder. "So why don't you hit the sack? Nobody cares. You're tired, so go get some sleep, seriously."

"Are you ... sure?" she asked, knowing the offer was a life raft she needed to accept. "I don't want to be rude, we haven't even had dessert yet."

"Yes, I'm sure—we're sure. Self-care isn't rude. Now go on, get outta here."

She exhaled, full of relief. "I won't be such a Debbie downer tomorrow, I promise."

Westley frowned. "Don't worry about us. Focus on yourself. That's what's most important."

She stood, slightly weak in the knees. Eyes shifted toward her and she pushed out one last smile. "I'm sorry guys. I'm calling it a night. So. Damn. Tired."

"Go!" Franny said. "Sleep. We'll have Amir tuck your lemon soufflé in the fridge for later."

Amir, the mention of his name livened a spark of betrayal, but she didn't have the energy. "That's great, thanks. See you all tomorrow."

As she turned to leave, Bibs piped up. "Wait, you had a book for me to borrow, yes?"

A book? Her mind was so sluggish it took a moment to register. *Right, the journal.* She shook her head in self disapproval. *You. Need. Sleep.*

"That's right," she replied. "It's just inside. One sec, I'll grab it."

Her feet led the way, an almost disembodied state arriving: parts shuffling, wires getting crossed, everything coated in hazy fog. She walked straight into the living room, still open to the night, and floated over to the couch. Her hand dipped between the cushions, where she'd left the journal.

The lack of contact rippled up and dispersed through her chest. She scraped the plastic couch bottom. Panic stirred as her body and mind reunited like a plug in a socket, electricity now flowing.

The journal was gone.

She dashed over to the other cushion and tried again, plunging her hand into the narrow gap. *Nothing.* Another empty slot. She stood in shock. What the hell? She'd left the journal wedged between the cushions, hadn't she?

Absolutely.

Yes. Yes, I did.

She'd been mindless, out of sorts, possibly reckless, but the journal was here, in this exact spot, and now it wasn't, which meant someone had taken it. She gripped the cushions and launched them across the room with unexpected strength. The exhaustion had suddenly vanished. Resources mobilized. Troops rallied.

Her chest throbbed and welled with pressure—something inside of her needed to release—*was* releasing. A cry fled her mouth, raspy with effort, as she flipped the couch onto its side.

The spongy underbelly stared back. No journal.

"WHERE ARE YOU?" she screamed, not intending to scream. Rapid-fire breaths came in succession as the air in her lungs wore thin.

"Aloe?"

She turned. It was Bibs—it was everyone, standing at the entrance to her condo. She knew exactly what she looked like, and could almost see herself in third person: feral and overheating, heavy breaths, wild eyes.

Shit.

Hot tears came, fast and streaky. "I've been robbed," she cried. "*Robbed.*"

"Oh gosh," Franny replied, rushing in for a hug. Aloe leaned into her chest: a frail prison of bones that smelled of seawater and floral perfume, then broke away.

Bob paced, visibly distraught. "Jesus, robbed? *Here?* What the hell did they take?" His eyes landed on hers. "Don't worry. Security will catch those mother fuckers. The whole place is surveilled. I mean, the *balls.* Seriously."

"Call your concierge," Westley offered. "Let's get an investigation underway, pronto."

Her stomach turned. Amir was the last person she wanted to involve, considering he was also a prime suspect. He'd lied to her, point blank, about a woman leaving Blue Haven, and the last time she'd seen the journal, Amir was standing two feet away. The book was obscured from view—but maybe not. Maybe he'd caught a glimpse and returned later to snatch it. He had access to her condo, after all.

She stared at her friends, each of them awaiting her response and direction. Her heart was still frantic, but the locus of control was starting to return—still a tornado, but a cyclone with boundaries and focus.

"You know what," she said, drawing in air, praying for composure. "I'm starting to second guess myself. Maybe I just misplaced the object I'm looking for."

Bibs gave her a side eye. "Is it the book?"

She nodded.

Bob threw his hands in the air. "You're missing a book? That's it? *A book?*"

Franny swatted him in the shoulder. "Enough. It's probably a very important book."

"I'm sorry," he said to Aloe. "Just judging by your reaction, I thought ..."

A moment of silence descended, bordering awkward. Four pairs of eyes watched and waited, with Aloe in the center of it all, a deconstructed couch between them. The heat of the moment was stifling. She pulled at her cotton shirt. The space tightened, pressing against her: a creature trapped in her own condo, by her own accord. And that's when the moment wavered, starting with Bob.

His teeth.

In a single blink, his gleaming white veneers faded to a fermented yellow, starting at the corners. Then came rusty brown, like a sweep of deck stain, followed by holes and valleys of blackness. Razor-sharp chips indented, enamel snapping from his mouth like peanut brittle.

She gripped the side of her cotton pants, looking for something to hold onto.

This isn't real. This can't be real.

"Aloe?" Franny said.

She turned, only to discover the same set of teeth—disgusting, offensive—forming in Franny's open mouth. "You look like you're going to pass out."

Am I? She leaned against the tipped-over couch, terror swelling. She struggled to conceal the horror of it all. This wasn't a moment of slight disturbance or exhaustion, but an atomic bomb, shattering her mental state.

I'm hallucinating.

I'm fucking hallucinating.

"Aloe," Franny said, suddenly in front of her. "Talk to me, please."

"I ..." She couldn't go on. The sight of Franny's teeth stole her words: turpentine yellow and decomposing, emitting an odor so foul she wanted to vomit.

Bibs grabbed hold of her arm, keeping her stable as someone in the background called for help—Bob or Westley, she couldn't tell. Images blurred. The fear thickened, filling her like tar.

"It's okay Aloe," Bibs said. "It's going to be alright."

She tried to nod, but her neck was tight, stuck in its current position. His voice was comforting at least—a small blanket of assurance.

It's going to be alright. She stared at Bibs, trying to communicate her gratitude, until ...

MY. GOD.

In a snap second, his face was drenched in blood. A gash jutted across his forehead with such depth she could see a peak of skull: ivory and dented. Thick, red syrup streamed into his eyes, coloring the whites a dark crimson.

The sight was so appalling her body thrashed, rejecting the image. She screamed—someone screamed. She couldn't differentiate what was happening to whom. The world had officially scattered apart, her sanity included.

Everything.

Nothing.

It ended with blackness.

Chapter Twenty-Eight
Day Six

"How are you feeling?" Doctor Marks asked.

The words fluttered like moths, just out of reach. Aloe cracked her tight jaw, sluggish. She glanced around the room: pale gray walls; inspirational throw pillows; a photograph of beach stones, half washed with sea foam.

If her emotional capacities weren't stunted with meds, she might have walked out. But alas, the groggy droll of sedatives kept her planted in the same green, polyester chair she'd sat in days before. Except this time, she was a real patient—one that required disabling with psychotropic drugs, apparently.

"Aloe?"

She focused on Doctor Marks, slowly coming around.

"I'm okay," she replied. "Embarrassed, but okay."

Doctor Marks pressed her lips together: a therapist's version of sympathy. "What do you think happened last night?"

Scenes replayed like flash cards. *The missing journal. A whirlwind of emotions. Mentally unraveling.* In the light of day, surrounded by peaceful Feng Shui and half numbed by medication, the events felt stoic and fact-like—save the ghastly hallucinations.

Teeth rotting before her eyes. A bone-deep gash, gushing blood. Those images still made her tremble, but they had the aura of a very bad dream. None of it was real, obviously, and probably induced by lack of sleep to some degree. She'd pulled all-nighters before, working back-to-back shifts at the diner, and had suffered mental consequences as a result: sounds bending, voices warping, colors bleeding at the edges. Never so extreme, but still. It wasn't outside the realm of possibilities.

Doctor Marks unfolded her legs and leaned forward. "Aloe?"

"Sorry," she replied. "What was the question again?"

"What do you think happened last night?"

"I was upset," she replied. "And I probably overreacted. I haven't been sleeping well, I'll admit that."

"Can you walk me through what you were thinking when I arrived specifically?"

She blinked slowly, buying time. Problem was, she didn't remember much of that, only what Franny had told her thirty minutes ago. *We called for help. Doctor Marks came—she administered something to calm you down, help you sleep. You've been having trouble sleeping, right? I agreed to stay with you overnight, but she needs to see you now, in the Hexagon.*

Franny's details were sparse for a reason. She was trying to be kind. Nobody wants to tell the crazy person how crazy she acted.

"Aloe." Doctor Marks leaned forward again. *How much farther can this woman lean?* "Do you want *me* to tell you what I saw when I arrived last night?"

No thanks. Of course, Doctor Marks was already answering the rhetorical question.

"I saw a woman in profound distress. Does that seem accurate to you?"

Her eyes met the window. Another balmy day in paradise. And here she was, in a psychiatrist's office. *How did this happen?*

"You aren't wrong," she admitted.

"My office is a safe space, Aloe. I want you to feel comfortable here. I won't betray your trust, I promise." Doctor Marks shifted back in her seat, crossing her legs again. "And we don't have to talk about your childhood."

Aloe bit her thumbnail. Realistically, she could use a few sessions of therapy—that was pretty obvious at this point, wasn't it? But even though Doctor Marks seemed nice, blind trust was no easy feat. *I won't betray your trust. I promise.* You know who else made a promise? Amir, and he was lying. Her mind wavered, too analytical for its own good. She felt sane at the moment—groggy, but keeping it together. Maybe her mental health was off around the edges, but there was something equally off about Blue Haven. There was a needle in this haystack, and she owed it to herself—and Eloise—to find the truth. No more beating around the bush.

"You saw a woman named Eloise," she blurted. It came out boldly, as she'd hoped, no room for objection. Her eyes glued to Doctor Marks. Any movement, subtle or otherwise, could speak volumes at this point. But the woman's face was perfectly still, a photograph across the room. After a five-count, Doctor Marks nodded.

"I did." She paused, clearly hesitant. "I shouldn't be disclosing this, as a matter of confidentiality, but I believe someone owes you an explanation. I know you read the journal."

Air fled Aloe's lungs in a swift gust. She couldn't hide her surprise. "How ..." she began, and then suddenly she knew. Doctor Marks had already told her, during their last session.

Everything is monitored.

"I ..." she continued, blubbering. "I have so many questions, I don't even know where to start."

Doctor Marks smoothed a swipe of hair behind her ear. "Of course you have questions, and I'm happy to answer them for you. I think your recent distress stems, in part, from this journal, so it's important we work through that. Together."

Aloe agreed. If there was a single source to blame for her recent spiral, the journal was certainly it: a blood thirsty mosquito, sucking happiness and enjoyment from all aspects of her new, perfect life.

"I need to know that Eloise is okay," she said. "That's what's been bothering me the most. Her journal was so ... *sad*. It's like she was trapped here, with all of her sadness, trying to escape. But she couldn't because ..." The paranoia kicked in. Was she sharing too much? Screw it. At this point, she needed answers. "It's like she wasn't allowed to escape."

Doctor Marks raised an eyebrow. "You think there's something sinister going on here, at Blue Haven? Is that correct?"

Aloe's cheeks bloomed with heat. *Well, when you put it that way ...*

"I don't blame you," Doctor Marks continued. "I currently have the journal, and I've read it myself."

"Wait, *you* have the journal?"

Another shockwave.

"I do, yes. One of the housecleaners told me she discovered it in your condo—initially assuming it belonged to you, until you informed her otherwise. It was brought to my attention because Eloise was my patient, as well as a resident. I'm still not sure how it ended up under your mattress, but it shouldn't have."

Aloe stewed for a moment, sorting her questions in order of urgency. "Okay," she said. "I need some clarity. Julian Bilbo told me that a woman left Blue Haven. Was this woman Eloise?"

"Yes, it was."

Her nerves eased slightly. One less body to keep track of. "Why did she leave?"

Doctor Marks sighed, neck dipping—a legitimate sign of disheartenment.

"I'm going to be open and vulnerable with you, Aloe, and I hope you'll do the same with me. It's not easy for me to talk about Eloise. She came to Blue Haven with diagnoses that pre-dated her admission: depression, anxiety—she wasn't well, but she was coping … until she arrived."

Aloe recalled her first few steps in Blue Haven: white sand like baby powder, an ocean view more spectacular than anything she'd ever seen, this wondrous feeling of being large and important.

"But this is paradise," she replied.

"Exactly. And for some people, paradise isn't enough. I think Eloise expected to come here and find ultimate happiness, but happiness isn't a destination."

Aloe related to this statement. She was young, newly rich, and living in the world's most exclusive condo complex—so exclusive they encased the premises with a giant wall. Yet, she'd experienced more internal chaos in the last five days than ever before. Sure, the day-to-day worries were gone (paying bills, affording groceries, fixing the goddamn radiator) but the larger, more perplexing questions remained. *What am I doing here? What's the point?*

Some people were inherently thinkers.

She was simply a thinker.

"So," Aloe said. "Eloise wasn't happy in Blue Haven, her symptoms worsened, and she left?"

Doctor Marks nodded; it was a flippy, off-kilter nod, not a straightforward *yes*. "I tried my best. I truly did. I encouraged her to write, and maybe that was my mistake. The journaling didn't help, obviously. Nothing seemed to help this woman."

The emotion in her voice was apparent, and Aloe felt sorry for Doctor Marks. At the end of the day, she was a human being like everyone else, not a robotic, sadness-processing machine. She genuinely cared about Eloise, just as Aloe had come to.

Doctor Marks continued. "Eloise needed more help than I was capable of providing in a limited, outpatient setting. She was escorted from the Blue Haven Facility and admitted to an inpatient mental-health center, where she ultimately ..." Her eyes averted, distinctly glossy. "Where she ultimately ended her life."

The grief was instant, like a slap, and Aloe yearned for a different outcome—even if she wasn't entirely surprised. The depths of Eloise's depression were boldly articulated in her journal. Aloe *still* cringed, remembering specific passages. Maybe that's why she'd gotten so attached to Eloise. She wanted to help her—just like Doctor Marks had.

But there was no helping her now. She was dead.

Aloe stared down, reflecting on the story as a whole. An emptiness settled. Was it really *that* simple? A sad woman entered Blue Haven, became sadder, left the facility as a result, and died by suicide? Toward the end, Eloise talked about being imprisoned, like she was here against her will, but what made more sense: a deeply disturbed woman had an altered view of reality, or Blue Haven was holding her hostage for zero gain?

Aloe certainly *liked* the latter story better—the one where Eloise fell privy to some larger, potentially ominous plot, and was still alive somewhere within the compound. But the truth didn't work like that.

She raised her eyes from the carpet and stared at Doctor Marks. "I was really hoping Eloise was alive. Honestly, at one point, I thought she was still here, after Amir first told me that no one had ever left—"

"Don't blame Amir," she interjected. "I told him not to discuss Eloise's departure with new residents. I wanted her memory to be dignified, not gossiped about or speculated upon. That's my fault. I encouraged him to lie, in part because I didn't think anyone would inquire so deeply. The journal was a wildcard I didn't anticipate; I assumed it was removed with the rest of her belongings."

Aloe paused, still hung up on finding the journal in her own condo. "I just don't get why it was stashed under my mattress. That doesn't make any sense."

Doctor Marks shrugged. "My best guess? Eloise broke into a vacant condo and hid it there, perhaps to avoid prying eyes—or her husband."

Right. The partner she'd referenced. "How does her husband fit into all of this? Eloise told Julian she was single and never married."

"She *was* single—and she claimed she was never married, but she was. She technically left her husband to come here, believing he was part of the problem. He wasn't though, and in her brief stay with us, she faltered between pulling him closer and pushing him further. We allowed him into the facility toward the end—a desperate attempt to remind her she was loved and cared for."

Doctor Marks combed her fingers through her hair. It was clear she didn't enjoy sharing these lingering details. "I think about Eloise every day," she added.

The tone of the room was solemn, like a funeral, and Aloe bowed her head. *A few moments of silence for Eloise.* Her heart tore for the woman, but somewhere inside, a small, selfish piece was almost … relieved.

It's over. Case closed.

There was nothing left to think about, really. Except …

"I'm sorry," she said. "This is slightly off topic, but there's no way Eloise's husband is still … here, right? He couldn't possibly be the man I spoke of earlier, the one that creeped me out?"

Doctor Marks shook her head. "Absolutely not. Trust me, a person can't just walk into Blue Haven. If he's here, we'd know."

Her chest lifted with relief. The steely eyed creeper was still a mystery, but she also hadn't seen him in a few days. Maybe he was security after all, checking in on her. Either way, she was less concerned by his existence—for the time being.

Doctor Marks glanced at the clock and folded her hands on her lap. "This has been productive. Our session is almost over, but I'd like you to come back tomorrow. Same time? Around eleven?"

Aloe nodded. "Alright, I can do that."

"Good. Now for the rest of the day, I'd like you to relax. Have you ever practiced mindfulness before? Deep breathing?"

Her eyes searched the ceiling. The words sounded familiar. "Maybe?"

"I'll program some guided relaxation onto your device. If you're up for it, I'd like you to try a few exercises. They're not difficult."

"Okay," she agreed, not opposed to the idea. She was failing miserably at unguided relaxation.

"And here." Doctor Marks passed over a bottle of pills.

Aloe froze. She wasn't a pill popper—not even close.

"I'm not comfortable with this," she said, surprised by her own assertiveness.

"It's just for sleep," Doctor Marks replied. "In case you need it."

She took the bottle and slipped it into her pocket. As much as she didn't want to take the meds, sleep was clearly an issue. She'd leave the pills by her bedside table, just in case. For a hot second, she couldn't help but think of Eloise, the words from her journal taking momentary flight.

Stash away the wife. Keep her quiet and contained.
Nice and drugged.

Chapter Twenty-Nine

"*Breathe in through your nose. Fill your belly with air.*"

Aloe did as the soothing voice instructed, pulling the ocean breeze deep inside her chest. *One Mississippi. Two Mississippi.* She awaited further instruction.

"*Breathe out through your nose. Place one hand on your belly. As you breathe in, feel your belly rise …*"

Her stomach expanded, the muscles taking on a jiggly tone. She repeated the exercise a few times, then tapped off her device. Overall, she felt lightyears better after talking to Doctor Marks, save what she'd learned about Eloise. The poor woman. Such a terrible end to an enthralling case—one that almost stole her sanity. She'd taken her sanity for granted, assuming it would always be there.

Now, she knew better.

She decided to try Gram—yet again—even if the very thought plucked a nerve. Six days inside Blue Haven, and not a single outside contact.

She activated her device with a quick tap.

"Good afternoon, Aloe," Amir said. "What can I do for you?"

The sound of his voice brought a tight, cinching guilt, right in the center of her chest. She'd been projecting a lot of anger toward Amir for lying about Eloise. Non-verbally, but still. He seemed like the sensitive type that'd pick up on that sort of thing. Based on what Doctor Marks had said, Amir was encouraged to lie. She couldn't fault him for being a good employee—for trying to honor Eloise's memory.

"Hi Amir!" She tried to be cheerful. "Can you please connect me with Gram?"

"Absolutely. One moment."

As the line started ringing, Aloe stood. Her body preemptively paced, preparing for another missed call. *Should I leave a message? What do I say at this point?* Her throat tightened with annoyance—the familiar wave of paranoia starting to rise—when suddenly Gram answered.

"Hello?"

"Gram?" she croaked, overcome with shock. "You're there."

A muffled laugh. "Hi Aloe. Where else would I be?"

"Jesus Gram." She was still pacing. "I thought ..." She stopped and drew a breath. *Breathe in through your nose. Fill your belly with air.*

"You thought what?"

"Never mind, it's not important. Just me, being silly." She grabbed a banana from the counter and peeled it open. "How are you?"

"I'm well. Yourself?"

The question stirred up a number of responses. Lately, she was a lot of things, though she settled with the generic, "I'm good, thanks."

The line went quiet for a moment. Aloe bit off a hunk of banana and tapped her fingernails along the counter. Truthfully, they weren't really that close, her and Gram—Gram being the flaky, self-aggrandizing sort that came into Aloe's life at eighteen, a solid decade after she could have really used her. Not Gram's fault; she didn't know Aloe existed. Somehow, they'd salvaged a relationship. "A" for effort.

"Gram," she said, breaking the silence. "You should see where I'm living right now. It's—"

Westley rapped on her window. She responded with a *one-second* finger. "Sorry, someone's at the door. I've been trying to get a hold of you for days, but can I call you back?"

"No problem. I'm just in the middle of packing, anyway. I'm heading to Florida! My flight is this afternoon."

"*Oh?*" She laid the banana on the counter and quickly glanced in the mirror. Good Lord. Her hair was a cry for help. She raked her fingers through a small section, getting stuck half-way. The texture was course and tangled—natural dreadlocks.

"Yeah," Gram said. "Think I'm ready for my snowbird wings."

"That's exciting," Aloe replied, her attention divided between Gram and combing through a forest of snares—a quick attempt to look somewhat presentable for Westley.

"Anyhow," Gram continued. "We'll chat soon, okay?"

"Sounds good."

Aloe prepared for their typical goodbye—a silly tradition they shared. The day they'd met, Gram was stung by a bee in the corner of her eye, causing it to swell shut. For whatever reason, this led to the nicknames *Buzz* (Gram) and *Bumble* (Aloe). Ever since, their conversations always ended the same: "Bye Bumble. Bye Buzz," and then Aloe would glow with warmth. As a kid, she'd never had a nickname. No one cared enough to give her one.

But Gram didn't say, "Bye Bumble." She just said "Bye."

The line went dead and Aloe's heart dropped. Gram never missed a Bye Bumble, and she could have used it, frankly.

She mulled some excuses. Gram was getting up there; she might have just forgotten. Or maybe she was preoccupied with packing. And then came another possibility, so ridiculous she almost laughed.

Maybe that wasn't Gram.

"Come on," she said out loud. Seriously? Of course it was Gram! But the idea—downright ludicrous, only seconds earlier—started to latch like an infection, gaining momentum.

Her heart livened. Conspiratorial? Yes. But that call was very unlike Gram—Bumble aside. Some of the finer details didn't make sense. Gram hated the sun; her dainty, Irish skin was ill-equipped to handle UV rays, just like Aloe's. The woman thrived in winter.

Snowbird wings. Gram wasn't a snowbird.

Rap. Rap. Rap.

Shit. Westley. She scurried to the side door and flung it open. "Sorry, I was just on the phone."

He gave her a quick and evaluative once-over. The heat of his eyes burned holes through her self-awareness. There was no taking back the image from last night: a spiral of strong emotions—couch flipped, breath heavy, screaming subdued (ultimately) by drugs. Her stomach pulled with shame.

"I'm so, *so* sorry about last night," she said, hoping to nip the topic in the bud.

"Don't apologize," he replied, pulling her into an unexpected hug. His embrace was so tight and warm she wanted to stay there forever. When they broke contact, he took a moment to stare at her seriously.

That part was more uncomfortable. "I came here," he said. "Because I wanted to make sure you're okay. For real."

"I am," she replied, the words rushing out of her.

His eyes narrowed. "Really?"

"Yeah, really." She spoke slower this time, more convincingly. "I saw Doctor Marks this morning and that helped. You were right to recommend her. I think the adjustment of living in a place like this— living a *lifestyle* like this—has taken a larger toll than I could have imagined."

Westley nodded. "I get it. I do."

"Here," she said. "Why don't you come in."

They congregated in the living room, Westley on one side of the back-together sectional, Aloe on the opposite. The windows were open, inviting the late afternoon sun. She debated changing the topic to something more comfortable, but it felt good to talk about her feelings with someone who understood the sorts of emotions she'd been having lately. Panic attacks, for example.

"I think," she said, forming her theory on the fly. "That I'm the type of person with a busy mind. I'm always thinking about stuff— even mindless stuff. Before coming here, I spent so much time planning for God knows what—the weekend, groceries, next year. Whatever. There aren't any distractions like that here, you know?"

"Very true." Westley leaned back, facing the ocean.

"Maybe a busy-minded person has more difficulty adjusting to this place, getting swept up in narratives that don't exist."

She was talking about Eloise, of course, without explicitly saying so. Westley nodded. Surely, he had no idea what she was talking about, but she was thankful he happened to be the type of polite soul that bopped his head to any beat.

A woman concierge approached from a few feet away, strolling up the beach with a tray of freshly squeezed juices. "Hi! We have mango passionfruit, strawberry kiwi, and lychee. Yes?"

Aloe nodded. "Yes, *please.*"

The tray came closer and Aloe grabbed a glass of lychee; Westley chose mango passionfruit.

They sat and sipped. The sweet, tangy lychee slipped down her throat as the sun warmed her toes. Less than twenty-four hours earlier, she was enduring a mental breakdown in this exact space, equipped with terrifying hallucinations that whittled her raw. Now, she was sipping on cold fruit juice, listening to guided meditation tapes, and fostering peace—with a friend. She tried to appreciate the moment.

"This is nice," she said.

"Too nice," Westley replied. "I'm going to fall asleep. Nap time for this fella." He stood and winked.

Aloe leaned back. Maybe she'd do the same.

"I'm really glad you're okay," he said. "See you tonight? We're thinking Tanto in the Hexagon. It's a Japanese sushi place."

"Love it."

He gave a quick wave, heading toward the door.

That was nice of him, to stop by and check on her. She smiled to herself—and then everything changed. The world rearranged so suddenly she couldn't make sense of it. Her eyes fixated on Westley's leg—the one he'd apparently injured. Concern filled her chest. *Holy shit, what happened?*

She stared harder, the details unmasking before her eyes. His knee was nearly severed, cut so deeply she could see his kneecap, jutting through at a strange angle—an angle bones weren't supposed to assume. Muscles peeled down his calf like fruit rinds, just hanging there, pink and glossy.

The sight was sickening and clotted her stomach. Lychee flavored bile rose up her throat as she clutched her glass, almost dropping it. The cry in her throat was muted by a larger disbelief. *What's going on? What's happening?*

She sat speechless, trying not to vomit as Westley continued toward the door. With each step, blood splattered from his wound, dribbling and dabbing, gushing at times.

And then he was gone, followed by a trail of burnt red.

She closed her eyes.

Fuck.

Chapter Thirty

Aloe pulled the silky black dress over her body, and then spun her hair into a top-knot—specifically to avoid brushing it. Sections had started to calcify, crusting over thanks to ocean salt and mousse and sweat, all bonding together. She blasted the whole mess with a douse of hairspray, hoping that would help.

This was a bad idea, going out to dinner.

She'd been spinning for hours: hands trembling over surfaces, feet pacing in various, aimless directions. *Walk it off. You're okay.* But she couldn't absolve the image of Westley's wounded leg: his raw bone, a grayish white, surrounded by gushing blood. The trail of red had since vanished from the hardwood, but she'd watched it for over an hour: shiny and dark, speckled, haunting every sense of her.

I'm going insane.

I'm legitimately going insane.

She swiped a crayon of pink lipstick over her lips and forced a smile.

No, you're not.

Suck it up, Buttercup.

In this exact, immediate second, she felt normal enough. A bit on the jittery side, but normal. Her feet were planted on solid ground. Nothing about her condo was unusual. The walls weren't shaking. Her fingers weren't forming into snakes. No signs of true insanity at the moment.

I'm fine. I'm fine. I'm fucking fine.

She stared into the mirror, addressing her reflection specifically.

You. Are. Fine.

She marched outside before she could think better of it, where Westley happened to be locking up his condo.

"Hey Aloe," he said. "Glad you're coming tonight."

Her eyes landed on his perfectly normal leg. No open gash. No gushing blood. *See? All good.* Still, her heartbeat slammed against her chest like a crane, mid demolition.

"Japanese, huh?" she said, trying to distract herself. "I've never really tried authentic sushi before."

Westley turned and grinned. "Sushi is my *favorite.*"

Aloe forced eye contact; it took every ounce of restraint not to stare at his leg, normal or otherwise.

"I'll show you the ropes," he continued. "I could see you liking tuna belly. It's a very subtle, delicate flavor."

She managed a smile.

"Hey kids!" Bob waved, heading up the cobblestone path with Franny. The dim light cast a shadow over his smile. Aloe squinted at his teeth: gray and obscured by darkness.

Franny skipped up ahead and pulled her into a bony hug. "Aloe, I'm so relieved to see you." The scent of her perfume was bold and nauseatingly floral: the familiar and comforting scent of Franny.

"Thanks," Aloe replied. "If it's alright with you, I'd prefer not to talk about last night." Typically, she wouldn't be so forward, but the last thing she wanted (or needed) was a rehash of yesterday.

Franny tilted back. "Of course."

Aloe focused on her thin brown eyes, like maple syrup. The teeth behind her fuchsia-glossed lips were white and normal, according to her peripheral vision; she refused to stare directly.

Bob caught up and gave her a head nod, his non-confrontational male way of saying, *Glad you've recovered from your moment of public insanity. Let's eat sushi.* He motioned toward the Hexagon. "Shall we? Bibs says he'll meet us there. He's still in the shower."

"Classic," Westley replied.

They walked as a group, and Aloe automatically found herself searching for the steely eyed creeper—the unidentified man she hadn't seen in days. He wasn't there as far as she could tell, but his recent absence—which should have been a relief—was suddenly the opposite. Her tongue slid across her teeth, back and forth, creating a pasty film.

What if he was never here?

What if I imagined him?

Palm trees swayed like onlookers, staring at her with suspicious and curious peepers, inviting an unwelcomed self-awareness.

Hair matted like a mutt. Wide, unfocused eyes. Haphazardly applied lipstick.

She grabbed her chin, orbited her neck, rubbed the tips of her fingers together. Her hands were going rogue, trying to grasp the ungraspable.

Franny gave her a nudge. "This probably sounds dreadfully pedestrian, but I sure hope they have a good California roll."

"For sure," Aloe replied. "I'm with you." Despite the pinch in her throat, her voice sounded polite, normal—*Right?* She searched Franny's face for concern, finding nothing. *You're seriously overanalyzing right now.* But those were just words, coming from a dictatorship being quickly overthrown by its people. Her sympathetic nervous system was officially done taking orders from above.

They mounted a few steps; Aloe focused on the ground, where there was less to see and dissect. Her ears frenzied with sound, nerves waiting, on edge. Adjacent waterfalls dripped, lights hummed, people's shoes flopped against the ground, voices babbled, bodies whooshed in the night.

Sweat dotted her forehead as they entered the Hexagon. The place was striking, per usual, but she couldn't focus. Lights shone thick from above, multicolored and moving. Music dominated, something Latin—loud and busy. *Great.*

"Friends!" Bibs shouted, just catching up. His V-neck was laughably low, which made her smile—until she remembered his bloody face: the skull-deep gash, carved into his forehead like a jack-o'-lantern. She shuddered.

Bibs smiled at the crew—until their eyes met, at which point he sighed and frowned, a well-meaning pity frown.

"Glad you're here," he said.

"Thanks," she replied, and then added, "I'm starving," begging for a topic change.

They piled into the elevator. *Up, Up, Up.* In the ten seconds it took to reach the ninety-seventh floor, Aloe tried her best to find composure. These people were her friends, and this place was extraordinary. Yes, something troubling had happened earlier with Westley—a disturbing sight—but the image wasn't real, and that moment had passed.

I'm fine. I'm fine. I'm fine.

She wiped her forehead, breezing by a swipe of crusty hair, its texture like a rose vine. *Pull yourself together, woman.*

The elevator doors opened and so came the view: a dark and lovely sky, lit with copper clouds and lingering dusk. Stars were everywhere, like glittery spray paint. The moon glowed pink and patchy, reflecting across the water.

"There's the money maker," Bob said. "That sky."

Music danced through the air, a jingle with distinctly Asian tones. A giant, golden cat dominated the center of the room: about twenty feet and protected by a small fence made of bronze chain.

Bibs posed beside the figure, giving a side tongue and rock-on hands.

"Man," he said afterwards. "I badly want a selfie with that guy."

Aloe laughed, finally starting to relax. Her body longed for chaos, but there was nothing to dissect, analyze, or catastrophize—not currently. *Thanks,* she thought sarcastically, her body like a disobedient child, finally starting to settle. *Thanks for calming the fuck down.*

A server in a blue kimono led them to a table. Aloe sat next to Bibs and Westley, admiring the open kitchen. The sightline was perfect, and she watched an assembly line of Japanese chefs working quickly and with laser focus. Around the kitchen, a moat of water brimmed with sushi boats—one of the cooler things she'd seen at Blue Haven.

"Okay," Westley said. "Who here has tried *actual* sushi?"

Everyone shook their heads—beside Bibs, who pounded his fork. "Bring on the monkfish liver! Extra points if that sucker is so raw it's still flopping on my plate."

Franny pulled her hand to her mouth. "Gosh, you're joking, right?"

Bibs winked. "Maybe."

Westley reached across the table and rested his hand over Franny's. "Yes, he's joking."

"Dear," Bob said, smirking at Bibs. "You should know better than to trust any words coming from that bloke's mouth."

Bibs laughed, ready to reply when a wooden boat of sushi arrived. One server placed it in the center of the table while another poured steamy green tea.

"Here we have *Toro*," the server said, pointing. "Also known as tuna belly, with oyster sauce and avocado. Torched mackerel with ponzu. Sea urchin wrapped in honeydew ..."

Aloe fumbled with her chopsticks, unsure how to use such tricky utensils. The spread was beautiful: shiny fingers of fish draped over rice; sauces drizzled everywhere; tight, precise rolls stacked in perfect lines.

When the server left, Westley translated the line-up into layman's terms. "For the newbies, I would suggest these guys right here, to start." He pointed toward the tuna belly.

Aloe attempted to grasp a roll with her chopsticks, ultimately stabbing it through the middle like a spear.

"I'm going primitive," she said, which drew a chuckle from the group. The validation was nice and her mood brightened. The tuna belly was far milder than she expected, soft and hardly fishy.

"Delicious," she said, going in for another. She glanced over at Bibs, who was helping himself to some of the more adventerous rolls, when she noticed his eye.

Her chopstick hit the table.

Every part of her seized.

Chapter Thirty-One

Aloe stared at Bibs, unable to properly digest the horror unfolding before her. His eye was a crude red—not partially, but fully: an exploded blood vessel. Every bit of white was covered in crimson spiderwebs. Her stomach shriveled further as the eyeball itself began to leak, like a water balloon deflating down his cheek in a pink, shiny stream, until there was nothing left but a hollow cavity. Veins tangled like barbed wire, exposed, as the gash reappeared in a single blink, parceling straight through his forehead.

She stared, gaping, at the table below, where a stream of blood was starting to pool, staining the fluffy white rice a dreadful, nauseating red. She closed her eyes, trying to stifle the image.

"Aloe?"

It was Bob. Her lids flipped open, strategically aimed at Bob—not horror-show Bibs—but the man staring back flipped her stomach. His skin was methyl yellow and shriveled like a dry apple; eyes listless, filmy. Matted facial hair clotted along his chin, gray and tinged with dust.

She couldn't hide the disgust on her face, each second exposing a shattering new discovery. *Am I dreaming? This must be a nightmare.* Her eyes traveled one place over, to Franny—or a version of Franny that lifted her sanity and tossed it aside. Franny's skin was an ashen form of jaundice, a shade of flesh that didn't belong to the living. Thin, patchy hair clumped like islands along her scalp, separated by baldness.

"Aloe," Franny said, her white, cracked lips parting to reveal a set of rotten teeth. "What's wrong?"

Aloe stood, aware of the eyes in the room, but desperate to get the hell out of there.

Here we go again. The insane woman, making another debut.

Unable to respond, she bolted toward the elevator, her body taking full control. Her mind stepped aside—a curious bystander, watching her own disembodied movements.

Fingers punch downward arrow.

Again. Again. Again.

Arms prying open elevator doors.

Legs leaping into furthest corner.

Body huddling while eyes soak in last view of stunned friends.

She looked away until the door beeped closed and the rush of downward movement stirred her stomach. *Holy shit.* Her reflection flashed on each surface of the chrome interior, and the sight of her own terror summoned a rush of hot blood. Every part of her trembled.

Ding.

The elevator opened and she dashed through the lobby, keeping her eyes on the tile floor. Amir was there, by the reception desk—she could sense him peripherally—but she refused to make eye contact.

Keep going. Don't you dare look.

She flew through the doors and into the night, breaking into a run. Her sandals thrashed against the cobblestone, threatening to snap, but she persisted. Everything was shadowy and strange in the dark—except her condo, lit and alive. Almost there.

Her thumb jammed into the fingerprint entry.

Come on! Come on! Come on!

As soon as the door released she fell inside, the safety of her own lonesome space a small relief. She struggled to breathe.

In through your nose. Fill your belly with air.

The guided relaxation advice from earlier was largely ineffective with lungs so abraded. She'd been gone fifteen minutes—maybe twenty. Was that all it took to go raging, irrevocably insane?

Apparently.

The events began to settle as a whole. Three undeniable moments of psychosis. Not one. Not two. But three.

Three.

It was silly at this point to blame stress or lack of sleep. These were legitimate, clinical features of something far greater, poisoning her mind.

And yet—

God, this is ridiculous. She gripped her hair, halting the thought in its tracks. Then a few seconds later: *What the hell.* Something about this place was off; she knew it in her gut—and she'd known it from the start. Her brain surged forward with ideas. Deranged ideas.

Or maybe not.

What if the horrifying images she'd seen earlier weren't hallucinations at all, but pieces of a larger truth—some sixth sense unclouding a great, uncommunicable horror that happened *here*, at Blue Haven, within these very walls. Surely, Eloise was a part of it. The steely eyed creeper: possibly the perpetrator—or maybe even a victim himself, coming to her as a ghostly mirage.

She treaded into the kitchen, keeping close to the walls. Her eyes pulled around the room, searching for cameras.

"I know you're watching me!" she screamed, not sure to whom. Did it matter? She was being watched—for her own protection, apparently. A small price to pay for freedom.

Freedom.

She almost laughed.

Blue Haven was the opposite of freedom: a tightly controlled community under constant surveillance, no ties to the outside world. How the staff here had managed to convince her otherwise—even for a second—was a true testament to their skilled deception.

Ugh. A sharp pressure rose up her neck, halting all conspiracies. Another headache, this one incapacitating. She continued along the wall, recalling with much gratitude the bottle of sleeping pills from Doctor Marks. Her heart lifted when she saw them sitting on the dresser.

She was, on some level, still skeptical about taking medication so willy nilly—*What* kind *of sleeping pill, and what dose?*—but the greater whole was desperate.

Please. Knock me the fuck out.

Now.

And so, she did.

Chapter Thirty-Two
Day Seven

Aloe's eyes bared open, heavy and sluggish. Everything was white—spotlight white, much like her apartment in Chicago. The gimpy sun porch, specifically, with its peeling wicker furniture and windows improperly installed in their frames. She used to nap there in the summer: a greenhouse of heat and light and flies. In the winter, she'd periodically glance at the frost-covered windows and bugs croaked on sills, venturing out a time or two for a cold thrill.

Her eyes strained to focus as the whiteness defined itself, creasing into angles and shapes. When her condo came into view, she sank. For a wonderful moment, there was a remote possibility that Blue Haven was a nightmare, and she'd been sleeping on the sunporch all along. As *if* she now craved her old apartment. *Oh, the irony.*

The tranquilizing effect of four sleeping pills was slow to lift; she didn't notice Doctor Marks at first, not until she spoke.

"Hi Aloe. I hope I didn't startle you."

The woman was sitting in the corner of the room, sipping from a mug.

"I think my startle reflex is on pause," she replied, her words coming out a bit clumsy. "You know that story about the tortoise and the hare? I'm currently the tortoise."

Doctor Marks looked contemplative. "And last night, were you the hare?"

Aloe winced. Lately, her life was unfolding like a series of benders. A regretful performance under the influence of temporary insanity followed by guilt and shame.

"I'm guessing that's why you're here?" she asked.

"Well, when you missed our appointment this morning at eleven, I did some digging."

Aloe glanced at her device. *Yikes.* It was three in the afternoon.

"Your friends are concerned about you," Doctor Marks continued. "*I'm* concerned about you, which is why I'm here, in your bedroom. To ensure your safety."

Aloe nodded, not disputing the point. They were right to be concerned. Hell, *she* was concerned. Each day ended worse than the last, a consortium of fear and paranoia cycling back and forth, without relent.

Was something sinister truly at play in Blue Haven? Her gut urged yes, but she had no evidence, just doubt and suspicion—and the inability, at this point, to discern fact from fiction. After the events of last night, she couldn't trust her own eyes—her own mind.

She stared up through the skylights, at the chubby clouds and rich blue sky. The end had come: a tipping point, and she knew it. The only way to stop the cruel, unrelenting cycle of mental torment was to leave.

It was time.

"Thanks for your concern," she told Doctor Marks. "Honestly, my initial instinct is to tell you I'm fine, but that's not true, because I'm *not* fine, and I don't think I'll ever be fine as long as I'm in here. I know this probably sounds ridiculous. Blue Haven is paradise, right? But I'd like to leave—I *have* to leave, for my own sake."

Doctor Marks blinked a few times. "I understand. These decisions are personal, but I wouldn't be doing my diligence as a psychiatrist if I didn't explore your desire to leave as a symptom of avoidance. I'm curious, do you think leaving Blue Haven will solve your current difficulties?"

Aloe sat fully, tugging at the black dress from last night, heavy with sweat. Sleep crusted in the corners of her eyes and she wiped them clean. She didn't dare touch her hair—the tightness and weight of which had gravitated to one side, stuck there like a hive made from concrete.

Doctor Marks leaned forward, her togetherness so apparent, by contrast: a pressed beige pantsuit, methodical blush, structured brown curls—the sort of curls a person ran pomade over, section by section, one spiral at a time. "Before you answer my question," Doctor

Marks added. "Let's backtrack. What *are* your current difficulties? I'm getting a sense that your recent distress is far greater than what you shared with me yesterday."

"Possibly," she replied. The need for psychiatric help was undeniable at this point, and disclosing her hallucinations to a professional was probably advisable. Still, the skeptic inside her could not be silenced. *What if this information is used against me?*

"I've been troubled by disturbing images lately," she replied, keeping the wording vague. "To do with my friends here."

"What sort of disturbing images?"

"Horror-movie stuff, I guess. Blood, gore, injuries. I have no idea why."

Doctor Marks sipped her drink; the impression of her beige lipstick formed a hook on the edge of her white mug. "Have you experienced any horrific ruminations like this prior to Blue Haven?"

Aloe shook her head.

"I see. So, it makes sense to you that Blue Haven is the issue, and leaving this facility will absolve you of your mental difficulties. Not terrible logic."

Aloe thought of Eloise, her departed … *friend*, honestly, is how she remembered her, even though they'd never met. Eloise ran from her problems, hoping they'd be different in a place like Blue Haven, except they weren't.

Aloe wasn't depressed exactly, just troubled by visions she couldn't understand. But weeks from now? Months? Sadness was a lot like ivy. Harmless at first, until it covered every inch of you.

She squirmed between the sheets, reeling with indecision. As her thoughts began to drift in line with Doctor Marks—*Stay, work out your problems*—she lifted the comforter and swung her legs to one side.

"Can you excuse me for a second?" she asked. "I have to go to the bathroom."

"Of course, please."

She skirted by Doctor Marks, pressing down the crumples in her dress.

Inside the en suite, with the door closed and locked, she pulled her lucky coin from the top drawer. It wasn't *really* lucky; she'd never leave a decision so important to chance or superstition. But chance, she knew, had a way of drawing out a person's real feelings. If you flipped the wrong choice, your gut would let you know.

She stared at the copper circle, rubbing it between her fingers.

Heads, I stay.

Tails, I leave.

Her thumb flicked the coin into air, where it spun before landing in her palm. She flopped it over, revealing the surface.

Heads.

I stay.

Her stomach pulled, sharp and harsh—an internal tug in the opposite direction. *Do. Not. Stay. Here.* She wasn't overly surprised by this reaction; her head and gut were at odds when it came to Blue Haven, constantly battling for control. Regardless, the point of this exercise wasn't to spiral deeper into confusion, it was to be decisive.

Trust your gut.

She stood, avoiding her reflection on the way out. No need to confirm her appalling appearance.

Back in the bedroom, she sat on the edge of the bed. "Okay," she said, rousing her shoulders, still sore and bent from sleep. "I appreciate what you're saying, about staying and working through my recent challenges." *Or whatever the hell they are.* "But I have to go. I hope you understand. I need to leave this place as soon as possible."

Doctor Marks gave a slow, single nod. "Alright."

Moments passed, thick with silence. The mood took an odd, almost chilly turn, and Aloe swung her feet impatiently. Now that she'd made up her mind, she wanted to leave *now*. Right now.

"So, what happens next?" she asked, surprised that Doctor Marks hadn't supplied any further commentary. "I can have my things packed in less than an hour if I'm able to—"

"Aloe."

The way she said *Aloe* was stern, assertive. "Is there any way you would reconsider? I really want to help you—and I truly think I can, but you have to let me."

"Thanks," she replied briskly, not interested in reconsidering. "I appreciate everything you've done, honestly. This isn't about you." She paused, shifting the mood away from impassive breakup. "It's hard to explain, but I don't feel … *right* here. Whether or not I have unresolved issues is another matter, and maybe those will catch up with me eventually, but right now—in this exact moment—my body is telling me to leave. I think I should listen."

"Okay." Doctor Marks sighed. "I can't stop you, of course, but we will need to make arrangements."

Aloe's chest drew forward. "Arrangements?"

"Yes, this is *Blue Haven*. You can't just hitch a taxi ride."

"Okay," she replied, worried by this new direction. "What do I have to do?"

"Well, we will need to orchestrate a proper exit interview, conduct a medical evaluation, discuss financial reimbursement, schedule your flight." She paused, staring at the ceiling. "I think that's all?"

"Timeline?" Aloe asked nervously.

"A few days, at least."

"*What?*" Her body jerked forward. "I can't stay here that long!"

Doctor Marks frowned. "I'll try and expedite the process for you, but this is new to us, having a resident formally depart. The only person who's left Blue Haven was Eloise, and under very different circumstances." She paused, her face emblazoned with concern. "Aloe, do you believe you could be a danger to yourself?"

"No," she replied, confident. She'd been seeing things that didn't exist, an obvious issue, but she wasn't *a danger to herself*. No risk of self-harm or anything like that.

Doctor Marks tilted her head, clearly trying to assess her honesty. How many of her patients had answered that question deceptively?

Was Eloise one of those patients?

Aloe leaned back against the headboard. Faintness swept through her like a draft. You'd think eighteen hours of sleep would relieve a person of exhaustion, but apparently not. She couldn't fathom any more days in Blue Haven—seven was enough, somehow rendering her a scared, shaking animal, hiding in her own condo. *What next?*

Eloise came to mind.

She rolled her shoulders, everywhere aching with fatigue and frustration. "So, I'm just supposed to wait this out? Is that the plan? *Please*, will you help me?"

Doctor Marks stood. There was something dragging on her gait—maybe the same exhaustion and sense of defeat Aloe felt.

"I'll do my best Aloe, and that's all I can do."

Chapter Thirty-Three
Day Eight

It was four in the afternoon and Aloe sat on the couch: stiff, unmoving, eyes darting constantly to her device, waiting—praying—for a buzz. She hadn't heard from Doctor Marks in twenty-four hours, almost to the hour. It was nearly 4 p.m.

She'd barely slept and the exhaustion, while crippling, had morphed into a hazy, sweeping lull, an almost euphoric edge settling. The *click, click, click* of the ceiling fan had become a timeless preoccupation, and she listened to the melodic rhythm pulsing like some sort of deconstructed jazz.

Her eyes shifted to the side door, the lack of visitors a great relief. Westley had come, so too had Bob, Franny, and Bibs, each stopping by at different intervals while Aloe peered from inside, too afraid and embarrassed to show her face. What was she supposed to say? *Sorry I acted like a complete maniac ... again, but your blood-seeping gash and leaking eyeball and half-dismembered leg and rotten teeth all very much concerned me.*

Instead of answering the door, she'd crouched in the corner: firm, planted, obscured from view. The last thing she needed was a glimpse of something terrifying, mid-conversation, or a full-serving of pity. To chase away the clash of feelings bubbling in her chest, she'd gripped her hair—tight, like a lasso—and pulled, again and again, her fingers barely secured around the crusty knot. The pain was sharp, wonderful.

Now, her stomach panged with hunger, except she didn't want to eat, the appeal of it gone entirely. She watched the ocean through a hairline crack in her otherwise shut-in space: windows covered and sky-lights closed, just a few pot lights on in the kitchen.

The ocean continued to coat the shore, ultimately pulling back into itself. An infinite cycle. *Those poor waves,* always trying to move forward, only to end up in the exact same place.

She shuddered, aware of the metaphor.

I need to get out of here.

Now.

She tapped on her device.

"Hi Aloe." It was Amir, and the sound of his voice both annoyed and relieved her. This was the fifth time they'd spoken today.

She went to speak, but he beat her to the punch. "I know you're waiting patiently. I still don't have any updates, but I promise, the second I find out anything more, I'll call you—"

Before he could finish, she hung up, expecting as much but hoping otherwise.

Her legs lifted and she started to pace, grappling with the weight of such profound, personal change in just over one week: everything stripped from her grasp—stability, security. Only days earlier, she'd moved through her life, assured by reality: a world governed by rules and physics, navigated through sight. Her eyes could be trusted. Seeing was believing.

Now though, she couldn't be certain of anything. *Question it all.* That was her new motto, thoughts included.

When it came to Blue Haven, there was so much to digest—too much. The eerie sparsity and isolation. A wall that kept them unknowingly hostage like figurines in a snow globe. Eloise's journal: a diary or prophecy? The steely eyed creeper: real, or imagined? Gram's strange behavior—perhaps not her grandmother at all. The hallucinations: delusions or premonitions?

Is something terrible going to happen?

Has it already?

Her body longed to hit reset, to return to a less complicated era days earlier.

She pushed her arms into a stretch, the muscles in her back loosening. "I can't do this anymore!" she yelled. The echo of her voice curbed the silence, its pitch almost unrecognizable. A divide was happening: her body and mind, disinhibiting from one another. Breaking apart like shifting continents.

She nibbled on her fingernails, long overgrown and chipped with polish. One by one she trimmed them down, spitting the scaly, crescent-moon remnants onto the floor. She continued to glance at her device, each minute an endless stretch of torture.

People often complained about time. *Slow down time! Where has the time gone?* Who knew the answer was so simple?

To slow time, all you need to do is wait.

Second by second.

And suffer.

Chapter Thirty-Four

Aloe opened the door and peered into the night. She couldn't endure another second of self-imposed quarantine. Hours had passed, and she'd done little but stare at her device, waiting.

Come on! Just buzz.

Please.

Fucking buzz already.

Get me out of here!

Sleep would have been nice, of course, but her body seemed incapable of resting. Too much adrenaline. Always. Even in the quietest, loneliest moments, it was still there: coursing through her veins, encouraging her to stay woke. *Look. Listen. Be alert.*

Now, she was incredibly alert. The air was sharp in her lungs and her feet slipped through the cool sand as she approached the vacant condos.

Her eyes adjusted to the dim glow of moonlight and, of course, the Hexagon, still illuminated, just faintly. Palms swayed, slow and spooky; everything else was still—as expected, at three in the morning.

The vacancy was nice, disinhibiting, and she prowled like a nocturnal animal, coming alive in the darkness. The chances of running into Bob, Franny, Bibs or Westley were slim, and as much as she loved her friends, she couldn't stand the idea of facing them—not now, after how she'd behaved.

The exhaustion in her bones had officially metamorphosed, like a werewolf at full moon. She wanted to howl, to feel the sound expanding in her lungs. The experience of energy, with all its dips and valleys, continually surprised her. Apparently, she didn't need food or rest.

The clouds seemed angry: sharp and large in the sky. She turned toward the ocean, where moonlight reflected across the water in one long, lovely beam, casting light like a spaceship, inviting her closer.

She sunk her feet into the warm liquid and considered a swim. *How far would I get before hitting the wall?* The other side existed, somewhere, waiting in the black, bleak beyond. They were encaged, all of them, and she almost laughed at the fact she'd paid twenty million dollars to come here.

Her legs pulled forward, slipping deeper and deeper, slowly deeper, until the water reached her waist. The black dress from days ago puffed against the surface like a sloppy umbrella and she kept going, becoming weightless, inch by inch.

When the water reached her neck she paused, overcome by a soft-spoken thought that landed gently, easily.

What if you just slipped beneath the water?

And that was all.

Days earlier, a thought like this would have shaken her immeasurably, but tonight it came like a piece of advice, and the idea of it almost eased her; a way out she hadn't considered. Not that she was prepared to do something so … dramatic.

Or was she?

She dipped a little further, letting her nostrils grow slick and wet. *How long would it take, start to finish?* Probably not long. Drowning was fast, wasn't it? A minute, maybe two. A few big gulps into the lungs …

"Stop!"

A voice rang through the air and she whipped around. Her heartbeat rumbled as a shadow by the shore came into focus.

The steely eyed creeper!

A moment passed before he turned, briskly, like he'd made a mistake calling out.

"Wait," Aloe yelled, her many apprehensions overshadowed by a need for answers. She sliced through the water, moving as fast as she could.

"Hey!" she yelled again, flopping onto the shore like a fresh calf. She cinched the heavy, soaking dress at her thighs and stood. "Hold on!"

The man glanced back, a look of dismissal on his face, then he picked up the pace.

She began to sprint.

Her feet whipped through the sand, soundless; her vision throbbed with speed as she gained on him. When her soles hit the cobblestone, he turned, eyes wide with shock. Her speedy arrival had surprised him, clearly, and for a moment he seemed panicked.

She leapt in front, blocking his body. Each breath was weak, shallow, but her muscles felt strong—ready to tackle this man, if needed.

"Who are you?" she demanded.

His face remained unreadable and she took in his dense blue eyes and rough skin. A few remnants of childhood acne pickled his cheeks. His hair was golden-gray, an aging blond, and something about him brought forth an agony so tense she clutched her chest. As quickly as the feeling came, it left.

"Who are you?" she asked again, this time less aggressively. He seemed—of all things—a little scared of her now. And maybe he was right to be. Something uncontainable and dangerous had been lit, and this fiery ball of emotion was not easily contained.

"I'm nobody," he replied. "I do groundskeeping and deal with tech issues."

"HA!" She laughed. "*Right*. I saw you watching me the other day, while I slept. What sort of *tech issue* was that about?"

"Watching you?" He stared at the sky, clearly trying to remember. "Oh, right. I wasn't watching you, I was fixing your router. I didn't mean to pry, but you left the blinds open and these places are all windows. I wanted to apologize, but you didn't seem very ... amenable."

Her skin tightened. She hadn't expected an answer so ... sensible. "Okay." Her mind spun, looking for other holes to poke. "Well, what are you doing out here so late? Why were you watching me in the water just now?"

"I usually work late. It's less disruptive to residents. I saw you out there and I was worried. I didn't want you going too far. I mean, it's dark out. Maybe I shouldn't have said anything. If so, I apologize."

She searched his face for anything revealing: a glance away, a hard swallow. Nothing. *Oh God*. Her head began to spin, filling with doubt. What if this man was exactly who he said he was? *Why would he be anything else?*

Her jaw clenched, embarrassment rising up. "*Oh*."

He frowned—textbook pity. His face was a sobering reflection of her own disturbance and she couldn't bear the sight.

Before he could say anything further, she turned and ran in the direction of her condo, feet pounding against the cobblestone. Her face throbbed with tight, hot blood. *I'm such an idiot.*

She jammed her thumb into the fingerprint detector and burst inside, instantly slamming the door behind her. The hard panting of her own breath echoed in the lonely space. The gasket of energy in her chest was nearing release, and she had no idea what that looked like.

"Let me out of here!" she screamed, in part referring to her own imprisoned body. She clawed her fingernails deep into her palms, enjoying the pain—a deserved punishment for her own discord. All the fear and suspicion and hatred she'd felt toward Blue Haven shifted inward; the revolver turning on herself.

What the hell is wrong with you?

She flopped onto the couch, repulsed by her own scent: damp and sour. A chill fluttered up her arms as the air conditioning cooled her wet skin. Every part of her was uncomfortable in some way: trillions of cells, shaking with friction. She imagined exiting her own body, becoming a formless mound of human Jell-O. Pathetic. Worthless.

As her body coiled to conserve warmth, memories surged forward—ones she hadn't thought about in years. Remnants of families she'd floated through. Billy with the silver braces. An older couple, she couldn't remember their names, but recalled their faces: bent and shriveled, like dried apricots. A nun named Belle. Horris, the touchy one, who smelled like old-world cigars. A hand moving in the dark.

These memories came in dodges, avoiding one led to finding another, until a pair of eyes prevailed. The surge of adrenaline stopped as their color sharpened: a light, vibrant blue.

Something about those eyes brought comfort.

A passage from Eloise's journal arose, a description of her son's eyes.

I still see his eyes when I shut mine: freakishly teal and arresting.

Aloe had no idea how these words were connected, if at all, to the vision in her mind, but it didn't matter. A *click* sounded, followed by a swipe of air. Her limbs stiffened.

Someone had opened the door.

Chapter Thirty-Five

Aloe stood, fingers shaking but the rest of her paralyzed. The steely eyed creeper—the man claiming to be tech support—was standing inside of her condo. The door behind him was shut. He came forward with caution.

"Don't come any closer!" She thrust out her arm, remembering the device on her wrist. She tapped its surface. *Pat, pat, pat, pat, pat, pat,* each press more urgent than the last.

The screen was blank, unresponsive.

"Amir!" she yelled, hoping he could hear her somehow. "AMIR!"

"It's alright," the man said, reaching forward in a careful, assuring way. "I'm not going to hurt you." His face was calm, unthreatening—a guise, surely.

She dashed to the back wall and slammed the button that opened her condo to the rest of Blue Haven. Westley was fifteen-feet away, at most. Her legs were tense and amped, ready to bolt toward Number Four. But instead of watching the partition of windows disappear, nothing happened.

She pressed the button again and again, slamming it with her palm.

"What have you done?" she asked, knowing the man must have tampered with the electrical system.

He took a step closer.

"HELP!" she screamed. "Somebody help me!"

"They can't hear you," he said.

Shit.

Shit. Shit. Shit.

Every part of her trembled: a human clothes dryer, reverberating. "Get the hell out of my house," she said, trying to sound confident, even though her voice box was strangled by her own heartbeat. She scanned the space for options, thoughts moving at a snappy, urgent pace.

Knives in drawer.

Vase on coffee table.

Dive through window.

She eyed the large pane of glass adjacent to the couch, and in a split-second moment of judgment decided to go for it.

Her legs dashed in long strides, driven by impulse. As she neared the glass, her knees sprung, propelling her through the air as she braced for impact—arms in, face turned, shoulders forward, legs back—ready to accept the jarring pain of severed glass, slicing through her skin.

Instead, a *thud* punched her side, and she collapsed onto the ground, lungs folding like a used tent. The force was blunt and she heaved for air.

"Oh my God," the man said, coming closer. "Are you okay?"

"Stop!" she managed, dizzy and still wheezing.

"Let me help you."

"Don't move!"

He stood his ground. She glared, thankful he was listening. The entire right side of her body throbbed, rocked by an unbreakable window. She was weak, vulnerable—and now injured. A quiet moment passed and she collected her bearings, trying to move past the pain.

"Get out of my house," she said again.

"I know you're scared," the man replied. "But I'm trying to help you, I promise." He paused. "*Please.*"

Her throat lodged. She swallowed hard, and that was all. Words seemed ungraspable.

"Look," he said, bringing a shiny black device—a tablet or something similar—to the forefront. "There's something you need to see, but I don't want to startle you. So, I'm going to move very slowly and set this on the kitchen island, is that alright?"

Every part of her body ached, further seized by confusion. She couldn't move, not even to nod.

"Alright," he said softly, taking one step. "Here I go, nice and slow."

He lagged forward, maintaining the wide-open stance of someone unarmed. When he reached the counter, he set down the slender tablet and backtracked toward the door, sloth-like.

His head tilted in the direction of the island. "Whenever you're ready."

She willed her body to liven, provoked by this strange turn of events.

"What's this about?" she asked, still unconvinced the man was trying to help her—that anyone was trying to help her. She hadn't heard from Doctor Marks in days. Her device was disconnected—no sign of Amir. Her condo was on lock-down. She was trapped, abandoned, left to fend for herself.

Her hand inched toward the heavy ceramic vase, the closest feasible weapon. It wasn't ideal, but at least it was something.

"It's a message from Eloise," the man blurted.

Her neck jerked. *Eloise?* "That's impossible," she replied. "Eloise is dead."

"That's not true," he said.

A throbbing pressure formed behind her eyes, coupled with the pain in her right side, now a dull ache. The confusion was unbearable. Who was a more trustworthy source of information: Doctor Leslie Marks, a respected psychiatrist, or a strange man who'd entered her condo and was seemingly holding her hostage?

"Why should I believe you?" she asked.

He glanced toward the counter. "Why don't you see for yourself?"

The tightness in her lungs eased. Could this man be telling the truth? Or was the tablet some sort of tactic—a way of keeping her distracted long enough to make a move.

On the other hand, if he *really* wanted to make a move, he hardly needed a tablet.

She had every right to assume this man was dangerous, but she'd been searching for answers, to the point of literal insanity. If the mysterious device contained any information about Eloise or Blue Haven, fetching it was worth the risk.

She slid across the hardwood, feather light and cautious, eyes locked firmly on the steely eyed creeper. She refused to break eye contact until the tablet was safe in her grasp. He looked different under artificial lighting, less edged with shadows. His eyes were an industrious blue and his stance was unassertive, almost timid.

Something instinctual—like a hunch, but deeper and more rooted—told her this man was here to help, as he'd said; but the fact remained.

Could she even trust herself?

"Who are you?" she asked.

He stared at the ground, like he wasn't sure how to answer that question. "I'm Jack," he replied.

A moment passed.

That's it?

"I need more than just your name. You're obviously not tech support and maintenance. So why are you here? What do you know about Eloise?"

He sighed. She could sense the exhaustion in his stance, a feeling she knew all too well. "I'm sorry. This is really complicated, but if you start by pressing on that screen, I think you'll find the answers you're looking for."

She brought her finger to the dark surface, then hesitated.

"Trust me," he said, and the softness in his voice caused such a familiar, unexplainable warmth she *did* trust him—for the time being at least.

"Fine," she replied.

She tapped on the screen, ready for some fucking answers.

Chapter Thirty-Six

An empty stage came forward: navy curtains, select lighting, followed by the words "Dr. Eloise Price" written in the upper left-hand corner. A title appeared on the screen. *"Overcoming the Unbearable."*

Aloe recognized the format—a TED talk.

A suited woman walked on stage with a wire-thin microphone strapped across her fine-boned cheek. Her hair was large, frenzied: curls left to their own devices. She was wearing a pair of thick-rimmed glasses and soft beige lipstick.

Aloe's jaw tightened; this small, pale, sharp-eyed woman—Eloise, apparently—was not who she expected. And yet, there was a pull of recognition in her gut; a strange sense of knowing without really knowing.

Eloise reached the center of the stage and beamed. She gave a quick, leaky smile, then addressed the audience, now quiet and awe-stricken, a definite sense of esteem diffusing.

"I want to tell you about a man named Jimmy," Eloise said, starting to pace. "I'll stick to the CliffsNotes here. Jimmy had a rough start in life. Unstable mother who liked uppers. Abusive, alcoholic father. Remarkably poor. Blessed with personality features one might call anti-social. *Impoverished upbringing*, in sum.

"Nevertheless, Jimmy made valiant attempts to move forward—onward and upward. He graduated high school, lived independently, and took a job in construction. He made friends—limited, but some. All very promising, until a single moment rendered these efforts insignificant. Six days after Jimmy turned twenty-nine, an improperly secured steel pipe dropped onto the hull of his back, fracturing his spine."

Eloise frowned for a moment.

"I started providing Jimmy psychiatric help a year later, after a suicide attempt. He was my first patient, and we were approximately the same age. His primary diagnoses were posttraumatic stress disorder, anxiety, depression, and chronic pain. We ended up working together for almost a decade—*nearly ten years*—exhausting treatment option after treatment option: various forms of psychotherapy, drug trials, brain stimulation, retreats, micro dosing—all to no effect. Negligible improvement, at best, and always temporary.

"In the end, Jimmy and I had a frank conversation—one of the more difficult discussions I've had professionally. He described his life as a hollow and meaningless trap; a painful course of time he could no longer stand to endure, despite everything we'd done. Blood, sweat, and tears. He asked me: *Doc, is this as good as it gets?*"

A look of devastation swept across her face.

"I told him we'd find something else, not to lose hope—that life is not a happiness factory, it takes work. But he knew as well as I did the answer was yes. We'd reached the bottom of the barrel; there was nothing left to offer."

For the first time, Eloise looked away from the audience and stared at the floor. "Jimmy took his life three days later."

After a long moment of silence, she returned with a weak smile. "Jimmy—and many other patients just like him—are the motivation for what I'm unveiling to you today. Thanks to a world-renowned group of doctors, neuroscientists, and developers—my esteemed teammates—we can offer marginalized, treatment-resistant patients suffering deeply from mental-health conditions a good life, *a fantastic life!* The sort of life they truly deserve."

Thunderous clapping began and Eloise paused to smile fully. Skin creased around her bright eyes.

"The pilot project I'm going to present to you, a facility called *Blue Haven*, is unlike anything the world has ever seen. It's a beautiful marriage of virtual-reality and neurotechnology that will provide patients like Jimmy *a new life*—literally, via alterations of visual and neural activity in real time."

Eloise shifted to one side, allowing a holographic image of a net-like structure descending over a three-dimensional brain to project upward from center stage.

"This is a neural net," she said. "A miraculous device that's implanted over the surface of the brain in order to stimulate and control brain activity. Specifically, we achieve this by utilizing electrochemical regulation and optogenetic beams of light in order to instantly improve mood, monitor the release of neurotransmitters and amino acids, maintain healthy profiles of functioning, and both eradicate and supplement one's own memories."

Eloise paused, letting the audience catch up.

"In short, once our neural net is implanted on the surface of the brain, invisibly hidden beneath the scalp, it attempts to turn a sick mind into a healthier one."

The three-dimensional brain began to pulse with rainbow-colored beams of light that flashed forward into the audience. People gasped and clapped as the holographic projection morphed into a human being, and began to walk across the stage.

"Wonderful, isn't it? Now, our neural net—despite its impressive capabilities—is not all Blue Haven has to offer. One cannot alter the mind, without altering the environment. We also offer our patients state-of-the-art virtual reality—created by some of the world's best 3D videogame developers—worn as a contact lens over the eye. The two devices in tandem are incredibly powerful, enabling us to upgrade the visual world in the eye of the beholder—even one's *own* appearance. *Imagine?* A mental-health facility that not only teaches the brain to function better, but does so in a beautiful utopia? In Blue Haven, this is precisely the goal: enabling people to not only move past their mental-health impairments, but thrive in an environment that's built to ensure happiness."

Eloise leaned forward, like she was letting the audience in on a secret.

"Why fix your old life, when you can have a new one?"

"—Temporarily of course," she added, after a pause. "Patients will ultimately transition back into society, after their brains have properly healed. Imperatively, their stay in Blue Haven—be it months or years—will not be a tumultuous amount of hard work and suffering, like therapy, but a wonderful healing experience filled with joy and abundance. In short, paradise on earth."

The video stopped mid scene.

Aloe shifted her focus back to Jack. He was quiet as she bridged this new information with the present moment. Her eyes darted, everything cast in a filmy haze of sudden doubt: the pearly countertops, a sherbet colored sky lifting through the darkness, a palm-fringed view of paradise unraveling.

Jesus.

Is any of this real?

She leaned onto the couch for balance, weakness ragging.

When Jack stepped forward, she didn't stop him; the fight in her was gone, replaced by an unexpected numbness: a body on overdrive, shutting down.

"So ... Eloise *is* alive," she managed, her voice bleak.

He nodded.

"Well ... where is she now?"

The reaction Jack gave was a disassembling of sorts, each feature breaking in unison. His silver-blue eyes glossy with tears.

"Sweetheart, *you're* Eloise."

Chapter Thirty-Seven

Two Months Earlier

Jack poured a heavy-handed glass of wine. He took a slug, the sort of gulp one might reserve for drinking water in a drought, and cringed at the bitterness. The sour-bodied elation was almost instant. A nice lift from his heavy, dampened mood. He was a lightweight when it came to alcohol; never much of a drinker.

He peered into the dining room, where his wife, Eloise—or Ellie, as he called her—was hunched over a scatter of papers. She twirled a pen effortlessly through her long skeletal fingers. He'd always been impressed by that seamless motion; her tell for deep thought.

For a while he just watched her, trying (unsuccessfully) to ignore the boulder of concern pressing against his chest. He was undeniably nervous. Their upcoming conversation would be unbearable: discussing Ellie's admittance to Blue Haven ... *for a second time.*

"How long have you been standing there?"

The question caught him off guard. He shook his head, returning to the moment.

"Sorry," he replied, unsure if a husband was obliged to apologize for standing in the vicinity of his wife, observing. It seemed like all he did these days was apologize. *I'm sorry none of this is working. I'm sorry we can't fix you.*

He approached the dining room table and sat. Ellie collected the documents in several piles, keeping them tight and rigid. She'd always had a dignified way of doing things, even now, her hair paradoxically slick with grease and dandruff, face patchy with dryness, a floppy sweater—*his* sweater, days-old—draped from one shoulder; her body trapped in a globe of sadness, keeping him at bay. He didn't care about any of this, and loved her all the same.

But he wasn't looking at his wife.

He was looking at major depression.

"I've worked out a new protocol," she said. Her mouth upturned, one of the first smiles he'd seen since her discharge from Seaside Recovery, an inpatient facility on the East Coast.

She'd stayed there for the better part of nine months, making insubstantial gains after the catastrophic failure that was Blue Haven, Round One. Seaside Recovery was his idea, and he'd sent her there against her will, hoping for a miracle.

By now, he knew better than to believe in miracles.

"*Oh?*" He took a long, lingering sip of wine. "And how does this protocol differ from the first protocol?"

Her eyes narrowed in response to his snappy tone. At one point, he'd agreed to be supportive, but that was easier said than done. Admitting a principal investigator to their own experiment seemed ill-advised the *first* time around, let alone the second.

She tapped a fat stack of documents, her fingernails bitten painfully short. The top page touted a title he'd read a hundred times over. Hell, he'd basically crafted it. *Blue Haven: An Experimental Pilot Project Employing Neurotechnology and Virtual Reality to Reinstate Normal Functioning and Instill "Happiness."*

"Unlike the first attempt," she began. "I'm recommending a more ... subtle tweak to my persona, for starters."

"As in?"

"I think I'd like to be myself, just younger. Twenty-five seems like a good age."

"Twenty-five? Are you sure about that? Weren't you awfully ... introverted and uncertain about life in your twenties?"

Ellie shrugged. "Who isn't? I think it'll be good for me. You can reconfigure my visual filter from old photos. Less memories to hamper. That will certainly make things easier on your end."

"*Ha.*" He didn't mean to laugh, but couldn't help it. The task ahead: experimentally reprogramming his own wife as a last-ditch effort to save her from herself was the antithesis of easy in every imaginable sense. *Easier on your end* was the understatement of the year.

"I'm sorry," he said. *There I go, apologizing again.* "This is tremendously difficult for me—you know that."

She frowned. "Trust me, I know."

Her formerly bright eyes, an almost seafoam green against the mahogany walls of their dining room, were now pallid, dull. In moments like these he could feel the powerful reach of her sadness, pulling him into despair. The photo hanging over the mantel—their son, twelve-years-old, at the end of Grade Seven—almost stole his gaze, but he refused to let it. There wasn't room for his grief in this household.

He reached for her hand: clammy, pale, malnourished—much like the rest of her. "So, we'll make you younger, but you'll still be … *you*, more or less."

She nodded. "Precisely. Less opportunity for neural rejection."

When it came to altering Ellie's persona, they'd been too drastic the first time around, giving her a new profession and an entirely contrived past: a single, successful lawyer from New York. They'd done too much too soon, and the experience was messy and difficult to manage—especially given Ellie's vast, insider knowledge and sharp mind. She'd spent her limited time in Blue Haven confused, quiet, and profoundly distressed, her brain lighting up like a Christmas tree.

He didn't doubt that the details of this "new protocol" were outlined methodically in the various stacks of paper positioned carefully around the table. Ellie was a brilliant, articulate woman, no denying that. But his mind longed for cracks, potholes—opportunities to talk her out of a second admittance to Blue Haven, or at least buy himself more time.

He winced, trying to look particularly concerned. "Have you thought about how your continued presence in the facility will impact our patients? As you know, once a person is admitted to Blue Haven, we can't suppress new memories in real time. We can't erase you, or your behavior, from their minds."

If there was any hope at curtailing what came next, appealing to patient wellbeing was certainly it. Ellie cared deeply about her patients—or she did, until she became one.

"I've considered this," she replied, pulling the middle stack of documents toward her. "Our numbers are small right now, so there's that. And I don't see my previous admittance causing much trouble.

The only person I really spoke to—and briefly, given my limited ventures—was Julian Bilbo, and he's doing extremely well."

She fished through some documents and slid over Julian's file—not that she had to. The offer was a formality, if anything. *Look, here's the proof.* Jack didn't need a briefing on Julian (or Bibs, as he went by nowadays) considering he'd been overseeing the man's activity in Blue Haven since Day One—and in Ellie's absence, no less. The cruel, darkly comical irony of it all being that Doctor Eloise Price—world-renowned psychiatrist and founder of Blue Haven—was secretly admitted to her own experiment on its opening day.

Such was the nature of mental illness.

No one was immune.

Jack pulled Julian's file closer, recalling the man's past—a tremendous tragedy.

Ten years back, Julian Bilbo had survived a catastrophic car accident that killed his wife and two daughters. Twins. Only six years old. *Six.* The driver of the second vehicle—piss drunk—survived unharmed. Julian was substantially injured: broken leg, internal bleeding, fractured ribs, a deep gash through his forehead, and a punctured eye. Over time, the physical wounds healed, but the emotional wounds did not.

The dragging feeling in Jack's chest lifted as he recalled more recent events. During Julian's intake session, the former Applebee's manager shared his love of opera. This resonated with Jack—and it challenged him. Making Julian's dream a reality had been one of the trickier aspects to program. Multi-user vocal adaptation: that wasn't his specialty. Still, the results were outstanding. And since entering Blue Haven, Julian Bilbo had flourished; the soft-spoken man with droopy eyes and inward gait was gone, replaced by a bright, dynamic fella with so much charisma.

Julian's case often reminded Jack—on his darkest days, when all the questions came out of hiding—that what they were doing was good. Because it was good, wasn't it? Julian's happiness was harnessed and contrived, unnatural, so to speak, but he was happy. They'd given him his life back, even if it was a different and temporary life.

Jack closed the file and pressed his fingers into his eyelids. "What were you saying?" he asked, the wine leaving him a touch flighty.

"I was just explaining that patient concerns are not an issue," Ellie replied. "Julian was the only person I talked to—barely. And besides, he knows me as forty-five-year-old Eloise, not twenty-five-year-old Aloe Malone."

Jack sucked in his cheek. "Aloe Malone?"

"Yeah, Aloe Malone, the name of my favorite book character growing up. I think it's pretty."

He smirked.

"What?"

"Was your favorite book character a porn star?" He couldn't help himself.

She rolled her eyes, but there was laughter inside of her somewhere, he was sure of it.

"You can read about the details later," she said, tapping the thickest stack of documents. "But—broad brushstrokes—leave my early memories intact. Get rid of college, med school; no sense reactivating all of that stress. My vetted contacts will be limited. I conveniently didn't have many people in my life at twenty-five, so I don't see myself reaching out very often, but if I'm persistent, guise a call from Gram—I'm sure that will distract me. Or give me a few solid hits of dopamine; I suspect I'll like that as well."

He nodded; the vetted contacts and calls were an opportunity for patients to connect with family and friends outside of Blue Haven—pending the memories of them had not been erased. So far though, no patient had contacted an outside party. Frankly, their support systems were generally non-existent.

Ellie searched the ceiling for a moment. "Oh yeah. I'd also like to try something a little bit more … traditional, so to speak."

"Traditional? How so?"

"Let's include my journal in the narrative."

He flinched, confused. "Journal?"

"Yes," she replied. "They had me write a journal at Seaside Recovery, remember?"

Jack nodded. *Right.* Ellie had written a journal as part of her treatment, and while the stay itself had been unsuccessful, she'd found the journal-writing experience surprisingly cathartic.

After an eternal moment of silence, he asked, "Why?"

"I think it might help me process things more … holistically. A blended approach. I'm optimistic it might shave down some of my recovery time."

He sighed. The ever-elusive *recovery time*. Months. Years. A decade. No one knew for sure.

"And if not?" he asked.

"At the very least, I think the journal will encourage me to see Leslie Marks. I've already spoken to her about prospective therapy targets, with hopeful emphasis on the childhood trauma piece."

He bobbed his head. It always baffled him that his caring, capable wife had endured such a horrific past. She'd only ever provided a glimpse, but he could hardly stomach the stories: foster homes without heat or proper plumbing, hands feeling in the dark, dinnerless nights and breakfastless mornings. He couldn't comprehend the neglect, particularly in light of his own childhood: a warm nuclear family along the Gold Coast.

When they'd met fifteen years ago, Ellie had virtually no one. Her only relatives, a flighty grandmother and closed-off aunt, had both passed. Her closest friends were patients. She spent all her time trying to fix people. Perhaps in light of that pursuit, she forgot to fix herself.

And then of course …

He turned to the portrait of their son, refusing to remember, then he looked away

The notebook struck Jack as a terrible idea, but who was he to object? He wasn't a psychiatrist; he was a computer scientist—and at least Leslie was involved. Doctor Leslie Marks was Eloise's long-time psychiatrist. They'd managed to recruit her as Blue Haven staff from the onset. If he trusted his wife with anyone, it was Doctor Marks.

He drained the glass. A choke damned-up his throat, followed by the sting of hot tears, waiting behind his eyes. "You know I don't want you to do this. I've said it a thousand times, and I'll keep saying it."

He pictured the first time he saw her, standing in line at Starbucks. She was thirty, commanding a stiff-shouldered turtleneck and plaid skirt. He knew exactly who she was. Everyone in the Chicago medical community did: *Doctor Eloise Price*, a young, gifted, forward-thinking psychiatrist. She'd finished medical school in two years, and held the number one *Top Forty Under Forty* spot according to the Chicago Tribune two years in a row. He was ten-years her senior: a CEO at a medical tech firm and wildly successful. But none of that made him any less intimidated. His hands shook as he approached her. He'd barely managed to ask her out for dinner.

Their story wasn't exactly a fairytale. She'd gotten pregnant by mistake, only a few months after they met. Though neither wanted children, Linus was an absolute gift. They'd made it work, despite the odds, building a family and career simultaneously. He didn't fall in love with Ellie as much as they grew into love, like a garden well-tended. And they had a wonderful life … for a while.

"My love," he said quietly. "I'm worried you're making the wrong decision."

Her mouth was flat. She was entirely unshaken by his sadness. *Emotional numbing*, is how she described it. Sometimes she couldn't feel anything.

She drew a deep, exaggerated breath. "I'm sorry. I wish things were different, but they aren't. I can't trust myself right now. I'm not sure what I'm capable of. But we'll get it right this time. I have faith."

He looked away. Her voice was oddly dense with emotion. On second thought, maybe he liked her better "numb." Ice over fire.

"Alright," he replied, knowing Ellie would get her way regardless; she was stubborn like that. "I want you to be happy. If this is what it takes, then okay. But I'm going to check on you in person this time. I refuse to watch you from behind a screen, like you're a regular subject in this experiment and not my partner of fifteen years. I need to see for myself that you're alright."

She sucked on her upper lip and he awaited her rebuttal. Ellie always had a rebuttal. But after a minute, she only nodded. "Okay."

Her eyes shifted to the photo—the one he'd been avoiding for over thirty minutes.

His stomach twisted, a longing so fierce he could hardly bear it. Linus had the most beautiful eyes—his eyes, but better. A clearer, brighter blue, full of light.

"Jack," she whispered, taking his hand.

He turned.

"Please don't wake me up until I'm better. I'm begging you."

Chapter Thirty-Eight

"It's deactivated now," Eloise whispered, referring to her neural net. In just under five minutes, Aloe Malone was gone. *Whoosh.* Like a gust of wind sucked from existence. Doctor Eloise Price sat on the edge of the sofa, knowing exactly who she was: a psychiatrist, a neuroscientist, the executive director and principal investigator of Blue Haven.

The back of her head throbbed—a rapid, pulsing sort of headache as the memories returned, diffusing like an aerosol and filling every part of her. Thoughts and facts and people and places. The process was astonishingly quick, and it surprised her—for a second time—how easily she could come and go, leave and return.

"How are you doing?" Jack asked.

"I'm ..." she began to reply, but the words escaped. At the moment, she wasn't much of anything. Her lids were dense, droopy. "I think I need to sleep."

He nodded, looking equally exhausted. *Oh Jack.* The rush of missing him was there, just messy, like white noise.

"I'm sorry," he said. "I put it off for as long as I could, but you were—"

She lifted a finger, interrupting. "I know. Let's talk about this later, when my head's on straight."

"Sure." He looked around. "Do you still want the virtuals on?"

She mulled. "There's no point. AMIR," she called out. "Go ahead and shut me down."

"Here," Jack said, handing her a pair of thick-rimmed black glasses. "You're going to need these."

As she propped them onto her nose, the world rearranged. From the sweeping white brightness rose a dull, ordinary apartment: khaki-colored walls, lumpy furniture. A bland, basic flat—precisely what it was, without a layer of virtual reality.

Eloise turned toward the wall of windows, now a steel surface, much like a garage door. Her hazy reflection in the metal was unsettling, the veil of youth now gone. The wells under her eyes were apparent, wrinkles grooving through her pasty skin. *Holy shit.* Her hair was a true monstrosity, tangled in clumps like a stray dog.

They walked through the side door and onto the beach: a quarter mile of fake sand, leading to an indoor swimming pool. She took one step, then another, dragging her feet over the soft grains. The veil had been lifted, exposing the other side of the movie camera—the behind-the-scenes machinery. She tilted her face toward a giant heat lamp, letting the adjacent tin fan blow a gentle breeze across her skin.

Without all the fluff, there was nothing extraordinary about this place at all: yellow sand, pale water, a blank horizon—nothing more than a green screen. She remembered the building before it had become Blue Haven: *Wally World*, an indoor water complex with poolside hotel suites.

She knew the facility was perfect during their first tour. Even without the pizazz, it was much nicer than anything typically offered to psychiatric inpatients. Those hospitals—or institutes—had always left her feeling ill. Shutting away human beings in sterile, sunless places. Ample security and select entry. Bland, boiled meals served on trays. That wasn't a life, and the idea that people dealing with mental disorders deserved less—simply because they were ill—was such a strange, unacceptable notion. In a truly just world, did they not deserve more, as retribution for their suffering?

Eloise stared at the blank wall, curving around the pool.

"I suspect there's a very nice sunrise happening, isn't there," she said, trying to stifle the weight of another failed admission—she'd deal with that later.

"Yes," came a voice. She turned to greet Amir, her all-time favorite psychiatry resident.

"Hi Amir," she said, giving him a weak smile.

He frowned, almost teary-eyed. "I'm so sorry, Doctor Price. I was really rooting for you this time. I had such a good feeling, honestly. This is partly my fault, I shouldn't have—"

"It's okay," she replied. "You did great. We'll review the details later, as a team."

He gave her a solemn nod. "Okay, sounds good."

Jack veered from the path. "I'm going to take the side exit, if that's okay. I don't want any residents seeing us together. Also, *please* put on a happy face. We'll work out later how to properly make amends."

Her stomach dropped. The evolving paranoia, the various mental breakdowns—all public. These episodes were disruptive and disturbing—and unfortunately, inerasable. Hardly the sort of reaction she'd anticipated, and the last thing she wanted for her patients.

What a fucking mess.

She followed Amir down the cobblestone path—not actual cobblestone but polyurethane, less upkeep. As they passed Westley's condo, he emerged looking simultaneously surprised and relieved to see her.

"Aloe!" he said.

The name caught her off guard. *Right. Aloe Malone.* "Hi," she replied, forcing out a big smile. "How are you?"

He leaned in, trying to be subtle. "Fine, but how are *you?* Jesus, I've been so worried. We all have."

"I know, and I'm *so* sorry. I'm doing better though—honestly. I know I've said that before, but I mean it this time. I'm working through my issues. I'm making progress."

Westley drew her into a hug. She felt so small and impish in his burly embrace. *Please, let me stay.*

"I'm so relieved to hear that," he whispered.

When she pulled back, he was smiling. He had such a bright, captivating smile—the sort that stuck with a person.

"Where are you headed?" Westley asked.

"Just taking a morning stroll, nowhere in particular. What are you up to?"

He pointed toward the Hexagon, probably one of the more pathetic looking features without digital enhancement, hardly more than a wall. It was Jack's idea, and a good one. What they couldn't achieve horizontally due to space and funding, they'd achieved vertically. The elevator didn't lead to hundreds of stories, it led to ten. Rooms were repurposed brilliantly. All of the restaurants, for example, took place in two spaces, by simply altering the set up and visual projection.

"Dinner later?" he asked.

"Actually, I'm going to sit this one out. Still trying to catch up on sleep. But please tell the others I'm doing much better, and I'll be making a public debut soon enough."

"Sure thing," he replied, and then he touched her arm. "Please take care of yourself."

Her heart sagged. She was going to genuinely miss these people. "You too, Westley."

After a few lingering moments, they parted ways. She carried on behind Amir, struck by the change in scenery. She may have designed this place, down to the grain of sand, but it was unusual being on the other side, after eight whole days in Blue Haven: the pitiful water features repurposed from Wally World, gurgling in sputters; the mechanical sway of robotic palms, like a parade float; the flat, green sky. It was mildly depressing.

On second thought, maybe she shouldn't have disabled the visuals.

When they reached the far north side, Amir opened the door to Condo Twenty-Three, a facade that portaled to the outside world. She followed him down the main hallway, keeping her eyes straight ahead. Colleagues were waiting in every direction—the main control room, the boardroom, their offices—but she wasn't ready to face a single one, nor did she have the energy.

When she reached the main exit, Jack held up her coat. "It's brisk outside. Bundle up."

"Right," she replied, remembering it was winter. She let him slip the heavy fur collar around her shoulders, already dreading the chill.

"Sorry," he offered. "I don't have a change of clothes handy."

She glanced down at her bare legs and sandals. *Awesome.*

As he opened the door, a gust of cold air rushed inside. She shivered, bone deep.

Don't make me go.

They hustled as a unit, him shielding her from the blustering wind—but not really. It burned her lungs and stung her legs all the same. She imagined an onlooker, wondering who she was: some disheveled, middle-aged woman with tumbleweed hair, blue flip-flops, and a two-thousand-dollar coat, hobbling through a parking lot. Luckily, they were on the outskirts of Chicago, surrounded by industrial space—there were no onlookers, no gawking pedestrians.

Jack stopped beside their black Suburban, flung open the door, and ushered her inside.

"Alright," he said. "Let's get you home."

Home.

The place they were heading was hardly home.

Chapter Thirty-Nine

Eloise dreamed that night for the first time in recent memory, and she dreamed of Linus. "Mom," he said. "Why do you keep looking at me like that?"

"Looking at you like what?" she replied, though she knew. The look was adoration.

There was so much to adore about Linus. He was a perfectly equal blend of his parents: creamy pale skin and strawberry blonde hair, like her. His dad's eyes, but lighter—almost scary light, enchanting and otherworldly.

In the midst of her admiring, Linus faced her square on, his expressionless face close to hers. She could smell his sweet, boyish scent: earthy, like springtime. "Bye Mom," he said. And that was it. Her lids snapped open and she was drenched in sweat, tucked beside Jack. His breathing was loud, labored, heavy with sleep.

She gently unbuckled herself from beneath his arm and found her slippers: two fluffy hedgehogs—a Mother's Day gift from Linus. She wandered to the bathroom, longing to watch the sunset or dip her toes into the warm ocean or be anywhere that wasn't cold and dreary.

Her reflection in the mirror was haggardly and she gawked at the state of her unbrushed curls, snarled into the shape of a boxwood. *Dear Lord, what have you become.* She stepped into the gray-tiled shower and turned on the water. The warmth against her skin was nice and also necessary; she tried to channel her focus, grounding her thoughts.

Exist in the moment. Take in the hot steam. Feel the water running down your skin, the hard tiles against your toes—wiggle them.

The effort was there, but her heart wasn't in it. Her heart was elsewhere, in happier moments from a past that no longer existed.

Lying careless on a beach.

Staring at her son, glorified by his existence.

Holding hands with Jack for the very first time.

Afterwards, she slipped into a robe and ventured to the kitchen, where she flipped on the coffee maker. It sucked up water like a choke and she waited, gazing up through the skylights. Their house was incredibly angular—an aspect she'd grown to hate. Too sharp, drastic, full of edges, the sort of architectural achievement that belonged in an art gallery, not a home. Everything was gray: gray walls, exposed concrete, varying shades of gray furniture. It even felt gray, like the air was heavy with melancholy.

The estrangement came slowly, rising from her toes and ultimately settling in her chest, like a weight.

Yesterday, she was a patient in Blue Haven—her own experiment. Today, she wasn't.

She'd woken in her bed, beside her husband of nearly fifteen years, and life had resumed—was resuming, even though she wasn't ready for it.

She dressed her coffee with honey and a swirl of cream, then popped a slice of bread into the toaster. At the counter, she nibbled and sipped, staring out the front window.

It was early—too early—and their Lincoln Park neighborhood was quiet: the odd pedestrian moseying by, cars inching along the slick road. At one point, she remembered liking this view: the boxy adjacent properties all lined up like stamps, tall and rectangular with black-rimmed windows and predictable layouts. Everything slim and smushed, close-knit. Small delicate trees and carefully trimmed hedges. A relaxed suburban feel to it all.

What had once appealed to her as a new buyer had long lost its luster. Now, she craved space, nature, water, sky. An unadulterated sightline. Places without people or things, reminders or memories.

A void perhaps, is what she craved.

It had only been twenty-four hours since her departure from Blue Haven, but she could already feel the emptiness invading her like it had before, seeping through the cracks. It was one thing to survive trauma, quite another to *continue* surviving, day by day, hour by hour, sometimes minute by minute. She leaned onto her palms, pressing her elbows against the cool quartz.

Another failed admission.

Fuck.

She wondered how a person so well-trained to treat and heal could entirely succumb to their own ailments; and whether this unto itself was a failure—professionally and personally—because it sure felt like one.

Jack stepped out of the bedroom, groggy-eyed.

"Let's move," she said.

"Move?" He rubbed his eyes. "Where to?"

"A house with less angles. A neighborhood with more space."

A quiet, sleepy laugh. "Sure, if you think that will help, then let's do it. Let's move."

She looked back out the window, at the frost-licked corners. *Would it help?* Likely not.

He wrapped his arms around her from behind, muscles tight against her shoulders. He was in good shape for his age—nearly fifty-five.

"We don't have to do this today," he whispered, referring to the team debriefing she'd requested last night.

"I'd like to," she replied. "Our patients need answers and it will be easier for me to participate while the residual effects are still ongoing."

He nodded. "I suppose that makes sense. Whatever you think is best."

It was well established that cortical stimulation of the sort provided by her neural net had some positive—though temporary—benefits when it came to mood and cognition. She had a window of opportunity before her mind eclipsed back into utter sadness, and she wasn't going to waste it.

She turned around and Jack stared back, a quiet stillness to his gaze, no obvious emotion. In moments like these she often wondered what he thought of her, and how his opinion had changed over time.

At one point, earlier on, he was unabashedly smitten. His eyes were full of desire and disbelief, and everything about her—from professional esteem to the swell of her hips—seemed to delight him. A shiny new toy, full of surprises. Obsessed was a strong word, but he was certainly enamored. She felt lifted and extraordinary around him.

Now, there was a different glint in his eye, a sort of exasperated relief. *You're here. You're alive.* She didn't doubt his love, but she couldn't easily discern the normal influence of time, which simmered the coals of any relationship, from the influence of her: the burden of her struggle.

Jack had seen her in all sorts of ways that husbands should never see their wives: paralyzed with grief, unable to stomach food; institutionalized; delirious; deadened with medication that made her drowsy and unresponsive; angry—at him, at the world; entirely repulsive, her pale, shiny skin unwashed and thick with body odor.

She—his once revered partner, sitting on a pedestal—had personally revealed the dark underbelly of human sadness, an abyss from which one cannot return. She'd fallen from grace, and there was nothing to do now but wonder.

Does he still see me as the person I was, or the person I've become?

"Do you want me to make you another coffee?" he asked, pointing to her empty mug.

"No, thank you," she said, standing. "I should get ready and head out."

"You're leaving *now*? It's five in the morning."

"Early bird gets the worm." She said it to be chummy, but Jack remained flat-faced.

"You push yourself too hard, Ellie."

Instead of replying, she kissed him on the cheek. He wasn't wrong, but today was important. Though it was the very last thing she wanted (or needed), she owed it to her patients—her friends. She had to make things right.

Chapter Forty

Eloise sped down Lake Shore Drive, heading for the office. She cranked up the music to distract her wandering mind from passing landmarks: each tied to happier memories, particularly of Linus. Her reflection in the rearview mirror was light-years different from earlier that morning. Surprisingly, it didn't evoke a jaunt of self-hatred, as expected. It had taken her thirty whole minutes to comb through those dreadlocks. She'd applied foundation, blush, and mascara. Lined her lips with a nude pencil and slipped on a pair of black slacks and a pinstripe blouse—sleek, professional.

She tried to enjoy the lovely murmur of self-esteem, the *umph* of bass pulsing up through her leather seat, the odd snowflake pelting her windshield. The sign for Wrigley Field caught her eye, and she looked beyond it. Driving was a trigger, often sending her mind adrift.

It was important now, more than ever, to stay focused.

She pulled off the highway and continued down side streets. Shops were just opening, and people ventured out into the day, cluttering the sidewalks with movement. A few turns later, the frenzy subsided. Buildings flattened, long and full of smoke stacks, the voids between them lengthening until she eventually reached Blue Haven: large and sprawling like a shopping center. She marveled at its size and plainness, how an entire world could exist within those walls.

It wasn't until she entered her office and molded into her cushy office chair that she finally exhaled. This room, large and full of light, was her safe place—one of the remaining few spaces that brought her a warm nuzzle of security.

At one point, she loved working for the sake of it.

Now, she worked as a desperate distraction.

She glanced at the large oval clock directly across the room.

One hour until Team Meeting.

Administration had printed five patient files and left them in a heap, as requested: Julian Bilbo, Westley Young, Bob and Franny Jennings, and herself—Eloise Price.

She arranged the documents into piles, enjoying the feel of paper against her fingertips. Despite all the technology in the world, she still preferred the texture of an eight and a half by eleven over holding another screen.

Each file began with a brief, up-to-date summary for quick reference, followed by the patient's current level of functioning. She started with Julian's, then moved along.

> PATIENT NAME: JULIAN BILBO
>
> *Mr. Bilbo, often referred to as "Bibs," is a 53-year-old former Applebee's manager who, prior to admission at Blue Haven, reported severe symptoms of depression following the deaths of his wife and two daughters. All three were killed in a car crash. Mr. Bilbo was substantially injured, though has since made a full recovery despite loss of vision in one eye as a result of impaled glass. The driver of the opposing vehicle was impaired; however, no charges have been filed. Mr. Bilbo attempted suicide on two occasions, and was still adamant on ending his life at the time of admission, during which he reported severe symptoms of major depression including low mood, insomnia and feelings of hopelessness.*
>
> CURRENT LEVEL OF FUNCTIONING: *High.* Mr. Bilbo is doing exceptionally well with the current regimen (see full report) and all mental health symptoms are presently abated.

She flipped to the next file.

> PATIENT NAME: WESTLEY YOUNG
>
> *Mr. Young is a 32-year-old former corporal of the U.S.*

Marines who presented to Blue Haven with symptoms of posttraumatic stress. Specifically, Mr. Young was perpetually haunted by a firsthand IED explosion that killed his sergeant, brother, and three fellow corporals. Though Mr. Young's leg was partially dismembered upon contact, he has since received considerable reconstructive surgery to achieve partial function. He continues to experience some periodic discomfort that is quickly relieved with neural net inhibition. Symptoms prior to admission include frequent, intrusive, and disturbing memories accompanied by vivid nightmares; difficulty falling and staying asleep; sporadic angry outbursts, and prolonged lulls of depression.

CURRENT LEVEL OF FUNCTIONING: *High.* Mr. Young is doing exceptionally well with the current regimen (see full report) and all mental health symptoms are presently abated.

Next came Bob and Franny.

PATIENT NAME: BOB AND FRANNY JENNINGS
Mr. and Mrs. Jennings are a married couple, both 65 years old, presenting to Blue Haven without permanent residence. The pair were referred by a third-party agency, Chicago Cares, a nonprofit seeking mental-health services on behalf of the homeless. It is estimated, though unconfirmed, that Mr. and Mrs. Jennings lived on the streets for twenty years, at minimum, presumably after the failed launch of several patents filed by Mr. Jennings. Case histories were difficult to ascertain given both individuals presented with dementia, as well as severe anxiety, social phobia, and chronic pain as a result of substantial tooth decay.
CURRENT LEVEL OF FUNCTIONING: *High.* Mr. and Mrs. Jennings are doing exceptionally well with

their current regimen (see full report) and all mental health symptoms are presently abated.

Eloise paused as she pulled her own folder near. This exercise—viewing her own file—always came with a sense of estrangement: doctor and patient, together in one body.

PATIENT NAME: DR. ELOISE PRICE
Doctor Eloise Price is a 45-year-old woman and the on-title director and principal investigator of Blue Haven, though her capacities have been limited as a result of profound distress following the death of her twelve-year-old son, Linus. Dr. Price first presented to Blue Haven with symptoms of depression that were unsuccessfully treated upon entry. She was subsequently admitted to an inpatient psychiatric facility, Seaside Recovery, due to a psychotic break, coupled with suicidal intent. Dr. Price was treated at Seaside for nine months, and discharged with minimal improvement. A second admittance to Blue Haven was attempted, and was not successful. Of note, Dr. Price has a substantial history of childhood abuse.
CURRENT LEVEL OF FUNCTIONING: Not applicable. Dr. Price has recently been discharged, and is no longer under the observation of Blue Haven.

She leaned back in her chair and watched the clock: the slow tick of the minute hand, inching forward. Her chest boiled with self-directed frustration as she remembered the hallucinations: Westley's half-dismembered leg, Bob and Franny's rotten teeth, the gash across Bibs's face—his eyeball, draining onto the tablecloth. Before her recent entry, she'd foolishly scoured every detail and photo presented in their case histories, out of sheer curiosity. She saw the post-accident photos of Bibs, the pre-surgical snapshots of Westley's leg, the true appearance of Bob and Franny.

Had she stayed in the dark on her fellow patients—as advised by her team, especially Jack: "Ellie, stop trying to work; you need to relax and take care of yourself"—the hallucinations she'd experienced in Blue Haven would not have occurred. There'd be no content.

Relax and take care of yourself.

Instead, she'd done the opposite, immersing herself in work, attempting (despite her broken brain) to catch up on the time she'd missed during her inpatient stay at Seaside, like she could return to her position unscathed.

She recalled the brief lull of normality: the quiet feel of her office after so much time away. The steady, predictable thrum of completing a task. A sense of importance, like she mattered. The joy and wonder of learning new information.

She closed her eyes and listened to the minute hand, clicking in her otherwise silent space.

Tick. Tock.

Tick. Tock.

Tick. Tock.

With each stroke her head began to clear, thoughts slicing away like a log of salami. Reality slipped beneath her awareness and she found a happy place: a Blue Haven sunrise, mid flair.

Bold streaks of fuchsia and turquoise sailing through the sky, followed by brightness.

A swell of soft clouds.

The calming lull of waves cushioning the background: a resultant *whoosh*.

She wondered briefly what the others were up to: Westley, Bibs, Bob, and Franny. Just waking up, or perhaps sleeping in. Another day cocooned in perfection. She already missed Westley's sweet candor, Bibs's wacky sense of humor, and Bob and Franny's cute dynamic. The bonds they'd formed in such a short amount of time surprised her, and they were real—even if nothing else was.

Her lids shot open. No more sunrise, just pale walls, covered in degrees—degrees that held little significance anymore. She soaked in the silence, waiting.

Soon enough, she'd be in a room full of others, all eyes on her.

Chapter Forty-One

Twenty-five people crowded around the boardroom table: doctors, programmers, research scientists. Eloise took a large gulp of coffee. Jack sat to her right. Amir, to her left. A few down, Leslie Marks tossed over a quick wave. "Hi," she mouthed.

"Hi," Eloise mouthed back.

It was strange being back inside this room—a space she'd spent months planning and decorating, selecting every detail, down to the color of paint: *Edgecombe Pewter*, a soft and smoky greige. Ultimately though, she'd hardly experienced the boardroom in action, a testament to how quickly life can change.

Her hand moved along the sleek glass tabletop, her spine nestled comfortably in the chair's flexible arc. Cool winter daylight flooded throughout, speckling people's blazers and dress shirts with polka dots of brightness. The air was thick with coffee and aftershave.

The first part of the meeting was dedicated to interdisciplinary team discussion, during which each patient's case was reviewed: a daily briefing, more or less, provided by their primary clinician—or *concierge*, according to residents, though there was no such thing as a "concierge" in Blue Haven. Every staff member was either trained—or being trained—in a mental health specialty, able and willing to intervene with residents, take detailed progress notes, and provide input into patient wellbeing. Compared to other mental health clinics, Blue Haven relied on a very unique and innovative business model. And that's why it worked—or worked for most, rather.

The round table began and Eloise listened intently, struck by how seamlessly the cases flowed. From her experience in other facilities, the case presentations of mentally ill patients with such pervasive disorders never involved words like *thriving* or *flourishing*. *Stable* was common. *Doing okay* was hopeful. *Doing well* was a triumph, usually temporary. The typical prognosis was an ebb and flow of bad to worse, with peaks of *alright*.

Hearing these uncanny outcomes made Eloise smile. Her life's work, invisible as wind and dreams, was finally materializing in the world—whether or not she'd been a part of it.

Her mood flattened as Amir's turn arrived. She could sense the weight of her own presence. The elephant in the room. All of Blue Haven's patients were prospering, except for one:

Her.

Amir glanced over, his forehead gleaming with sweat. He smoothed the non-existent wrinkles from the breast of his blazer, clearly uncomfortable. And she didn't blame him. Who on earth wanted to talk about a person's mental unraveling while they happened to be sitting one seat over?

"I'm happy to start the discussion," she said. "Do you mind?"

Amir's shoulders dropped with relief. "Please, go ahead."

She smiled at the row of faces, trying to lighten the mood. This was her team—her employees, technically—and these forthcoming moments would only be awkward if *she* was awkward.

"So, here we are." She paused, and then added, "Again," to be funny.

This drew a few warm smirks.

"I'd foremost like to thank you all for participating in my rehabilitation journey. As I've said before, this is a very unique situation and opportunity for all of us, and it hasn't been easy." She looked specifically at Jack, but didn't linger. "I'll read through my file in more detail, but for now, I thought we could discuss some of the larger pitfalls."

An eerie silence unfolded. She waited a few seconds. "I'll start. The journal was a bad idea. I didn't anticipate the amount of fear and paranoia it would provoke, or how resistant I would be to exploring these emotions in therapy."

Leslie leaned forward. "Agreed. The journal was one of the more challenging aspects to manage, and it was difficult—near impossible—for us to improvise a cohesive storyline in your absence that was consistent across multiple staff members. It felt … disorganized, like we were trying to write a television series in the middle of the broadcast. We couldn't keep up."

"Fair," she replied.

Doctor Ronda Fairchild lifted a hand, the "cleaner," who was technically a neuropsychologist. "For example," she said. "I didn't expect you to drill me so thoroughly about the journal. I made a split-second decision to feign a language barrier, but the damage was done. I could tell this simply added to your suspicion."

"And when you confronted me about past residents," Amir said. "I had no idea what to say."

"Me neither," added Rayla Fortum, the social worker stationed at Le Boutique. "I had no clue when you asked about other staff members, you'd done so out of suspicion, because you were wary of Jack."

Eloise nodded, seeing her second admittance for what it was: a complicated tapestry gone terribly awry. "I underestimated myself, for sure."

"We were hoping," Leslie added, "that Eloise's fictitious death by suicide would act as an almost subconscious permission for you to move forward as Aloe Malone. We wanted to provide closure, but you continued to spiral. And a hit of neurotransmitters can only go so far …" She paused, taking a sip of water. "Jack's presence inside the facility was another misstep, in my opinion."

Jack leaned forward, a huff slipping between his lips. "I won't watch my wife on a screen, like she's a contestant on some reality show."

Beneath the table, Eloise laid a hand over his. His muscles were tight, rigid.

"All of this aside," she said, "there's a puzzle piece we're clearly missing. Something that makes me different and less responsive to this treatment than our other patients. Perhaps, instead of continuing to rehash the challenges, we can discuss what actions are required to provide closure to our current residents."

Leslie nodded, slow and deliberate. "Yes, I agree, let's talk about how we can rectify their distress and concern."

Eloise couldn't ignore the jerk in her chest. *Rectify their distress and concern.* In other words, the hardships *she'd* placed on Westley, Bibs, Bob, and Franny—and for what? She was hardly recovered.

"I'll make it right," she said. "I'm not sure how, but I will."

Rayla raised her hand. "If I may? What if you simply return in good spirits and disclose that you're leaving—something pressing, like an ill family member."

Around the room, people nodded, a consensus forming.

"Alright," Eloise replied. "That sounds reasonable."

She kept her face steady, even though her chest flapped with enthusiasm. *I'm going back*—temporarily, but any amount of time in Blue Haven seemed better than her current reality.

Escapism was a concept she knew well, being a psychiatrist: the desire to seek distraction and relief from difficult circumstances. As far as coping went, escapism was largely discouraged by professionals. But if one were to unpack the concept, to consider the word *escape*, as in, to break free of confinement or control, was it really so terrible? Did people not deserve to escape from the brutal hardship of life, if a better life was possible?

She looked out the large, modern window. Tiny flakes of snow drifted, swirling in blusters. The cold, barren world awaited—and so did everything else: the tight grip of anxiety that would soon come; the guzzle of depression, sucking her dry. *Linus*, and all the lovely and toxic memories tied to his existence.

Escapism.

Maybe she was escaping. But who the hell could blame her?

Chapter Forty-Two

"Christ Almighty," Bibs said, his voice booming. "You look incredible."

Eloise stepped out of her old condo, a silk gown flapping at her heels. Amir had arranged a group dinner at Da Vinci, an art-inspired Italian restaurant in the Hexagon. The plan was to meet at her condo, Number Five, and go from there. Bibs was the first to arrive.

She smiled. The pull of her lipstick was tight and cakey. "Now *this* is a moment," she replied. "Julian Bilbo, first on the scene. In all my years ..."

He clobbered her with a tight hug; a bright, zesty scent wafted from his neck. "*In all your years*. Please, you're a kid."

Her head spun before she remembered. *Right, Aloe Malone.* As far as Bibs knew, she was only twenty-five. She squeezed him a little tighter, her arms digging into his soft, squishy shoulders before releasing.

"I've been worried about you," he said. "I mean ... God, I was starting to think something awful had happened." His dark, kind eyes glossed with tears. The agony was palpable and her stomach seized with guilt.

"I'm so sorry I worried you," she said. "I'm okay, I promise. I know I've said that a few times already, but I'm on a new medication for anxiety and I feel wonderful. Good as new."

He leaned over and kissed her on the forehead, a paternal sort of energy that was unfamiliar but so, so lovely.

"Now let's talk about *this*." She waved her finger over his outfit, referring to a black and white pinstripe suit, paired with a crimson tie and glossed-back hair. A chain dangled around his neck, featuring a diamond palm tree. "Al Capone meets the Tropics?"

He winked. "Bingo. What else would I wear to an upscale Italian restaurant?"

She laughed, then took in a deep breath of humid night air. The moon hung low and large in the sky. A perfect night, per usual, and she was thankful for the active virtuals that brought paradise to life, right before her eyes. She'd barely left, but missed the bright heat of day and fresh heat of night. Outside of Blue Haven, it was snowing. The air was so cool and dry it had already started to crackle her skin like desert plains.

As Bob and Franny strolled up the cobblestone path, hand in hand, Eloise waved. "Hello!" she called out, smiling. She was putting on a show tonight: her very best self.

"Hi!" Franny replied.

The pair looked suited for an awards ceremony: Bob in a navy, double-breasted tuxedo and Franny in a sparkling ankle-length dress with a peek of cleavage. The dark bronze color lifted her hazel eyes, though Eloise couldn't help but wonder what image lay beneath the visual filter altering everyone's perception: a second-hand suit and old prom dress, most likely, donated to the facility and put on display in Le Boutique as something rare and extraordinary.

"Hey kiddo." Bob smiled and she instinctually shuddered, remembering the haunting visions from days ago—only now she knew the origins behind the perturbing image: Bob's *actual* teeth, a haggard display of half-rotted chicklets, hiding beneath a fake reality.

"Wow," Eloise said. "You both look incredible."

"This old thing?" Franny replied. Her eyes were traced with navy liner, cheeks rosy with blush. She linked arms with Bob.

It was hard to imagine these two as anything but a ritzy, retired duo, spending their golden years in paradise—though Eloise knew better, of course. She wondered what kind of experiences lay nestled somewhere in their white matter, hidden behind dementia. Living under a worn tarp, perhaps. Shivering and trembling and starving. Witnessing the sort of violence that occurs in the darkest alleyways. Feeling the sort of fear that lingers in a person's soul and starts to define them.

"Happy you're out tonight, kid," Bob said.

Eloise returned the smile. "Me too."

"Are you sure you're ..." Franny began, wincing with concern.

"Yes," she replied, ensuring her voice was firm and sturdy. Her friends had reason to doubt her wellness. She'd declared *I'm fine* on a number of occasions and behaved otherwise. But not this time.

She took Franny's small, delicate hand in hers; the skin along her knuckles was so thin, like a moth's wing. "I know you're worried and I appreciate your concern. But really, I'm doing well—more than well." Eloise upheld the non-verbal behaviors she knew professionally evoked trust: unwavering eye contact, physical touch, stillness, a steady voice.

"Good," Franny replied, seemingly convinced.

Westley stepped outside, half-tangled in a button-down. His dark, sculpted abs gleamed briefly in the moonlight before he covered them with a shirt. "Sorry!" he apologized, still doing up the last few buttons. "I hate being late."

Eloise nodded; his military background was peeking through. The personality features enforced through service were stubborn and difficult to simmer—even with a neural net.

Bibs glanced at his device. "You're hardly late. Two measly minutes."

"What can I say?" Westley replied. "I'm a punctual guy." He gave Bibs a quick jab, then hugged Eloise with real, legitimate force. His untampered strength was almost painful but she didn't mind. "Glad you're here," Westley whispered.

As they walked towards the Hexagon, Eloise reflected on the giddy, childish elation in her chest. Whether this emotion was a by-product of her fritzy nervous system or a legitimate feeling, she didn't know—or care. Hope broadened through her like a waterfall, spilling into the night, and she surrendered to the enchantment of this special place, real or not: the splatter of stars like freckles in the night; the slow dance of palm trees; the marbled water, lit by the moon and blue as a lagoon.

The Hexagon glowed softly and she marveled at its brilliance. They had Universal Studios to thank for the acuity and sharpness of this particular illusion. A public-relations move, really, and while she was grateful for the funds (even if they were a one-time donation), it astounded her that, for the budget of a single movie, they could afford to admit a dozen more patients.

These sorts of realizations made her criticize—with fury, and yet, an eye for opportunity—how society glamorized certain industries without limit, while neglecting others completely. Who was more deserving of this lavish lifestyle, a person with acting skills, or a man like Westley, who'd served his country and—in return—lost his sanity?

She pushed away such thoughts as they entered the Hexagon, letting the friction in her chest subside. Amir was waiting, smiling. "Welcome," he said, giving her a wink.

Tonight, the lobby blazed red: cherry-colored lights shone from the floor and ceiling, creating a velvety, royal ambiance. The windowed walls were covered in glowing damask patterns—chrome, gold, silver—and a red carpet led to the elevator. Briny, bold flavors hung in the air: rich sauces and red meat, a preview of what was to come.

"It smells incredible in here," Franny said.

"Sure does," Bibs added. "I would like to welcome tonight with a song." He drew a large belly breath and everyone waited—well aware of what came next.

The sound was long and large and wonderful. Eloise let the moment travel down through her spine and into the souls of her feet, where it lingered.

When Bibs was finished, he took a bow. His cheeks glowed, dramatic and rosy against the red lighting, and she couldn't help but marvel at the gift they'd given this bereaved man. She wondered briefly what life awaited him otherwise: collecting ends-meet unemployment, surrounded by the ghosts of his late wife and twin girls. In truth, he'd probably be dead, his life taken by his own hands.

"That was incredible," she told Bibs. "Your voice is really something."

He shrugged. "The Lord Almighty blessed me with the pipes of an angel. What can I say?."

Chapter Forty-Three

Da Vinci was housed in the same large space as all the other restaurants: on the third floor. It was an event space, in its day (business retreats, wakes, conferences, weddings), and if one were to peak under the hood of virtual reconstruction, it hadn't changed a bit: beige walls, ten-foot ceilings, two-thousand workable square feet. A boring, vanilla room.

When the elevator doors opened, however, there was no trace of ordinary left. All at once the view came in every direction: a dark, cosmic backdrop.

Eloise moved closer, the stir of wonder in her stomach undamped by knowing the truth—it was *that* beautiful. The moon was bright and telescopic, effervescent as a lamp in the sky. Stars scattered in nests of peach, mandarin, and fuchsia, coming together in cotton candy swirls.

"Holy shit," Bibs said, pointing to a painting on the far wall. "That can't be … real, can it?"

"It can," Amir replied. "And it is. Flown in from the National Museum in Krakow, just for this evening."

Eloise evaluated the portrait of a pretty young woman holding a ferret-like creature. *Lady with an Ermine*, by Leonardo da Vinci. Not real, of course, but what did that matter? The awe inside of Bibs *was* real, and he deserved that feeling.

They found their table in the center of the room, a stately design made from dark slabs of ebony wood. It matched the Tuscan ambiance: exposed stone, flickering candelabras, a ceiling covered in ivy.

Their server (not actually a server, but Clarise, one of the psychology residents) came around with water, fresh bread, and a dish of olive oil. "Welcome to Da Vinci," she said, filling Westley's glass. "I'm sure you've had a chance to admire *Lady with Ermine*, our first surprise of the evening."

Bibs laughed. "*First* surprise? Like a famous painting by *my man* da Vinci isn't enough. You folks spoil us."

Clarise grinned. She had a calm, methodical aura; soft eyes and acute awareness of her body language. This would serve her well as a psychologist. "Tonight's chef is Italy's own Massimo Bottura."

Bibs gasped. "*No.* He's like … the most famous chef in Italy."

Clarise nodded. "Only the best!"

"Seriously?" His eyeballs projected outward like a cartoon character. "Seriously! This is truly something. I have to meet this man afterwards. I must shake his hand."

Without pause, Clarise smiled. "Of course, I'll arrange it."

Eloise lifted a brow, imagining the behind-the-scenes scramble that would now ensue: assigning someone the role of Massimo Bottura, outfitting them with the chef's visual filter, the exact tone of his voice.

"Can you believe that?" Bibs said, just beaming. He reached into the center of the table and took a slice of bread. Eloise followed. It appeared to be focaccia, dense and speckled with rosemary and olives.

She took a bite. *Mediocre.* The crust was overdone and the pillowy insides were too heavy. It was perfectly fine, but without neural enhancement, there was nothing extraordinary about the loaf at all—probably someone's first attempt, given the kitchen staff were all members of a youth rehabilitation program. Produce often came as a donation, with an expiration date looming or slightly passed. Still, the food program at Blue Haven was a successful partnership on all fronts: low waste, low budget, sustainable, and it supported the local, at-risk community.

"This bread is sublime," Westley said, soaking a second slice in olive oil.

Eloise nodded, pretending to agree. She imagined the taste with a buzz of neural stimulation, elevating the flavors and textures: salty crust, fluffy interior, briny olives.

"Reminds me of my time in Florence," Bibs said, going on to describe the dazzling architecture, esteemed galleries, and pasta so fresh it made a person weep.

Eloise listened with absolute fascination, not because Florence itself was so enthralling, but because Bibs had never actually been there. These memories—much like the time he'd spent at famous opera houses, performing for fame and royalty—were implanted: enforced repeatedly while his brain was in a lucid, dreamlike state.

Guided imagery under the right conditions was remarkably effective, and watching it unfold in real-time with such vivid recount (the mouthfeel of a single rigatoni; wild lavender growing under ancient archways) reminded Eloise that reality wasn't objective, but figural: a notion in people's heads, subject to change.

"Sounds like quite the trip," Franny said afterwards. "Bob and I went on the loveliest Mediterranean cruise just before we came here …"

Another delusion, and Eloise found herself imagining Bob and Franny as they were a few weeks before admission: living behind an air-conditioning unit, starved and delirious.

Amidst the travel stories, courses continued: scallops and peas in browned butter, a twirl of fresh spaghettini, saucy osso buco over creamy risotto. Eloise ate, applauding the effort, but was more preoccupied with decoding her patients-turned-friends. The psychiatrist in her noted the abundance of clues hiding in plain sight, the hints of nonverbal behavior that spoke louder than words and were far more genuine: wide glossy eyes, forward facing shoulders, lively hand gestures, leaning in with engagement. These people were happy—*really* happy, and while this brought her joy, of course—it was the point of her life's work, after all—her chest pinched with jealousy. Not the bitter, vengeful sort, but the quiet and droopy kind; the kid at the back of the class wishing to participate.

"You're quiet tonight," Westley said as dessert arrived.

"Sorry," she replied, realizing she'd lost track of her primary purpose: mitigating damages and closing the loop. "You're right. I have some difficult news to share."

Bodies shifted. Franny's eyebrows came together like a car crash. "I thought you were doing well."

"I am. I really am. Unfortunately …" her voice trailed, "Gram is quite ill. I don't have much in the way of family, so I need to be with her, which means leaving Blue Haven. Hopefully not forever, but for the time being. It's not what I want, but family comes first."

Faces fell. "Well that royally sucks," Bibs said. "Though I get it. The cost of kin."

His voice was slightly apathetic, not intentional, but thanks to a series of light beams deactivating the memories, or engrams, of his wife and children. Bibs had paid the ultimate price for family—a price not explicitly mentioned when a person decides to have one. Eloise knew this cost with devastating familiarity: you can love your spouse and children with every piece of your soul, give them the world—perhaps more—but that doesn't mean they won't die.

The table was quiet for a few moments, save the tink of forks cracking into creme brulees.

"I'll come back," Eloise blurted, already imagining Jack's reaction (that thick vein in his forehead, raised and ready). The rest of her team was probably reeling—*Oh God, not again.*

"I sure hope so," Bob said. "We'll really miss you, Aloe."

"I'm going to miss you all so much," she replied, and she meant it. Her heart bloomed just being there. Seeing their faces: the most unlikely cast of friends.

Except now it was over. They would stay, and she would return to the real world: a place that didn't organize itself around her happiness or anyone else's.

A place that didn't give a shit.

§

The walk back was quiet. When they reached Number Five, bodies shuffled into a semi-circle of droopy faces. Eloise stifled back tears—an unexpected reaction. Her emotions were all over the place. She wanted to stay, of course, but hardly anticipated the force of her longing, sharp and visceral like a tide pushing her toward these wonderful people instead of away.

Blue Haven was the happiest place on earth, and she cursed her mind for being what it was: a goddamn saboteur, destined to keep her sad, desperate, and miserable.

She hugged them each one last time—Bibs, Westley, Bob, and Franny—then slipped into her condo and closed the door. She leaned against the wall and whispered, "Okay Amir," into the omnipotent void. Her visuals flickered off and she stood in the drab, ordinary space. For the first time since leaving Blue Haven she truly dreaded what came next with every cell in her body: the resumption of normality and all that came with it.

She'd started all of this with a vision and simple premise. If happiness became a commodity, it should be awarded to those who need it most.

And now, against all odds, she was among the neediest.

Chapter Forty-Four

Raindrops pelted against the window: drizzly, bleak. The sky beyond was streaked with fog, painting the world with cheerless haze, like a coat of primer. Eloise took a sip of tea; the mug was warm in her hands. The rest of her shivered.

Fucking February.

Outside, the streets were quiet, the sky drenched in darkness. She dragged her fingers along the slick kitchen island. Back and forth, back and forth.

An entire month had passed since The Last Supper, as she'd come to think of it, like the painting by da Vinci: the five of them seated together. Bibs embodying the Italian mobster Jesus.

The thought made her smile. Overall, her mood had been decent, considering. A six out of ten, perhaps a six-point-five, thanks in part to her busy schedule. Self-imposed, but necessary: eleven-hour work days. *Early to bed, early to rise*, as the old saying went. Something her grandmother might have voiced, if she were a different grandmother altogether.

One. Entire. Month.

It was hard to believe time had passed so quickly, and in hindsight, most days came and went without much thought or refection: a steady swipe of events, zipping by.

Except tonight.

Tonight, was another matter entirely. Her mind seemed keen on poking and prying, stirring up something to think about—anything besides sleep. She'd tossed and turned for nearly an hour before coming into the kitchen, her thoughts diverting from work-related quandaries (*perhaps, if we positioned my net deeper into the cortex …*) to her personal life.

Jack was the current topic. A fire with plenty of fuel.

Their first few days together had been … quiet. Jack was clearly timid, unsure how to resume being her husband. And she couldn't blame him; the scenario was unchartered for most. He'd stop in the middle of a sentence, holding back, leaving her to wonder what exactly he wanted to say. Everything about him was softened, dulled, like he was walking on eggshells—scared she might deflate if pressed too firmly.

Would she?

Maybe.

He'd since evolved to be slightly more forthright, but still reserved—the sort of reservation she was now starting to question. *Is he unsure, or holding something back?* Those were different types of silence.

Jack had always been guarded, but lately he was … different, in ways she couldn't place but sensed. There'd been a few moments—a turn of phrase, an odd gesture, a whitewashed stare—that left her wondering if he'd been overtaken by extraterrestrial life: his behavior was *that* striking. And yet, so brief and insignificant she'd quickly recovered.

You're being stupidly analytical, Eloise.

Perhaps she was, but there was no denying a drift had formed between them, mysterious and fleeting, like a secret.

Still, over the past few days they'd fallen back into something like love, just a little more jaded. Last night, she awoke to find him sliding over her half-dressed body, a spirit in the night. They'd moved in sync, out of habit, quenching a drought-long thirst. The resulting form of lovemaking was tender—for the most part—though it became evident through the odd thrust or hard grip that they weren't just making love; they were making a small, ferocious bit of hate—not unjustified.

Jack had sent her (kicking and screaming, no less) to an inpatient facility.

She, in turn, had tried to erase him from her memory not once, but twice.

When it came to harboring resentment, they had their reasons.

She took another sip of tea, barely lukewarm. Outside, the rain accelerated, sheeting down in torrents. It was 3 a.m.: an ungodly hour to be sitting at one's kitchen island, drinking shitty tea, but she was sick of trying to sleep, troubling as it was.

Steady sleep was often the first to go, replaced by an unpredictable cycle of drifting and waking. Never feeling fully rested. People underestimated the importance of a good sleep, how quickly a sturdy mental landscape could tumble into oblivion without proper shut-eye. Lack of sleep, she knew—rain weeping down, clock ticking faint echoes in her large, angled house—was just the beginning.

Her neck pivoted and she met the photo of Linus, cased in a thick walnut frame, glass glinting in the limited light. He looked handsome, healthy, alive, his navy polo tremendous against his pale skin, eyes almost three-dimensional, reaching out.

And then came a wave grief so sweeping she was nearly drowned by it. *My sweet boy*, she mouthed, letting the room fade until it was only her eyes and his eyes locked in the dark.

The heavy, sunken feeling was impossible to ignore. It wasn't a single trauma that had broken her, but their summative weight. Tempered glass slammed over and over, then tapped perfectly along one side and voila! instantly shattered. She owned a suitcase of memories that was far too heavy for one person to carry—psychiatrist or not. At one point, she was proud of her strength and resiliency, but that day had long passed. Nowadays, she was just as fragile as anyone else.

She chugged the last of her cold tea and shut her eyes, *hard*, inflicting enough pressure to burn. She longed to activate the machinery in her head—the neural net capable of inhibiting the pain entangled with her thoughts—but it wasn't that simple. As much as she wished it were true, it was impossible to erase the past without changing the present. It only confused people, poking holes in their mind like a slice of Swiss cheese. Novelty and loveliness and distraction were required: a perfectly controlled environment like Blue Haven.

She leaned back against the chair and faced a piddly pot light wedged into the kitchen ceiling, imagining a hot beam of sunshine instead. She tried to pull out a positive thought from her sadness, like tug of war.

The briny ocean breeze.

Waves rolling forward like poetry.

The soft skin on Linus's palm.

These thoughts did little to lift her slipping mood, and reminded her instead of life's emotional inequity. Short of mechanically altering neural hardware, there was no form of happiness as strong, pervasive, and overpowering as the notes of grief in her heart. The two emotional valences—happy and sad—had different floors, different ceilings, and their intensities were incomparable.

She stood and strode to the bathroom, the tiles cool on her feet. The dismal light was almost soothing as she carefully unlatched the medicine cabinet. Her fingertips danced over a small pharmacy's worth of bottle caps, and in the end, she tossed back a sweet cocktail of sedatives.

That oughta do it.

Her weight on the bed roused Jack and he flopped over, a human pancake, his breath a mix of warmth and toxicity. "Are you okay?" he asked.

"Yes, I'm fine," she whispered, knowing those words were a lie. His arm hooked around her waist and she allowed the uncomfortable heaviness of his elbow to push against her abdomen.

"I love you," he said, his voice half asleep.

"I love you too," she replied.

Silence came, longer and louder in the dead of night.

She loved him, yes, and he loved her, but that didn't erase the queasy feeling in her chest that something stood between them.

Something worth investigating.

Chapter Forty-Five

✦

"And then what happened?"

Eloise leaned back, closing her eyes. She was in the middle of a session with Doctor Leslie Marks. *Prolonged exposure*: a common therapeutic approach for PTSD whereby traumatic memories are gradually revisited.

"He came into the room," she replied.

Leslie interrupted. "Active tense—you know the drill."

"*Right*, right. He enters the room and it's dark—but not dark enough. I can make out his whiskers, glinting like needles, and his bulbous nose: frumpy, troll-like. An alcoholic's nose. Though I suppose I don't know this yet, being ten. At any rate, *wake up*, he says, coming closer. His breath is vicious—so strong it stings my eyes. I freeze, and his face scratches up my cheek like sandpaper. The friction intensifies, growing painful, until—"

"Stop. How are you feeling?"

Eloise opened her eyes. The first time she'd approached this memory in session (years ago), she'd felt panic—a whole stampede of it, trampling everything else. Then came anger, fear, shame—the usual suspects, each taking their turn in the spotlight. That was the point of prolonged exposure: stirring up pain and watching it linger, confronting it safely in a beige room with parlor chairs and a trusted voice. The alternative was avoidance—the kindling of fear.

She took a few seconds to evaluate her emotions, but there was little reaction: pulse normal, chest unwound and open, skin tempered, comfortable. This memory—dreadful, almost unspeakably horrific—roused nothing. Instead it came to her like a story in a book, or a movie on television. She was more the observer than the narrator. *Detachment*, was the proper term.

"I don't feel anything," she said. "Just numb."

Ironically, the hardest part about the slew of mental illnesses that had come to define her was not sadness or grief or soul-sucking misery. It was the opposite: an emotional flatline that came and wiped away her emotions—good and bad—like an eraser over chalk. How could a person live without feelings?

Leslie was statue-still and quiet. A topic change was coming—the sort of insight that came from many years of being treated by Doctor Leslie Marks. During this time period they'd grown close, blurring lines and complicating matters, but also simplifying them. Rapport was always deepest between friends.

"How are your meds going?"

Eloise sighed. "This is incredibly embarrassing to admit as a psychiatrist, but my adherence is terrible—has been for a while. Recently, I've tossed back the odd benzo here and there, but that's it."

Leslie's eyebrows dashed together in confusion. "You haven't been taking your medication regularly? Like, ever?"

"*I know*," she replied, her cheeks flushing with warm blood. "I'm a terrible patient; I should heed my own advice. I'll work on it, I promise—though I'm currently exploring different options. *Between meds*, let's call it."

For a moment, Leslie stared out the window, collecting thoughts Eloise could not decipher, and then she nodded, refocusing. "Be honest. Do you want to go back to Blue Haven?"

Eloise glanced around the spacious, ivory-walled office. In a sense, she was back, at least physically. Only twenty feet away the door to nothing and everything awaited: four wonderfully happy patients, living inside of a perfectly catered paradise: Bibs, Westley, Franny, and Bob—all of whom she'd been monitoring regularly. Tweaking and modifying, stimulating and inhibiting, providing input into narratives she knew would bring them joy. *Can we have some famous opera singer visit Julian? Is it possible to re-create a sunset cruise for Bob and Franny? Can we modify and broadcast highlights of Westley's fictitious NFL career?*

Her job—insofar as she could perform it, for the time being at least—was to keep them happy, and she took that job very seriously, though she couldn't deny the longing in her heart—a desperate, if not guilty, desire to be among them. Was it selfish to want this? Or an act of self compassion? Personal gains aside, would her continued re-entry into the program not strengthen the overall project? So far, she was a stain on their record of success. An outlier that needed correcting.

All at once she thought of Linus. The scent of his buttery skin and soft hair. He'd always smelled the same, ever since he was a baby: bright and salty, like the seaside.

"Yes, I want to go back," she replied. "I think about it almost every day."

"Do you *think* about it, though? Pragmatically?"

"No, I haven't fleshed out any details. I mean, I'd return as Aloe, naturally. I'm sure that would appease the others. And absolutely no notebooks, or any other creative schemes that may rouse my own suspicion and doubt. I suspect if we recalibrate the placement of my neural net along the premedial—"

"—So, you have thought about it."

"In passing, I guess."

"I see. Have you talked to Jack?"

Her nerves flinched. "God no. I think we both know what he'd say."

Leslie tilted her head, curious as a parakeet. "How is Jack, anyway?"

"He's fine." The reply came automatically, though it was more assumption than anything. Jack was always fine. A sturdy piece of driftwood floating along the sea of her instability.

"That's a relief," Leslie replied.

A relief?

"Is there a reason you're relieved?"

"No. No of course not. Just checking in on your support system, is all." The words came quickly. Too quickly?

Yes, based on the slant of Leslie's left eyebrow, a quick glance at the clock, her thumb tapping against her knee. She was holding something back.

Something to do with Jack.

Eloise steadied her reaction, though her mind filled with theories. For the first time, Leslie's uncanny beauty came to the forefront. Her large, almond eyes fanned with dense lashes. Perfectly arched eyebrows and rosebud lips. The remarkable symmetry of her features: everything well placed and contoured. A striking single woman, in sum—not the type you'd happily leave with your husband. And yet she had. *Twice.*

Please, she told herself, shaking off the notion. But part of it stuck, like a note pinned to her subconscious. She considered pressing further—asking questions that would either put the theory to rest or liven it further—but their session was nearly over, and frankly, she didn't have the energy. There was a time and place for this investigation to proceed, but it wasn't now.

"Well," Leslie said, smiling. "That's a wrap." She buttoned up her cardigan. The material looked soft, expensive. "I do hope we're getting somewhere."

"I hope so too," Eloise replied, doubtful. When it came to trying variations of cognitive behavioral therapies, she'd given up hope. Not that such interventions didn't work; she was a psychiatrist, after all, and had used psychotherapy regularly in her practice, before all of this. Perhaps it was her own insight that made such techniques less effective for her, personally. She wanted to be hopeful—*maybe this time?*—but the realist in her prevailed. Her only chance at happiness was two rooms over, in Blue Haven—if only she could solve the missing link.

She stood and pressed her wrinkly slacks, wishing she'd taken the time to iron them, particularly in Leslie Mark's shadow: the muse of work attire—with impeccable bone structure, at that. "What are your plans for the rest of the day?" she asked.

Leslie grabbed a mint, carefully prying it free with her long, groomed fingernails. "Intake. We're preparing interview materials. I'm sure you've heard, but we're hoping to admit our first addictions patient."

"*Oh?*" She hadn't heard. "That's great." Her voice was flat, a little snippy, despite her best intentions. Blue Haven was building the capacity to help more patients with increasing diversity, and the results were promising—great accomplishments, truly—but her personal lack of involvement in higher-level decision making stung. Blue Haven was *her* baby, and she was still the executive director, on paper at least. Not that she could blame anyone. They'd done—and continued to do—an exceptional job in her absence.

"I'm sorry," Leslie said, clearly picking up on her tone. "You know," she paused, looking up at the ceiling, like the words were tumbling down from the sky. "People work here for a lot of different reasons: to be on the forefront of discovery, to have their name beside *Blue Haven*—the first of its kind in the world, to witness history and be a part of it, to help people. Personally though, I work here for you, because I think you're an extraordinary woman with an extraordinary mind."

Eloise looked away. "Please."

"Seriously," Leslie continued. "What you're doing here today: showing up, being honest, allowing us all to take part in your recovery, unveiled. That level of vulnerability is brave. It's damn brave, and I hope you know that."

"I appreciate the words," she replied, feeling a tinge of guilt for considering moments earlier that this woman—her therapist and friend—was capable of having an affair with her husband. "Anyway," she turned toward the door. "Same time tomorrow?"

"If you're up for it," Leslie replied, smoothing her sweater. The motion drew attention to her curvy figure: small waist, vivacious hips. Eloise livened with jealousy, the sort of instinctual rouse that came from standing in the shadow of a younger, more beautiful woman.

The notion of an affair was dramatic. She could see this, plain as day. But she also imagined Jack standing in her shoes: lonely and bereaved, abandoned, angry. And Leslie, so lovely and warm and gorgeous and smart—much like his wife, before all of this.

Even if he hadn't acted.

He certainly must have considered it.

Chapter Forty-Six

As soon as the door clicked open, an aroma wafted: garlic, fresh pasta, the sharp tang of citrus. Eloise shook the powdery snow off her hat and coat, then tapped her boots against the step. Jazz oozed in the background, soft and sleazy.

Jack swung around the corner. "Hi, welcome home." He looked handsome in a fitted olive dress shirt, a stemless glass of white resting in his palm.

"Hi," she replied, taking it all in. "What's going on?"

"I'm making dinner for my wife. Here, let me take your coat."

She arched a brow as he kissed her on the cheek; it lasted a few seconds longer than a simple peck. "I wanted to surprise you with a nice evening."

A grin pulled at her lips. "That's sweet," she replied, the coat slipping off her shoulders. Jack tossed it on a hanger and she admired him—perhaps for the first time since her release, just over a month ago. There was cadence to his movements, a swagger achieved in partnership with his good looks. Not traditionally handsome, per say, but a tamed sort of ruggedness: the texture of his aging skin; thick, salty blonde hair tousled with pomade; large, soft lips; childish dimples.

"What's on the menu?" she asked, following him into the kitchen. Her bones soaked up the warmth from inside as Jack rushed to the stove. He drained a colander of steaming noodles, then carefully selected a few spices from the open shelves that existed on every wall of their kitchen. She hated those shelves, everything on display: mismatching mugs, vials of oil, cookbooks with clashing spines—maroon, pink, brown.

"Tonight, we're having lime cappelletti with seared scallops."

"*Mmm*," she replied. The dish was a favorite between them, something they'd first tried in Brazil. Jack was a good cook. She often forgot how well he knew his way around the kitchen. Over the past few years, they'd seldom eaten together—on account of being seldom together.

He slid a glass of wine across the island. "Italian chardonnay. Quite good."

She took a sip, savoring the sharp, bright flavor, followed by a gulp. The liquid melted through her body, muting everything—in a good way. "This is going straight to my head," she said.

"I bet. When was the last time you had a drink?"

"Gosh, *years?*" The ever-changing gurney of treatments did not bode well with alcohol, and so she'd abstained. "Actually wait, I think we shared a bottle after Seaside, before Blue Haven, round two."

Jack nodded. "Yes, that's right." He filled his glass and splashed a little more into hers. He began to hum. Was he tipsy? Perhaps. Or just exceptionally upbeat.

She sat at the counter, letting her body exhale.

"How was your day?" he asked.

"Fine," she replied. "Not overly productive, but long and tiring nonetheless."

After her session with Leslie, she'd spent the afternoon in the main control room: a giant, humming space that broadcasted the happenings of Blue Haven like live-stream TV. Elegant pieces of hardware monitored neural responses in the background, requiring some oversight, but little. People moved around her like spirits as she sat and watched, tracking the movement of Bibs, Westley, Franny, and Bob, wishing she was among them.

She'd spent a long while monitoring Bibs in particular, as he read a book on botany, for sheer pleasure. She imagined the world through his eyes, wondering—less with curiosity than longing—what made him so different? Why she continued to land on one side of the wall, while he, content as a jaybird, thrived on the other?

"You look tired," Jack said, breaking her daze.

"I am. Sleep has been ... a challenge."

He frowned and she regretted sharing. "I had a session with Leslie today," she added, feigning optimism. "We're doing primary exposure again. She's still convinced my childhood experiences are a root cause, so we're revisiting. I'm also hoping to try *maledropam*—that new medication they're trialing in Canada. I emailed a colleague in Ontario about it."

"That's promising," Jack replied, his whole face aglow.

"Yes." She took a gulp of wine, large enough to burn her throat. Under different circumstances—were Jack not trying to procure a lovely evening, and her talent for arguing not drowned with exhaustion—she would have voiced that the most promising option was the facility they visited daily; the one he'd helped her create.

Jack salted the scallops and placed them gently into a hot pan, each hissing as they landed. He talked about his day—*I met with Michaela from accounting to review financials and funding. Did Leslie tell you we're admitting an addictions patient? Anyway, I'll be part of the interview panel, so I prepped.* The words washed over her while she sipped and nodded, sipped and nodded, her heavy brain not capable of keeping pace. As she drained the glass and poured another the exhaustion stupefying her thoughts lifted, replaced by a poke of excitement.

"Can I help with anything?" she offered.

Jack waved her off, simultaneously gathering two porcelain bowls from the ghastly, disorganized shelves. He snapped a pair of tongs, *clank clank clank*, and this action, for some insensible, alcohol-fueled reason, made her laugh.

She watched him curl the pasta, spinning and spinning. Next came the scallops, perfectly browned. He finished the dish with grated parmesan and extra lime zest.

"That smells fucking heavenly," she said.

Jack smirked. "Do you think *fucking* and *heavenly* are oxymorons—biblically speaking?"

"I think fucking and heaven go well together." She winked, unsure what was overcoming her, but definitely not disputing it. She hadn't felt the giddy pulse of flirtatiousness in recent memory.

Jack gave her a twisted look, clearly amused, and then he carried the bowls to the table. She followed, a touch unstable on her feet, but managing.

They sat across from each other and Jack lit a few tealight candles.

"We have candles?" she asked.

"As of today, yes. I thought you'd appreciate the ambiance."

"Thank you—this was all such an effort."

Too much effort?

Stop it! She scolded. Extravagant gestures were out of character for Jack, but she refused to ruin a nice evening with unnecessary skepticism.

She took a bite of lime cappelletti, and the flavor was everything she remembered, perhaps more: creamy, surprisingly zesty.

"Did you brown the butter?" she asked.

"I did. I was wondering if you'd notice."

"I quite like it. Adds depth."

Her knife slipped through the scallop, perfectly cooked. She closed her eyes and took another bite, hoping to liven a memory from years ago (that seaside bistro in Brazil—one of their first trips as a couple), but instead there was only the impression of Blue Haven. The experience of food there was like nothing else, and Jack's cappelletti brought forth a similar joy, just muted. She could easily be sitting at a Michelin-star restaurant, Bibs performing an impromptu solo, the others quiet with awe, a million stars in every direction, the best of everything just within reach.

"I missed this," she found herself saying.

"Me too," Jack replied, misinterpreting her statement to mean dinners with each other—which, to be fair, she also missed. Her focus shifted, narrowing back to their house with all its angles and open spaces. She twirled her fork with pasta and tried to enjoy the moment, uninterrupted by thoughts of Blue Haven.

Ordinary life just couldn't compete.

Jack's hand landed over hers and the touch of his skin stirred a breeze of lust—unusual, for her. She loved Jack. *Of course* she loved Jack. But their relationship was complicated. Most days, she was simply incapable of loving. The urge, the principle, the *theory* behind it was there, but the feelings wouldn't come.

"Hey," he said, and then he held up a finger, standing. "One moment, I have an idea I'd like to propose. But first, drinks!"

Seconds later, he returned with another bottle of wine, red this time. He uncorked it with a smile—strong, sturdy. Jack had a fantastic smile; it reminded her of a handshake. Some had perfected the handshake—authoritative, the correct amount of pressure; Jack had perfected the smile.

He filled their glasses, the odd drop oozing down like blood. "There, that's better," he said, lifting his glass.

She met him half-way—*clink*—and then took a sip. Luscious and full-bodied, sweet yet tart. "So, you were saying?"

"I was?"

"Yes." She laughed, noting the faraway look in his eyes. He was adorably spacey, a drunk frat boy. "You said you have an idea you'd like to propose."

He stared up at the ceiling, through the skylight and into the night. "Oh yes! I have a slightly wild proposition for you."

"Wild proposition?" She took another sip, drowning her inhibitions. *Death by pinot noir.*

"Let's go in the hot tub."

"What?" She nearly spit out her wine. "Seriously? *The hot tub?* We still have one? And it works? I mean, it's been … years."

"For you, maybe. I like a good soak now and then."

She pictured Jack sitting in a froth of water, all alone, staring into the Chicago cityscape from their balcony, his expression glass-still and utterly depleted. The image of his loneliness was shattering: a cleaver to the heart, straight down the middle. And then she felt nothing at all, and was both troubled and relieved by the sudden absence of emotion.

She glanced outside, where freckles of snow splattered the window, whisked occasionally by a gust of air.

"It's so cold though."

"The water will be warm, I promise. Come on." He reached out his hand, inviting. "Like the good old days."

The good old days. They'd had some, yes—a shared life that came hard and fast. One minute, it was puppy love: dinners on verandas; hand-held walks through the city; lazy Saturdays, cocooned together on the couch. Then suddenly they were living in a mid-century modern with far too much space, creating an empire, and raising a child. They hardly even knew each other. She knew Jack's body, yes—knew his swollen pecs, brilliant eyes, rough patches along each knuckle, earlobes like teardrops. But she hadn't known his soul. This, she'd become acquainted with over time, layer by layer, and it turned out to be a good soul: kind, attentive, supportive, nurturing—everything she wanted in a partner.

And then tragedy struck, and it wasn't about discovering souls or falling deeper into love. It was about surviving.

She took a gulp of wine, pushing these thoughts from her mind. Her body was humming, a silly mood arriving. Times being what they were, she couldn't afford to waste it.

"Alright," she said, sending Jack a smirk. "Let's get in the damn hot tub."

His cheeks flushed and he grabbed their glasses with one hand, wedging the bottle under his armpit with the other. Before they scurried up the stairs, he turned back and winked. "Clothing optional."

Chapter Forty-Seven

E loise tossed her wrinkled slacks in a heap and flung her white sweater across the bedspread, where it curved and stretched like a cloud in the wind. Outside, on the balcony, Jack was opening the lid to the hot-tub. A plume of steam billowed into the night.

Despite his *clothing optional* comment, she slipped into a black, one-piece bathing suit. They had neighbors, after all, and though she was technically drunk, she wasn't nearly drunk enough to skinny-dip around strangers for the sheer sake of it.

She mistakenly glanced in the oversized mirror, taken by the sag in her skin. Not anywhere specifically, just an all-over tug. Gravity being gravity. She was thin, the sort of figure that looked nice in clothing but not exposed. Not *nice* thin: frail, old-boned and droopy, with patches of eczema and blotchy sunspots. A drastic change from weeks ago, when she was living in her twenty-five-year-old body: everything tight and smooth and porcelain. Breasts with vivacity. Two inches of breezy space between her thighs.

She pictured Leslie Marks: a decade younger, but aging far more gracefully. Still glowing with youth. Eloise stared at the furrows of her cleavage, spaced and textured like an elephant's hide.

The sliding door *swooshed* open and Jack popped his head in. "You coming?"

She grabbed a towel, her wine glass, and whatever dignity she could manage. "Yes, coming."

When she reached the door, a gust of frigid air cleared her lungs.

"Holy shit," she managed, her teeth already starting to chatter.

"Well hurry up then!"

Jack pulled her into the steamy lagoon. Her legs entered the swirling water, followed by her waist, torso, breasts, shoulders, chin. In five seconds flat, she was instantly more drunk. Still, in stark contrast to the days and weeks before, she liked everything that was currently happening: lights coming from beneath in a prism—pink, purple, blue—obscured by movement; the strong medicinal smell of chlorine; the coolness on her face but warmth everywhere else; the neurons in her brain slow and lax; Jack gazing at her like he used to, unabated by worry.

She leaned in and kissed him, noting the surprise in his eyes, so close to hers. His lips were cold and still, but only for a moment, until they moved in sync.

"This was a good idea," she stated afterwards, sinking into a plastic, preformed seat.

The jets blasted onto her lower back, easing the tension that hardened her muscles like bone. Jack found her hand beneath the water and squeezed it—a small thrill. Perhaps they would make love tonight—*love*, without the hate.

"We used to come here all the time," Jack said, and then he paused, adding, "Or we tried to." He chuckled and she did too, remembering. When Linus was a baby—and well into toddlerhood—he'd slept terribly, waking often with loud, shrill cries. She swore that boy had a relaxation radar. The second she was neck-deep in hot water, a glass of wine poured, the stress of the day slipping away: *Muh-waaah! Muh-waaah!*

They took turns, robing in towels and mincing to his crib with wet feet.

"It's okay sweet boy," she'd say, rubbing his back until he dozed off.

Twenty-minutes later, half a glass gone: *Muh-waaah! Muh-waaah!*

And so it went, back and forth and back and forth, their footsteps dotting the hardwood like bunny trails, moments of triumph and turmoil mixing interchangeably, sporadic sips and quick soaks—all worth it, to hear Linus's soft breaths, watch his eyes close in sleepy defeat, the love in her chest just blooming. He needed her and she needed him and the three of them needed each other in ways that fulfilled and completed a cycle, like the conversion of nitrogen.

In some ways these memories seemed like just yesterday; in others, a lifetime.

"He would have been sixteen," Jack whispered, not to her, but into the night—perhaps to Linus, somewhere in spirit.

The plummeting dread was sudden, like a trap door, and she clutched her rock-hard stomach.

Today was her son's birthday, *February 26th*, and she had forgotten.

"Oh my God," she whispered. "I didn't even …"

"*Shhh*," Jack said, bringing her into his arms. His embrace was tight, like he was trying to hold her together before she could fall apart. "I shouldn't have mentioned it."

Tears came—weird, drunken, spluttery tears. "Yes, you should have!" She was livid with herself. "It's our son's goddamn birthday and I didn't even realize. Why didn't you say anything earlier?"

"I wasn't sure you wanted to remember."

"*Of course I want to remember!*"

He paused. "Okay, I'm sorry."

Tectonic plates of emotions collided in her chest. She wanted to remember as much as she wanted to forget. How could it be that everything she loved and feared existed so closely; that losing one, meant losing the other? Linus's quiet voice whispered in her mind, the last words he'd spoken to her—to anyone.

"Mom, it's okay."

The hurt was so deep and forceful it rallied through her like a crescendo from one of Bibs's many performances, reverberating in every cell. And then all at once the feeling drained, suctioned away, and she was empty and numb. Her emotions were clearly malfunctioning, on the fritz. The rapid, bipolar landscape of ups and downs and nothings was impossible to process. She drew in her wine glass and chugged, livening whatever drunken buzz she could savor, sucking the last drops of contentment from the evening like a sponge.

"Let's talk about something else," Jack said. "I know you're not a fan of winter, but isn't it great out here? I mean, what a view."

She nodded, though she disagreed. The view was nothing to gawk over. Their swanky Lincoln Park neighbors cluttered the horizon with their tall, skinny houses. Puny maples dotted teeny-tiny lawns, half grown and stiff with winter; neatly trimmed hedges swelled in the darkness like burglars. Eerie balms of light beamed from street lamps, illuminating gusts of snow suspended in the sky. While the city lay beyond—prominent skyscrapers with glowing windows and chrome surfaces glinting in the moonlight—the halo of light smothered the stars, leaving them faint or invisible, nothing much to see in the dark, dark sky but some gray, low-lying clouds.

Compared to Blue Haven, the view was hardly worth speaking about.

She gave her head a shake. *Stop thinking about Blue Haven.*

But she couldn't.

"I want to go back," she said, the words flying from her mouth like they had a mind of their own.

Jack was quiet, and for a while it was only the whizzing of jets and stillness of night and air flooding into her lungs. As time passed, she began to wonder whether she'd said those words aloud—*I want to go back*—or just thought them.

"I know," he said softly.

She slid deeper into the water, reminded of her last day at Blue Haven: how sinking into the ocean seemed reasonable, if not pre-ferred—a stark reminder that her recent admission was an ultimate failure.

"I don't know what else I'm supposed to do," she said, "besides keep trying. Blue Haven feels like my only chance at something like happiness. And I want to be happy."

His hand smoothed along her back. "I also want you to be happy."

"And Jack, it's *so* lovely there," she found herself saying. "I was able to appreciate more this time around. It's like nothing this life can offer. The sky, the water, the air—living in a protective bubble. Although … I suppose the bubble wasn't so protective for me, personally." She paused, recalling the deep distress she'd felt being inside of those tall, transparent walls—just regular walls, in reality: a visual illusion they'd constructed in the event a patient (herself, apparently) ventured to the outskirts.

She stared at the sky, fog rising like a frown in the night. The idea that happiness awaited in any capacity seemed wishful, if not mirac-ulous. She was an exception to her own solution. And maybe she de-served to be miserable, for believing she could figure out the human brain and remove the pain and suffering tied to human existence. This was her retribution.

"Maybe we can't play God," she whispered.

"*Can't?*" Jack replied. "Or *shouldn't?*"

His eyes met hers and she noticed a sad form of endurance she hadn't seen before, or perhaps overlooked: running out of steam.

She wasn't sure what to make of it all: the question he'd rephrased, her recovery—or lack thereof. The wine was sharp in her belly and her thoughts were heavy with hot, drunken exhaustion. She closed her eyes, reminded of her conversation from earlier, with Leslie, an implication left lingering: something to do with Jack's wellbeing.

Her lids shot open and there he was, staring at the sky.

"How are you doing?" she asked. "Really?

His eyebrows furrowed, like the question was some sort of puzzle. "You never ask me how I'm doing."

A lump formed in her throat. Not a lie, by any stretch. And perhaps the implications, so simply alluded to in a single sentence—*You never ask me how I'm doing*—had branched into something larger and uglier than she fully understood.

"I'm fine," he said, and then he drained the last of his wine. "Thanks for asking."

Chapter Forty-Eight

Eloise kept the alarm close, on vibrate, so the murmur against her skin wouldn't rouse Jack awake. Four in the morning came unpleasantly: a headache splitting through her skull, mouth parched. The exhaustion was sweltering, like a full body heat, and every part of her begged for sleep.

She reached into the bedside drawer and found some Advil. After tossing them back with a dry gulp, she dragged herself out of bed and into their cold, dark en suite, where she flocked to the tap and sucked back mouthfuls of water. Nothing had ever tasted so good.

She wiped her chin and flicked on the light. The reflection staring back made her cringe: saggy eyes full of crusted sleep; the pores on her cheeks large and puckered, like pie-crust; an overall paleness that bordered pallid. She filled her hands with cold water and splashed herself awake, letting the droplets slide down her face and pool along her hairline. She smoothed the wetness over her flyaways, then pulled back her half-kinked, half-curled strands into a bun that smelled strongly of chlorine. *This is as good as it's going to get.*

Jack was still dead asleep, sprawled like a starfish and snoring in loud, labored groans as she snuck past him toward the closet. Inside the doorway, she paused, leaning against the frame. The night before lingered, its impression bittersweet: a lovely dinner, a nice buzz, some quality time with Jack. But after she'd slipped into bed, and her thoughts started to spin, the problem became apparent.

It wasn't that she'd forgotten Linus's birthday, or that Jack had lied about being fine—unsettling as those moments were. It was far more subtle.

She'd expressed a desire to return to Blue Haven.

And he hadn't tried to stop her.

He always tried to stop her.

Last night, he'd hardly even reacted, which got her thinking. Maybe he didn't care. Maybe … he actually wanted her gone.

She paused, trying not to get ahead of herself. Jack's lack of dispute is what prompted her to arise at this ungodly hour. The evidence was starting to surmount. Not an if, but a what. The man was hiding something, and she was going to discover the truth.

Her closet was dim and she pawed around, taking the first outfit that met her grasp: a pair of winter leggings and a navy oversized sweater, balled with fluff from the wash. Not the most professional attire, but *screw it*. What did the world expect of her at four in the morning, hungover?

Her body slipped through the darkness, out of the bedroom and down the hall, the harrowing light from a single spot light leading the way. The wide, oversized tiles were cool on her thinly socked feet, sending goosebumps up her arms. When she reached the end of the hallway, prepared to continue, a tug in her chest made her stop.

She turned and shone the light onto Linus's door: white and grooved, marked with a train-shaped board made from walnut and adorned with a baby blue "L." It was a gift from a patient, just before Linus's birth.

She traced her finger over the "L" and closed her eyes. Her chest rocked like the hull of a ship, stirring with motion. Even though time had passed, his absence—the crater-sized hole in her heart—was no less afflicting. The grief had not dulled or shapeshifted or lifted in its brutality. Still it came, the waves of heartache, over and over.

Her hand cupped the doorknob, smooth and chrome. *When was the last time I came in here?* She couldn't recall, and perhaps that's why she entered like a gust of wind. One rotation, a small creek, then a human *swoosh*.

What she expected to find was an exhibition of her son, perfectly preserved and on display like a museum. His bedsheets half ruffled from the last impression of his warm, living body; fuzzy monster slippers with emphatic googly eyes tossed in the corner; his desk scattered with papers and pencils and half-finished sketches; a computer screensaver dancing with multicolored bubbles; posters on the wall of sports heroes she didn't know, or care to know, but had purchased and mounted nonetheless; a black, graphic hoodie slung over a chair, still wafting with his boyish scent. At one point, the little pieces he'd left behind had become her lifeline.

This time, as she stepped inside, there was nothing. Not one thing. She took in the four empty walls. The space was so small and vacant it seemed more like a closet than a bedroom. For a moment, she questioned everything. Had she entered the wrong room by mistake? Or been thrust into some alternate dimension where there was no Linus, and he never existed? Her breathing quickened as a thrum of pressure mounted in her temples.

She left immediately, unable to stomach the loneliness.

At some point during her recent treatment, Blue Haven or Seaside, Jack had cleared the space of Linus's belongings. He'd even plucked the tacks from the wall. *The fucking tacks.* Anger blazed through her like an open burn, and she found herself marching back to their bedroom with the intention of waking Jack—demanding answers.

What the hell have you done? Where did you put his things?

Her hands trembled as she imagined the encounter. Jack's heavy, confused expression, the fight that would certainly ensue, rousing far more than the state of Linus's bedroom.

She stopped in the doorway, heaving air. *What good would any of that do?* She eyed his cell phone on the console, blinking red and needing a charge. In his drunkenness, he'd forgotten to plug it in. Her anger switched gears and she tiptoed over.

She took the device in her hands and entered the passcode.

Scroll, scroll, scroll.

First came the texts: sparse and months apart. Either he'd deleted messages, or had very few to begin with. She wasn't sure how to feel about that—pissed, or empathetic. Her fingers tapped on recent calls, and just as she absorbed the name—*Leslie Marks*—over and over again, the phone went dead.

She closed her eyes and took a breath, overcome with stupidity. Her gut had pointed her in this direction yesterday, and she'd chosen to ignore it.

She placed the phone back on the console and left the room, trying to make excuses. *Maybe Leslie was trying to get a hold of me instead?* After all, she barely used her cell phone. *Perhaps they had a work matter to discuss?* There were innocent reasons for repeated calls, surely.

At the front door, she slipped on a thick wool coat, simultaneously stepping into a pair of clompy boots. Her movements were tight and controlled as she passed through the garage, staying quiet. Adrenaline was starting to murmur as her headache receded, the Advil kicking in.

Her plan wasn't nearly as dramatic in principle as it seemed to her thumping heartbeat: searching Jack's computer at work. Her early departure wasn't even suspicious; during periods of wellness, she was a known workaholic, spending long days at the office—the odd night.

Still, thrill flickered as she backed out of the driveway, glancing at their house in the rearview mirror: sharp-edged and peculiar. The windows were large and dark-rimmed, modern and cold. Perhaps it was less the house she dreaded than the memories hardened inside.

Either way, the sight of it urged her to run.

And Blue Haven was the only destination she knew of that made sense.

Chapter Forty-Nine

The streets were vacant and frosted with early morning snow—not much, just remnants from the night before, hanging on. Eloise turned onto the highway, Lake Shore Drive, and merged among the whizzing headlights: early risers, late nighters.

Normally, she drove to work on autopilot, but today, Linus overtook her thoughts, stirred to life by an empty room. Her anger toward Jack broadened as she absorbed the passing landmarks. *There's the sign for Lincoln Park Zoo. Wrigley Field is just over there. Coming up to Montrose Beach.*

She pictured Linus involuntarily, livened by the passing locations—memories demanding to be felt. So many firsts. Like the first time he saw a real tiger and the magnificent look in his eyes. Or their first Cubs game, Linus far less excited about watching baseball than eating a footlong hot dog. He was four—finally allowed to devour an entire esophagus-sized choking hazard without having it sliced in two. "I want this every day," he'd joked, with his gummy smile and front tooth missing, a streak of ketchup across his pale, soft cheek.

Oh God.

Montrose Beach.

The memories here were endless. She pictured Linus in all his forms: a bright, chubby infant, eating mouthfuls of gritty sand; a waddling toddler, streaking down the boardwalk with his bum cheeks bright as moons; a little boy, building slanted sandcastles; a bigger boy, his hair mop-top shaggy and shoulders starting to broaden.

The summer before he died, Linus had learned to surf, and she recalled the vivid sense of amazement she felt watching his thin, agile body sail over waves with grace and focus. He filled her with pride and love and wonder—emotions that only came flatly now, like a sheet of paper, shadowed by his absence.

In hindsight, it had happened both quickly and with excruciating slowness. Six months short of his thirteenth birthday, the diagnosis came: a Wilms tumor. She'd actually sighed with relief, fearing Linus's recent symptoms (constipation, abdominal tenderness, frequent vomiting) foreshadowed something far more serious. Not that cancer wasn't serious, but the doctor within her rose to the occasion, full of facts: Wilms—a rare, cancerous tumor in the kidneys—was highly treatable. The five-year survival rate was ninety-five percent. Linus would be fine.

She'd revisited this moment on many occasions, and wondered if something deadlier, like a brain tumor, would have spared her the false sense of hope she harbored for months.

"Am I going to die?" Linus asked.

She'd laughed in response—*laughed*. "Sweetheart, you're not going to die. Think of it like a rock inside of you. We'll take out the rock, and everything will be perfectly alright."

Except the rock, as it turned out, was laden with anaplasia: rapidly dividing abnormal cells. And the rock, as it turned out, was not *a* rock, but several, clotting inside of his lymph nodes and spreading throughout his body.

Within weeks, the prognosis pivoted, steep as a cliff—so quickly she couldn't adjust. The hope within her fired onward and upward, emboldening beliefs that were no longer true.

She clung nonetheless.

Hardly any children die of Wilms. The survival rate is nearly everyone.

And then one night—one of his last—Linus turned to her, a paleness settling in his skin, ashen hues unpacking beneath his eyes, appetite all but gone, and he asked, "Mom, am I going to die? Be honest."

"No," she said. "Of course not."

And she truly believed it, *still*, her mind clinging to a delusional form of hope.

Days later, she was sitting beside Linus's hospital bed, their hands intertwined, and suddenly he was gone. Just like that. Snow fell outside, a bone-cold day in February, and it seemed the whole world had gone dull and dead in one final breath.

He was one week short of becoming a teenager.

She sat for hours longer, cradling his hand in hers, staring at his still and perfect face—paper-thin lids, feathery eyelashes, his hair still fringed with baby-soft wisps—until the warmth of his skin was gone and she couldn't bear it. For reasons that escaped her—probably shock, disbelief, maybe symbolism—she took a picture of their hands clasped together.

Over the years she'd memorized every detail of that photo: her maroon polish, chipped on the thumbnail; sterile white hospital sheets, creased in the background; Linus's short, thin fingers; the unnatural color of his skin—waxy, a pale yellow. She'd seen that color since: a waterlogged leaf in autumn, a rich bearnaise sauce, a colleague's blouse, and it made her stomach lurch. *That's my dead son's hand.*

She loved him immeasurably, but Linus haunted her—all of her memories did. A lifetime's worth of pain she'd tried to dam but couldn't. Some people's lives were simply too much.

More snippets flooded in as she gripped the steering wheel. Her absent, drug-addicted mother. Dead, yes, but still managing to incite a forcefield of anger and resentment in her chest. The peeling paint walls at *The Ardenson Home for Boys and Girls*. She could still smell the redolence of staleness and piss, seeping from her bedsheets.

The memories began to move faster, and she braced through the rapids.

The boy who touched her, slipping his yellow-nailed hand beneath her pants and up her shirt. The sour-breathed man who also touched her—and made her touch him back, his beard so abrasive it reddened her pale skin for weeks. The stories of her patients, stirred to life by her empathy: murders and accidents and illnesses so distressing her own heart ached.

Her son's cold hand, wrapped in hers.

When she reached Blue Haven, her face was soaked with tears.

It was 5 a.m. and the parking lot was nearly empty. She found her spot and dashed through the bitter, sweeping wind. Her nerves pepped as she scanned her swipe card and entered the mostly quiet building, trying to forget the terrible commute.

She hurried to Jack's office, boots clopping against the tiled floor. Select office lights peered through door cracks—eager colleagues, the night staff. She wiped her hands across her thick sweater, suddenly aware of the nervousness boiling in her chest. Though it wasn't a matter of getting caught. She had a thousand excuses to be in Jack's office, using his computer.

No, the adrenaline bursting through her arteries had more to do with what she might discover.

Chapter Fifty

Eloise slipped into Jack's office and closed the door. She had no idea what her husband was hiding, aware on some level it could be nothing, and her radar for dishonesty and hypothetical affairs was tainted by paranoia. Still, her mind grappled with the prospective scope of Jack's secrecy.

A pebble? An asteroid?

She rushed through the giant space, busy with technology. The walls were filled with screens, monitors, degrees, awards. Jack's desk was comically futuristic, almost satirical with its sprawling chrome design and minimalist detail. *I don't want a desk, I want a spaceship*, he'd said, clearly trying to fulfill some boyish vision of success. And behold, a spaceship was exactly what he'd received.

His chair was equally unnecessary: high-backed and padded; silver, white, and navy. Comfortable, but ridiculous. She roused the mouse, watching the screen come alive. This computer was practically Jack's existence, the paintbrush to his programming artistry and a peak inside his head. She placed her thumb on the fingerprint access, which allowed her entry—as both his wife and business partner—and then she waited. The black screen slowly uncovered icons, folders, and a background photo that simultaneously stole and shattered her heart. It was Jack and Linus, a candid picture of a lazy Sunday afternoon: the two sitting in gaming chairs, glancing over from the heat of virtual battle to smile for the camera.

She'd taken that picture, not believing it to be spectacular by any stretch; and yet, here it was: a moment she'd give anything to return to. A moment so meaningful to Jack he'd chosen to stare at it every day for hours.

The sky started to brighten, just enough to motion her fingers into action.

She scrolled and tapped—*click, click, click*—delving into file after file. Nothing seemed extraordinary or out of place, not even the sight of her own file, *Eloise*, considering she was technically a patient.

She opened the folder, expecting it to be largely like the others— *protocols, assessment reports, progress notes*. She'd already read her file front to back, every single word. These personal details were her only clues, her only remnants of hope toward one day achieving recovery.

As her eyes glazed over the documents for completion's sake, she quickly realized this was not the same patient record she'd scoured in detail, but a collection of new information she'd never before seen.

Her rapid, methodical brain sprung into action, eyes flowing over the words and figures like quicksilver. As seconds passed, dread expanded in her chest. Her lungs grew tight, tense.

My God.

She'd come here with vague suspicion, but this—*this*—far exceeded any realm of possibility.

She gripped the side of Jack's elaborate office chair. The heat of betrayal rose up through her, and the room became small, suffocating. Outside, the sun rose over the horizon, forming a bright line of fury. She turned away from the office window, seeking darkness, somewhere to hide.

Her husband was asking questions he wasn't supposed to—seeking answers he shouldn't find. Her heartbeat quickened with realization.

Holy shit. Does anyone else know about this information? The possibility that Jack had discussed—or heaven forbid *shared*—any of this content made her break an instant sweat. She reached again for the computer mouse and pulled up Jack's work email: an overwhelming dump of data. She frantically sorted by attachments, subject lines, eyes moving at the speed of light.

And then she stopped, deciding to search by sender.

Leslie Marks.

The lengthy yield, combined with the calls from earlier, made her blood boil. She imagined the two embarking on a passionate affair, sabotaging Blue Haven while she rotted away, neuron by neuron. Her stomach curdled as she pictured Jack in the hot tub, not lonely, as she'd envisioned him earlier, but occupied by a gorgeous brunette—her *fucking therapist*. He'd cleaned out Linus's room because he was moving on, erasing the past and starting a new life.

How could they?

She paused—*erasing the past and starting a new life*—refusing to acknowledge the irony. Her hand seized the mouse, trembling. *I'll ruin them! I'll ruin them both! …*

Breathe, Eloise. Just breathe.

She took a thoughtful breath, returning to reality: to a world composed of facts and truths. Jack and Leslie were colleagues. *Of course they conversed*—they had reason to.

She scanned the subject lines. Nothing abnormal. And then Personal Request caught her eye and she double clicked. The e-mail, dated shortly after her recent admittance to Blue Haven, was from Jack, and inquired about therapy providers.

She followed the resulting thread, predominantly from Leslie.

Hi Jack. Thanks for reaching out. Certainly, I have a number of colleagues I can recommend. Any particular specialties, therapeutic alignments, or other details I should know about? This information will help me narrow focus.

Leslie: *Hi Jack, just wanted to follow up as I haven't heard back from you in a few days, but I know of an excellent psychotherapist with recent openings. Please advise if you're still interested. Her name is Doctor Mia Hartley. Check her out on Google.*

Leslie: *Hi again. I left Mia's card on your desk. Just checking in to ensure you received it? I applaud your forward thinking, and believe Mia would be a wonderful fit for Eloise if her current stay at Blue Haven goes South. Sadly, it appears to be heading in that direction, doesn't it? I've spoken to Mia briefly, and she has some innovative thoughts on psilocybin. I'm hopeful!*

Jack: *Hi Leslie. Sorry, I've been meaning to reply, just busy. The request is not for Eloise.*

Leslie: *Oh, my apologies. I just assumed. At any rate, I still offer my highest recommendation for Mia Hartley.*

Eloise scrolled down to the next email, from just last week.

Leslie: *Jack. Thank you for being honest with me today. I hope you didn't feel cornered or pressured; I realized afterwards that I came by your office uninvited and perhaps you were avoiding me for a reason. You've been through so much. Naturally you're struggling! Entirely understandable. I truly believe speaking with someone will help you immensely. Please let me know if there's anything else I can do. You have my continued support, as a colleague and friend.*

And then came one last e-mail, sent only yesterday.

Hi Jack. Your office door was closed. I've tried calling—many times. We need to speak. I'm concerned about you. I've been filling Eloise's prescription at your request, but have reason to believe this medication may be serving a different purpose. Please connect with me as soon as possible.

Eloise lifted her hand from the mouse, the narrative coming together like beads collecting on a thin string. Leslie's tense, confused expression from yesterday around medication non-adherence. The missed calls on Jack's phone.

Guided by instinct, her hand traveled to the side of his desk. She gripped the drawer handle, and slid it open. After ruffling through a stack of paper, a tangle of chargers, the odd pen, she ultimately found what she sought and feared: a plastic bottle.

The label, of course, belonged to her.

Valium.

Her shoulders dropped. *Oh Jack.*

As she closed the drawer, an item of substantial weight rolled forward, its impact rippling against her fingertips. She reached behind the first compartment and gripped a cool, glass bottle.

A twenty-six ouncer of gin, half drunk.

No.

No, no, no, no.

This made zero sense. Jack—her Jack—was incapable of addiction. He barely used over-the-counter meds! And when it came to alcohol, he was a cheap, occasional drunk, hardly able to stomach the hard stuff, let alone at work.

Then again, his behavior was certainly *off* lately, and she'd suspected something different about him from the start.

The anger rallying in her chest began to simmer. On the one hand, she was furious by what she'd discovered on Jack's hard-drive, coupled with Linus's empty room—how dare he. But it broke her heart to know Jack had resorted to substance abuse, as means of coping.

Her eyes squeezed shut. The pressure in her temples was ramping back up, the hangover returning. She longed to disappear, to become nothing more than a particle of air: unthinking, unfeeling, so light and insubstantial she could float away. This was her fault, wasn't it? Since Linus's death, she'd been a passive, selfish wife, hoarding grief to herself like a commodity. She'd hardly paid attention to Jack's suffering, too consumed by her own.

She stood from the desk with shaky knees and continued toward the door unsteadily. It was all too much, the tangle of emotions trapped behind her rib cage, unable to properly release.

Her husband: an addict.

Her son: dead.

Her future: completely hopeless.

Faces surfaced in the hall, floating by in a daze as the office hummed with arrivals.

"Good morning," a voice came. She turned to great Amir, spritely and smiling, though his cheery expression faded when he noticed her own—whatever it was; she'd lost all sense of self-awareness.

"Shit, are you alright?"

She went to speak, but nothing came, not even air.

Chapter Fifty-One

For what seemed like eternity, Eloise simply stood, her mouth gaped and wordless.

"Jesus Christ, Eloise," Amir said, pulling her into the nearest room: the control center. The touch of his hand on her skin was like a gust of wind, so light and fluttering she hardly even noticed it. He shut the door and a halo of brightness rose all around. She turned toward the large screen. A striking peachy sunrise was unfolding inside of Blue Haven. Turquoise clouds blossomed as the sky untangled from darkness: swipes of lavender, streaks of highlighter yellow, plumes of navy. The sense of calm was instant, the beauty unspeakable.

"Wow, that's lovely," Amir said, and then he faced her straight on. "Okay, now tell me what the hell is going on, *please*."

She continued to stare at the screen, envisioning a warm breeze dancing through her hair; the faint heat of morning, just warming up; all of her problems eradicated, swept from her mind like a tide—only to return again and again, refusing to drown, refusing to die.

It was all so unbearable she nearly wept. The data on Jack's computer—collected and analyzed by *her own husband*, the same husband who'd secretly turned to booze and narcotics—was a new layer of upheaval, shattering her world to bits.

And despite it all, Linus was gone. *Still*. Gone.

"I ... I can't," was all she managed before the tears came, gutful and violent. For a split second, Amir stared with shock, then he drew her into his small frame. The moment was uncomfortable—though she didn't resist.

"Breathe," he encouraged, and she tried, reminded of the mind-fulness exercises she'd attempted in Blue Haven. *Breathe in through your nose. Fill your belly with air.* She recalled the warm, salty ocean breeze filling her lungs and the distinct calm of dopamine flooding through her cortex.

As her heart steadied and air arrived more readily, she released from Amir and turned away. Her cheeks burned with shame—even if that shame opposed everything she stood for. People shouldn't have to apologize for their mental health, in the same way they wouldn't apologize for breaking a leg. And yet, she found herself apologizing.

"I'm so sorry Amir. This morning has been … a challenge. I'm not coping well."

"Don't apologize," he said, his voice soft and soothing, the thera-pist in him shining through. "Would you like to talk about it?"

"Not particularly, if that's alright." She was too fragile at the moment: glass bones, tissue-paper flesh. Instead, she turned toward to the screen and watched the sky, now brilliant with light. The blue of day had arrived, leaving pastel streaks that disappeared toward the edges: seafoam green, Easter pink, sherbet orange. An ice-cream sundae morning.

Separate monitors hummed with human activity and she found her people: Bibs, Westley, Franny, and Bob. Bibs was lying in bed, sip-ping an espresso, smiling at nothing in particular. A housecoat tucked around his chubby frame.

Westley was standing on his patio, arms outstretched and chest facing the sky. A look of peace settled across his face and he was hum-ming. She recognized the tune: *Amazing Grace.*

Bob was making pancakes. Batter splashed down his apron and Franny was chuckling. "Do you think any will make it onto the plate?" she asked. He smiled and kissed her on the cheek.

They were happy—*so* happy. She'd done something good for the world, tremendous even. And yet, the data she'd just seen shook even the sturdiest places inside of her.

For years she'd been guided by the same unwavering principle: that technology and science could fix the broken and serve the disadvan-taged, if only the right people with the right priorities took charge. She'd found those people, she'd even married one, and they'd come so far.

But perhaps her idealism had silenced the inner skeptic, avert-ing her attention from the questions she'd normally ask, under different circumstances: *What are the consequences of controlling people's brains? You've well discussed the benefits. Tell me more about the risks?*

She brought her finger to the screen and stroked Westley's calm, upturned face.

"Maybe we *shouldn't* play God," she said, the words from last night tumbling out of her.

"Pardon?" Amir replied. She'd almost forgotten he was standing there, her mind partly detached and lost in a dream-like state of exhaustion.

"Do you ever wonder, Amir, if what we're doing here is right?"

He turned his head to one side. Silence passed, and continued to pass, and then he shook his head. "Sorry, it's just taking me a minute to process all of this. I've never seen you doubt the direction we're moving. It's a little out of character for you."

"Ha," she replied. "*Out of character.* I'm not sure I know my own character anymore, to be honest." She rubbed her eyes, the skin tender from tears and lack of sleep. "Look at me, I'm a human irony: a doctor and her own patient. It's pathetic."

Amir frowned. His face was so young and bright, absent of loss and pain, fear and failure. She longed suddenly—a motherly instinct coming through, branded into her skeleton—to protect him from all that awaited, instead of crying on his shoulder like a child. She cringed, imagining what he must think of her—a true fall from grace, as with Jack. For years she'd been Amir's mentor, and he looked to her for advice and wisdom. He was so eager to rise up the ranks, to hold what she held.

"I wish you hadn't seen me like this," she said, aware the veil had been lifted; the sad, broken woman waiting beneath a slew of post-nominals and declarations could not be unseen.

"Eloise," he said, so gently she nearly wept all over again. "My impression of you has never changed. I think you're a goddamn hero. I always have."

If the tenacity had not leaked from her spirit like a broken faucet, she may have kindly rebutted. *I'm no hero, dear Amir. I'm a cog in my own wheel.* Instead, she was quiet until he spoke.

"*Maybe we shouldn't play God.* That's what you just said, wasn't it?" She nodded.

"Well, as far as I see it, based on all of the suffering in this world, I think somebody should fucking try."

Chapter Fifty-Two

The front door wedged open and Eloise woke. The sofa was tight against her frame and for a moment she stared up through the skylight, watching the snow land on the pane of glass, feather soft and quickly melting, unsure where she was. The darkness stretched before her like a void, a space she yearned to enter.

Swallow me up, please.

Making me nothing.

Sounds sprung from the kitchen and she sat, details returning like an echo. Jack was just getting home; she was in the living room.

She'd passed him in the hall at work—her leaving, him arriving—but that was their only encounter since last night: a quick head bob. It seemed much longer ago, those moments in the hot tub, like they were two entirely different people staring drunkenly into the winter sky. Then, as far as she knew, they were on the same team.

Now?

Based on his hard-drive, Jack had become the opposition.

She stood and began to walk, utterly unprepared for the conversation that awaited. She'd returned from work with bold intentions: scour the medicine cabinet for further evidence, canvas the house for alcohol and drugs, search the basement for Linus's belongings—the contents of his room she longed to touch, smell.

Instead she had done none of these things. Moments after walking inside, she'd crashed on the couch and fell asleep.

A pot clashed in the kitchen and she carried forth in Jack's direction, her mind heavy with sleep. She dragged her feet across the hardwood, stopping at the dining room table. Their plates were still soiled from the night before: dried bits of pasta, two sloppy forks, a sad forgotten scallop, shriveled like a prune. The scene resonated with her for some reason, this neglected dinner. A metaphor she couldn't place.

Years ago, she would have prepared for this argument, five minutes, maybe ten, enough time to form a sharp and articulate opener, line-up each dispute like a series of bottles at a gun range.

Ping. Ping. Ping.

Knock 'em dead.

Their fights were never willy-nilly. Not a wobbly collection of tits and tats, but a tree-diagram of carefully planned words: no corners left unturned; no places to hide. She almost always got her way.

Now though, her thoughts scattered like dust in the wind, and it took real, cognitive effort to channel her arguments. *The secret data. Prescription drugs. Booze. Linus's room.* By the time she got to the kitchen though, she was running on smoke, impulse, emotion.

As she emerged from the shadows, Jack turned. "*Oh,*" he said, clearly startled. "Hi. I figured you were in bed."

"What have you done with his things?" It came out barky, jagged.

He stared at her sideways. "Nice to see you also." He turned back to the stove and stirred a pot. "I'm heating up chili. Would you like some?"

"I asked you a question. How dare you. How *fucking* dare you touch my son's belongings." The gusto in her voice was unexpected, uncontrolled.

"*Your* son. Right," he replied, turning down the burner. "If you're talking about Linus's room, that was ..." he paused, staring at the ceiling with thought. "A year and a half ago. Yes, his room has been empty for ... five hundred and forty days. Please don't raise your tone with me."

A year and a half? Her chest pulsed with guilt, but she refused to dwell. "I'm not a child," she replied. "Don't talk to me about *raising my tone.*"

She waited, expecting a combative reply, but he only nodded, returning to the pot of chili.

This was hardly the Jack she remembered—far too complacent. Normally he put up a good fight. She sat at the island, unsure how to proceed.

"Jack, please tell me you kept his things," she said. "*Please.*"

He stopped stirring, though he didn't face her. "I donated everything."

A moan came from her chest, filling the room with sorrow. "Why? *Why?*"

"Goddamn it, Eloise," he turned, the anger on his face arriving now. "Because you were gone. Because I didn't have the luxury of erasing the pain in my head. And because every day, there was pain. Linus's room didn't feel like Linus anymore, it felt like loss. I didn't need another reminder of loss." He reached for a bottle of caramel-colored booze. "You have no right," he said, filling a tumbler. "I know you've suffered and I hate that you've suffered, but I've suffered too. You abandoned me. *You erased me from your memory*—twice—and you erased Linus, so don't you dare guilt trip me about cleaning out his room."

He took a large gulp, another. "I kept his baseball glove," he added. "It's in the front closet."

She imagined that glove, the weight of it in her hand, the soft edge of worn-down hide. The last tangible piece of her son.

Jack was right of course. Her anger was unfounded. She'd expected the impossible: for Jack to remain a strong, unwavering pillar of support, immune to his own grief; for Linus's memory to stay hidden within walls, a ghost she could visit on occasion, fully and without restraint, slow to come and quick to leave, happily returning to a pain-free paradise.

She hadn't wanted to erase Jack and Linus from her memory. It was a matter of survival, a surrender to sickness.

"I know you harbor a lot of resentment for what I've done," she said. "And for what I continue to attempt, I suppose, with Blue Haven, but I do so out of desperation. I've apologized a thousand times, Jack. I'm not sure what else I can say. I'm sick. My brain is broken."

"Yes," he replied, a cool edge to his voice. "But who broke it?"

Her gut hardened.

"I know you searched my computer," he added. "I checked the security footage."

She leaned against the counter, suddenly faint. The tapestry of their argument was weaving in a new direction. The accused becoming the accuser.

The arguments riled in her mind. *You're treating me like a case study without my permission! You're trying to ruin Blue Haven! You're stealing my prescriptions! You're an alcoholic!*

She thought these thoughts, but couldn't bring herself to speak. The look on Jack's face was hard and full of truth; there was no rebutting it.

"Here's what I know," he said, taking a fast swig. "Three years ago, we lost our only son. You became depressed—of course you became depressed; we both did. Linus was our light, our life, and suddenly he was gone. You think I don't know your pain, but I do. Perhaps I didn't wear it so brazenly, but I wasn't spared, that's for damn sure."

He paused, eyes glassy and distant, then he reined in focus, clearly determined to make a point. "Ellie, you and I both know you barely tried any form of conventional treatment before Blue Haven came up as an option. One measly antidepressant? A few sessions of therapy?"

"Sure," she replied, owning up to her lack of effort. "But Jack, I'd been to therapy before, for years, and it just seemed so silly in light of—"

"I know," he interjected. "Why nibble on a crumb when you own the whole cake. I get it. The facility was shiny, new, accepting applicants—and you were deeply bereaved. But you can't deny that corners were cut. You used your power and influence to admit yourself to Blue Haven. You convinced the team, and you convinced me."

Her chest folded in with guilt. Was she deeply depressed after Linus's death? Yes, of course she was. But had she also taken the easier road simply because she could—regardless of whether there were more appropriate candidates? Yes. That was true as well.

Jack took another drink; the folds of his skin were harsh in the dim light. "At any rate, Blue Haven didn't work. In fact, you became *worse*. Dark and terrible traumas from your past, suddenly livened, like they'd happened just yesterday. Events I couldn't imagine."

She closed her eyes and tried to suppress the demons Jack spoke of: piss-soaked bed sheets, smelling of sulfate; surfaces swathed with dust and mildew; children everywhere, all the time—a cast of rotating characters; those brash, unmistakable whiskers, scratching up her cheek, scraping her raw.

Dark and terrible traumas from your past, suddenly livened, like they'd happened just yesterday.

She wished it weren't true, but the memories spoke for themselves. Jack took her hand, large and rough, and her lids flashed open. There he was: her husband. The man who'd loved her despite everything. *For better or worse.* And they'd certainly tested the limits.

"After Blue Haven," he said, "I had no choice. Inpatient treatment was the only option: a place that would keep you safe from harm. *Self-harm.* And here we are again. Every day you're a little bit worse, running on fumes, the crash inevitable. You're already starting to scare me."

She turned away, sickened by the thought of scaring her own husband, even though she was starting to scare herself.

Jack rolled his neck and shoulders, letting loose. She noticed the release in his movements, a chemical sense of calm. The effects of booze were washing over him—likely coupled with narcotics.

"The problem is," he said. "On paper, everything adds up, like a chain reaction: Linus's death, a traumatic past, all coming together to fuel a steep and continuous decline. You're not getting better and sometimes that happens to people—we've seen it a million times over. Sometimes, people get worse, regardless of their efforts. You believed this narrative, so have our colleagues—and I almost believed it, or I did for a while. But something wasn't right, Ellie. Ever since Blue Haven, you've been so ... different. I just had this feeling in my soul. I was driven by something, you know?"

She nodded, a gulp forming in her throat, tight and uncomfortable.

"So yes, I started looking at the data differently, paying close attention to changes in your brain function as a result of neural-net activity: patterns of reorganization, structural and functional connectivity, pairing these with overt symptoms, your observed behavior. And do you know what I found—have continued to find?"

She looked away, refusing to speak the words out loud, like keeping them silent and unspoken might change the truth.

"Ellie," he said firmly. "We pretend to know everything about the human brain, but we don't. Our neural net doesn't enhance cognitive function, it *seizes* cognitive function. In Blue Haven, people's brains don't need to regulate emotion and memory, because we're doing it for them. And do you know what happens as a result?"

"Dependency," she replied. "But we anticipated this to some degree." As a doctor, she was entirely familiar with the concept of dependence. When medicated, the human body quickly became reliant on external supplementation instead of internal regulation, creating dependence. Textbook medical school.

"Yes, but this isn't regular dependence," Jack added. "This is dependence like I've never seen it before. Stubborn, self-sabotaging behavior to the point of collapse. Blue Haven robs the human brain of its intrinsic ability to regulate emotions. You can't give someone nirvana, and then take it away."

She didn't need Jack to explain the implications, though he did. Without neural-net activity, her brain was glitchy, dysregulated—failing, quite frankly. "That beautiful, three-pound organ, as lazy as it was resourceful, craved Blue Haven like a—"

"It's a drug, Ellie," he said. "Let's call it what it is. Perhaps the most complex, expensive, and revered drug in human history, but a drug nonetheless. Blue Haven is like heroin ... on heroin."

She rested her elbows on the counter, holding her face for support.

Drug. She hated that word. Blunt and harsh, far too simple. Blue Haven was far more than a smooth, round pill. A *sanctuary* was how she envisioned their facility. A place of beauty and justice and healing. Blue Haven staved people's pain and brought pleasure in return.

Blue Haven is good. We're doing something good.

These thoughts, at one time so certain she'd stake her life upon them, were suddenly dotted with question marks. Worse, the results harbored on Jack's computer would end Blue Haven indefinitely. No governing ethics body or funding agency would support the admittance of patients into a rehabilitative program that ultimately made people sicker.

Her chest rolled as she thought of their current patients—her friends. The time she'd spent in Blue Haven was a small fraction comparatively. And if this was the result *for her*, what terrible hell awaited the others? After all they'd been through, only to come out a hundred times sicker—unimaginably sick. Each of them—herself included—had become trapped in a cycle of addiction, apparently stronger and more superior than any known to date. And there was data to prove it. Data that belonged to her husband—of all people.

Her lip began to quiver. The fate of Blue Haven—and her own fate, the two now inseparable— depended on Jack. She watched him carefully, the way his almond eyes narrowed, the odd face muscle flinching. He was waiting for a response, but she didn't know what to say. Her thoughts dragged, coming and going.

"How long have you known all of this?" she asked, breaking the silence.

"I was suspicious at the start of your first admission, which is why I was especially reluctant about your second entry. Now, all of my hypotheses are confirmed."

"And you're sure?"

He sighed. "I'm a data scientist, Ellie. The data doesn't lie."

Her skin began to flush, hope evaporating from her pores like heated water. The tone of their argument had shifted—less an argument than a truth bomb. Once again, she could feel the edge of sanity slipping from her grasp, the locus of control disappearing.

"What happens next?" she whispered.

"Ellie," he said, the sad, soft tone of his voice an answer unto itself. "You know I can't keep this a secret. We can't move forward as planned. We're not fixing people. *We're destroying people.* They may be happy for now, but what we're doing is the antithesis of therapy."

Her head bobbed in response. *Of course.* Jack was a pillar of integrity, and the doctor inside of her—the one who vowed to *do no harm*—was, of course, alarmed by the findings. But discontinuing Blue Haven meant everything she'd worked for—including the prospect of happiness for herself and her friends—would vanish. Headlines would follow, her last impression on the world a bold, capitalized **FAILURE**.

She wanted to collapse.

It was all too much too fast. Her head began to spin, desperate, delusional, seeking some sort of solution. This wasn't the end. This couldn't be the end.

And then she saw the knife resting on the counter, followed by a voice—her voice, but not really, rising from a place she'd never visited before.

Stop him.

Chapter Fifty-Three

E loise inadmissibly loved her husband. It was the sort of love that ran deep: magma flowing beneath the earth's crust, keeping the world afloat. They'd been through so much together—more than most couples could even imagine, from birthing an unexpected child, to building a company, to experiencing unfathomable grief. Growing, expanding, deteriorating. They'd done it all. Jack was a part of Eloise's skeleton, the fabric holding her in place.

And yet, taking his life seemed remarkably easy. It came to her in a detached, factual way. A thing that must be done. She walked toward the knife, robotic and overtaken by forces she couldn't control and didn't care to—so depleted, at this point. Her hand clasped the handle of the weapon while Jack poured himself another scotch, his back turned.

She lifted the blade into the air, tightening her grip. The carotid artery, running up his neck, would be the fastest. One clean slice, and it'd all be over with.

She came around his right side, moving quickly—no time to overthink. Her elbow linked around his shoulder, the knife close to his skin, and then she pulled her arm in one steady motion.

But something caught her wrist—his hand, and she saw his shocked reflection in the metal backsplash. He'd seen her coming.

All at once her arm twisted backwards and his burly shoulders encaged her own. Suddenly, *Jack* was holding the knife, its piercing tip inches away.

"You ... you just tried to kill me," he said, his voice shaky with disbelief. "Ellie, *you just tried to kill me.*"

The mention of her name—*Ellie*—seemed to shatter the spell of ambivalence. Reality arrived, her true self rising from within.

Oh my God.

I just tried to kill my husband.

Every part of her convulsed, unable to believe how close she'd come to making the biggest mistake of her life. "Jack ... I ..." she stuttered. "I don't know what's happening to me."

He set the knife on the counter. "This isn't *you* Ellie. I know this isn't you. It's not your fault—your brain is broken."

The tears came with overwhelming strength, and she cried so hard every molecule of oxygen leaked from her lungs. When she finally caught her breath, her attention refocused on the knife, resting on the counter. *You know what you need to do*, a voice said. She nodded, and before she could think better of it, she untangled from Jack and lunged toward the counter, grasping the knife in one swift motion.

Finish what you started, the voice whispered. *Just do it already.*

"Ellie," Jack said, panicking. "What are you—"

She positioned the blade against her *own* carotid artery. "I'm so sorry Jack."

"No," he replied. "Listen to me Ellie, do not—"

"This is what I want, darling. It's over for me. I'm so terribly exhausted. Keep the others in Blue Haven—let them be happy. And let me be with Linus, please."

Tears tumbled down her face while Jack took one step closer. "Stop. Please don't do this, Ellie. Put the knife down."

She flexed her arm, ready for it all to be over with. God she was tired. Her life had become a grueling cycle of trying to heal—trying to achieve something like happiness, peace, or contentment in the absence of her beautiful boy. At one point, she'd wanted to change the world. By now, the fire in her belly was smothered to cold ash.

She closed her eyes and imagined the afterlife, everything inside of it forced to static, like white noise. It called to her, this noisy nothingness, and she wanted to be a part of it. For the first time in recent memory, she thought of Linus with joy and longing, his existence untethered to heartache. *Don't worry sweet boy. Mommy's coming to find you.*

"Goodbye my love," she whispered.

"No!" Jack yelled. "Ellie, I know why Blue Haven isn't working for you. We can fix this."

She paused, the vision of Linus dissolving in an instant. "What?"

"*We can fix this.* Trust me. Just put down the knife and we'll talk."

She watched him closely. Was he serious? Or simply saying what she wanted to hear out of desperation?

"Promise you're not lying?" she asked.

Jack nodded, and without waiting for her to accept his offer, began describing specific areas of her cortex that remained highly active in Blue Haven, despite continued suppression, as well as profiles of dream activation that demonstrated a consistent pattern—reinforcing and strengthening a preoccupation that lingered into wakefulness, at least subconsciously.

As he spoke, she lowered the knife, holding it by her side.

"I know I don't need to explain what these cortical regions and networks are involved in," he added. And he didn't. She knew well they were associated with affection and guilt, specifically.

"What does all of that *mean* though?" she asked.

"Well, as far as dreaming goes, you're dreaming of ..." An almost bashful look crossed his face, his stark blue eyes brightening. "You're dreaming of me, Ellie. I can tell, because the activity profile in your dreams exactly matches what your brain produces when you see me physically, in person. My working theory is that, unlike our other patients, who have seamlessly integrated into Blue Haven, you've left someone behind you care deeply about, and this haunts you."

She turned her head, taking in Jack from every angle: his stiff jawline and broad shoulders, the nape of his neck, small but penetrating eyes, freshly shaven skin (he never allowed stubble, for her sake). He was a good man—far better than she deserved—and her love for him was real, even when the rest of her rattled with insanity. This much she knew.

She thought of her most recent stay in Blue Haven, this time with a different lens. The panic attacks, her obsession with Eloise, the constant paranoia, a continued sense of confusion, like she was missing something. She'd faulted these emotions to the journal, to the character of "Eloise," she'd regrettably created, but now she saw a strong case of transference.

Half of her brain was trying to find Jack.

The other half, erase him.

It all made so much sense. Paradise wasn't paradise without her husband. He was the Bob to her Franny, and she needed him to be at peace.

"My brain couldn't let you go," she whispered, stating the fact of the matter. On some intracellular level, there was a Jack-shaped void in her Swiss-cheese brain, a piece of her longing for love.

Even still, she could hardly stomach the person she'd become since—and what this person was capable of. She looked down at the knife, still tight in her grasp. *You nearly murdered your own husband.* The metal blade dropped to the floor and she took a step back, knowing she couldn't be trusted with sharp objects.

"So now what?" she whispered.

"I have a plan," Jack said, his voice full of truth. "Everything is going to be alright."

Chapter Fifty-Four

Two Months Later

Jack stood in the empty room of his late son, the baseball glove firm in his palm. He usually ventured here to remember.

This time, he was saying goodbye.

He imagined what physical remnants of Linus still remained in this room, all these years later: a flake of skin or dandruff, a stray hair, the faded impression of his bare foot, a fingerprint left on the window pane.

The family who'd purchased their house—a pair of surgeons from New Jersey—had a young daughter, and he imagined this small girl filling Linus's room with her dreams and belongings. Such thoughts evoked joy and misery in equal proportion. Memories, large and small, rose up through him like a vine: helping Linus with his homework, assembling train tracks around the perimeter, countless bedtime stories, the look of peace on his son's face as rest took hold, the soft texture of his brilliant blonde hair, always parted to the right.

Jack tried his best to become these memories, to relive them in his mind with vivid clarity. Because as of tomorrow, they'd all be gone.

It had taken some convincing, but the team had ultimately accepted his entry into Blue Haven—as anticipated. He was a legitimate candidate, after all: an alcoholic and a drug addict—not to mention the compelling evidence he'd produced about Ellie. Using a subset of data from recent analyses, he was able to successfully argue that her rehabilitation hinged upon his own. They were a packaged deal.

He clenched his shaky fingers, the effects of withdrawal starting to set. Becoming an addict had not come easily to Jack. He never enjoyed the hazy wash of substances, preferring his reality sharp and raw over blunt and dull. Dependency had taken real effort: careful planning and full dedication; involving Leslie just enough to support his forming narrative, so she could unknowingly vouch for his drug-seeking behavior and mental health collapse. The experience overall was generally unpleasant, but what other choice did he have?

As soon as he'd discovered the truth about Ellie's neural net, he knew Blue Haven—with all its plans for growth and expansion—would end one way or another. Of course, he could've hid the data or erased it, kept everything a secret, but the truth would come out eventually. It always did. And besides, that's not who he was. He simply couldn't live with himself.

Yet sharing the full breadth of data he'd discovered would have come at an inconceivable cost. If Ellie's only hope of recovery was readmittance, and Blue Haven was no longer …

The mere thought left him nauseous; his love for her was still a thriving force, after all these years, and he couldn't bear to lose her.

His final plan—merely twenty-four hours from initiation—was their only opportunity to be together. He had everything ready, prepared, staged. Tomorrow morning, they'd both be admitted to Blue Haven—*temporarily*, as it stood, like all of their other patients, though his plan was far from temporary. Their house was sold and their belongings all spoken for. In a week's time, an encrypted email would deploy to team members with *all* the data he'd collected, revealing the risks of neural net exposure for long-term brain functioning. New entry into the program would halt, but given the immense harm associated with deactivation, their current patients—himself included—would remain. There was no option otherwise.

He'd suggested in this email a number of ways in which Blue Haven's now permanent residents could still benefit the scientific community—salvageable projects, so to speak. It wouldn't be a total wash, though certainly not the outcome they'd envisioned years ago. Frankly, how the team moved forward was of little concern to him, given he'd no longer be a part of it.

One room over, Ellie stirred. Sheets ruffled and a long, exasperated breath leaked, then all was quiet. Jack glanced at his watch; it was

3 p.m., and she was still in bed. His heart welled, imagining her head-space. They had a caretaker now: a round-the-clock set of eyes that kept Ellie comfortable and settled, away from sharp objects and other items that could be used for self harm. Over the past few weeks, her symptoms had escalated to a new low, and she'd morphed into a being that was hardly human. The depths of her suffering and mental torment left Jack devastated, as before, but this time he was encouraged.

Stay with me, darling. We're going to a good place.

He dragged his fingers over the baseball glove, returning to Linus. The only detail that left him truly, deeply bothered was Linus. Erasing his son's existence was not a decision he'd taken lightly, particularly given the narrative of their new Blue Haven story: Ellie would return as Aloe, and he a younger version of himself. They would meet as they had in real life—less memories to alter—and marry shortly thereafter.

Essentially, he was going back in time.

To a world without Linus.

In many ways this felt like a disservice to his late son, and he struggled to accept it. But at the end of the day, he had to save his wife—something Linus would have wanted, too. Jack had never formed a strong opinion on the topic of religion, but he suspected it was, at best, a metaphor. He found some comfort in the idea that Linus didn't live in the sky or the past, but a place in his heart—a place from which he could never be erased.

"I love you, my boy," he whispered, drawing the glove to his chest. "Until we meet again."

Chapter Fifty-Five

Sunshine beamed through the expansive windows, streaking the floor with light. A hot breeze drifted through the open concept condo like clean smoke. Aloe rolled back her shoulders and took in the dewy scent, sliding her slipper into the warm beam's path.

Another day in paradise.

Across the room, Jack sprawled along the sofa with a book. Beside him, steam rose from a white mug. She vaguely remembered his body lifting from the bed, the soft kiss he planted on her forehead before sneaking out.

She leaned on the counter and simply watched, unable to help herself. He was truly admirable, sitting in a beam of morning light: lips slightly parted; his jaw tight with concentration; sunshine gleaming off his youthful skin, brightening his ash-blonde hair. This man—her *husband*, a word that still felt foreign on her tongue—made her weak in the knees.

Seconds ticked by and her chest lit with gratitude. She'd left Blue Haven to care for her ill grandmother, but Gram had already passed by the time she reached Chicago. Though something good had come of it all, because one day later there was Jack, standing in line at a coffee shop.

His crystal-blue eyes stole her heart and they'd married not long later—before her financial compensation from Blue Haven had been processed. The decision to return was practically scripted, if not serendipitous, and she couldn't deny fate. She'd shared the idea with Jack and he'd agreed in a split second.

Now, she knew they'd made the right choice. For two entire months—and counting—their lives had been pure bliss, and she'd never been happier.

"Good morning, wife," Jack said.

She smiled. "Good morning, husband. How did you sleep?"

He folded the book and stood, stretched. "Fantastic, per usual. There's coffee on, by the way." He motioned toward the counter where a full pot awaited. "What's on the agenda for today?"

She filled a mug. "I was thinking we could go for a swim, relax for the afternoon, and then tonight have dinner with the crew? At our place, but on the beach. Let's enjoy the night air. Rumor has it another celebrity chef will be joining us tomorrow, so we'll be inside for that."

"Wow, *another* celebrity chef? That's two in a week! These people spoil us."

She smirked, glad to see him impressed. "That's the idea."

As Jack approached, heading toward the coffee pot, she flung her arms around his wide shoulders. He jolted at first, surprised, then took her embrace and chuckled. "I wasn't expecting that."

"I know, I'm sorry. It's just … *Oh Jack*, I'm so happy. My life feels so … complete here." As soon as she said it, an unexpected waver came, like she was forgetting something, the moment itself wrapped in a strange deja vu. But within a second all was forgotten and she carried on.

"I'll get dressed. Be back soon."

She kissed him on the cheek and then skipped off to the bedroom.

Excitement bubbled everywhere as she flung on a white bikini and covered it with a loose, flowery sundress. She wrapped her apricot hair into a braid, tossed on a floppy-brimmed hat, then glanced in the mirror, pleased with herself. Her eyes and skin were so bright, alive. Young. Lucky in love. Living free in paradise.

Could life truly get any better?

She floated back into the living room, where Jack was waiting at the island.

"Amir brought turnovers while you were getting ready," he said, lifting one to her mouth. She took a bite, savoring the buttery pastry and apple-pie filling.

"*Damn*, that's tasty."

"Right?" He wrapped his arm around her waist, and the contact of his skin sent a flutter up her arm. "Let's take breakfast to go," he said, grabbing another. "Shall we?"

She smiled, and with that, they headed toward the beach.

§

The sunset came like a masterpiece unfolding: an almighty painter layering long, whimsical brush strokes across the sky. The warm blue of day faded, leaving glorious blasts of coral and violet, marbling into the distance.

Aloe gasped at the beauty. "Breathtaking," she said.

"Absolutely," Jack agreed.

A few feet away, Amir was helping other staff members erect a beachside tent. Crisp, white linens draped over a rustic frame, subtly flowing like ghosts at dusk. Candles were arranged in prisms, wedged casually into the sand. Tonight, they were having surf and turf: wagyu beef and fresh-caught lobster, plus a few other surprises along the way, per usual.

She tousled her cotton dress, creating some air flow. Hot, sticky daytime lingered and she looked forward to the coolness of night. As Amir arranged the table setting, Westley emerged from his condo— just in time to join Bob and Franny, walking up the cobblestone path.

Aloe stepped forward but Jack strode ahead, drawing their guests into a big hug before she had a chance. A smile spread across her face. She loved watching Jack interact with her friends; they'd all become so close in such a short matter of time. One big happy family.

"Hi everyone!" she said, unable to contain the excitement in her voice.

"Howdy," Bob replied, pecking her on the cheek. "I dressed in my finest attire, just for you." She had to laugh. Bob was wearing a red T-shirt cluttered with cartoon pictures of fast food: hot dogs, hamburgers, French fries. "Where the heck is Julian?" he asked. "He's gotta see my new get-up. That clown is finally rubbing off on me."

"He's not here yet," she replied, simultaneously hugging Franny.

"Please ignore my ridiculous husband," Franny said. "Bob had that so-called *get-up* tailor made at Le Boutique. Waste of material, if you ask me."

As the couple took their seats, Westley gave Aloe a solid squeeze. "Hi friend," he said. "What's on the menu tonight?"

"Surf and turf!" she replied, and then added. "Wagyu beef, lobster, and all the butter you can handle."

He grinned. "Perfect."

They sat, darkness closing across the sky like a curtain. The soft glow of candles intensified and a galaxy of stars came forward, slowly at first, then all at once.

Small talk bubbled. Aloe bobbed her head and laughed along with the rest of them, but as time passed, she quickly started losing focus. *Where's Bibs?* He was usually late, but not *this* late. When a server arrived with an amuse bouche—cured salmon, fresh roe, and a nori cracker—her heartbeat scampered.

A familiar panic rose up her spine and she stood, frantic. Bibs was prone to a fashionably late entrance, but he never, *ever*, missed an amuse.

"I'm just going to pop over and check on Julian," she said, trying to keep her voice light and casual.

Jack offered to join, but she gave him a hand wave. "No need. I'll be back in a second."

Steps later, a figure evolved in the distance. "There he is," she said, her heart easing. "Pushing the boundaries of acceptable tardiness." She laughed a nervous laugh, then quickly recovered from the unusual bout of anxiety. Julian was fine—of course he was. *Why wouldn't he be?*

But as he neared, a second figure materialized: a small woman with sleek, shiny hair, glistening in the limited light. She was young, Aloe's age, with gorgeous almond eyes and dewy skin. Asian, perhaps Filipino.

A seventh chair arrived, carried by one of the concierges.

"Friends!" Bibs said. "Look what I found!"

The woman's thin red lips parted and she smiled. .

"Hi everyone. I'm Amelia."

Chapter Fifty-Six

Amir thumped into Jack's ridiculous space chair, now sitting at the head of the control room. He watched the group of patients interact: Bibs, Westley, Bob, Franny, Jack, Eloise—and now Amelia. He could have been there in person, seeing it all unfold, but he much preferred a screen: the lovely, two-dimensional flatness, dotted with microscopic pixels; the soft hum of neural activity whispering in the background; the unnecessary encumbrance of dissecting human cues—tone, eye-contact, posture—totally eliminated.

The group liked Amelia, based on their neural feedback. *Of course they did.* She was friendly, beautiful, full of joy ... now that she'd become an entirely different person. Formerly a fifty-two-year-old nobody named Peggy Budge, Amelia was the first patient in Blue Haven who technically wasn't a patient, just a deeply unsatisfied woman longing for change.

Chronically disappointed, is how Amir would describe Ms. Budge: single, frumpy, quiet, unattractive. Average, essentially. A woman with very little to offer the world. She had nothing to lose and everything to gain.

Blue Haven, for Ms. Budge, was a miracle, and she'd delightfully chosen her own appearance, backstory, and personality characteristics. "I want to be beautiful," she'd said foremost. "And skinny! *God*, I'd love to be skinny. Small-boned and just all-around tiny, you know? And more confidence please! Not too much—I want people to like me, of course ..."

Through a few extensive interviews, they'd created the perfect avatar for Ms. Budge—who, as of this evening, no longer existed. *Abracadabra!* Bye-bye, now.

Convincing the team to shift gears was hardy a task. Without Eloise or Jack pushing their own personal agendas, members were surprisingly quick to pivot. And they hadn't entirely abandoned ship, they were simply tweaking Blue Haven's focus.

Primary prevention.

Why wait until people were a lost cause? Why not focus on the window before serious mental health consequences—a decision that was not only smart, but profitable. Board members loved the concept, and Amir had been awarded acting director because of it.

Ingenious. Innovative.

And importantly.

Marketable.

The original business model for Blue Haven was hardly a business model. The problem with focusing exclusively on mentally ill patients was simple, though unfortunate: people didn't overly care—at least not people with money. And why would they? There was no *corporate* angle to pitch or sell, no opportunities for growth. Such time and effort, advancements like nothing achieved by humanity thus far, and for what? Six measly individuals.

But that was then. *Now?* They were going places. They had company buy in, sponsors, and a way forward that made better sense. Why restrict the world's most innovative neurotechnology to the sad and broken? Shouldn't *everyone* be given access to a place like Blue Haven, should they desire?

And desire they did. The wait list for Blue Haven was enormous—and growing. Their current facility would be full in a month, and then onto the next one: *Green Haven?*

Or perhaps just *Haven?*

Yes, Haven.

Simple, elegant.

Haven on Earth.

Haven on Earth!

Goosebumps prickled up his arm. *Holy shit, the perfect byline.* He could already envision their brand: the look and feel of it.

His cheeks lifted—he couldn't stop smiling. *Thank God* he'd searched Jack's computer and intercepted the teamwide communication auto-timed to distribute. He'd physically shook upon learning about the neural net's degenerative effect on emotional processing and regulation. Jack was right to be concerned, and his actions were admirable. But what Jack failed to see was the *utility* of their creation, despite its shortcomings. The neural net only became a problem when disconnected. *So why disconnect it?* Why not let people live an entirely blissful life in Blue Haven—or whatever Haven existed in their neighborhood. Soon, there would be plenty of other facilities.

Amir leaned closer to the screen, watching Eloise pull a glass of soda to her lips. He traced his fingernail over her cheekbone, wondering if she'd be proud or appalled. Either way, she couldn't blame him. He was doing exactly what she'd taught him to: climb the ladder, rise to the occasion, be smart, think outside the box.

In fact, she'd said it herself—the new corporate tag, straight from the mouth of its original CEO, the new posterchild for admission.

Why fix your old life,
When you can have a new one?

Acknowledgements

Foremost, I owe you one, dearest reader. Thank *you*, for taking the time to finish this book, amidst the infinite number of other tasks you could've otherwise entertained. Of course, I hope you liked this story; but I also hope—and with far greater sincerity (it's just a book, after all)—that you're able to find contentment. Somewhere along the line, I think many of us (myself included) have managed to confuse happiness with pleasure, and journeys for destinations. May we all learn to untangle, unwind, and appreciate.

Many thanks to my wise and wonderful editor, Lou Aronica at The Story Plant, and the other skilled Story Plant team members who contributed to the publication of this book. Specifically, Allison Maretti (associate editor), Stacy Mathewson (copy editor), Nick Clements (proof reader), Sonya Maretti (proof reader), and Elizabeth Long (marketing). I appreciate each of you.

To my literary agent, Travis Pennington at The Knight Agency: you're a superstar. I'm beyond lucky to have such standout representation and diverse talent in my corner. Thank you for using your graphic design prowess to craft the perfect book cover, and for everything else you do, always.

I've been blessed with the support and enthusiasm of so many wonderful folks over the years. Cindy McDowell (high-school English teacher) and Dr. Ken McRae (graduate-degree supervisor): thanks for your wisdom and inspiration. A lucky grasshopper, I was. Endless gratitude to all of my friends, family, and colleagues; but particular thanks to Felicia Ketcheson (colleague/friend/fellow writer), and my dear friends Amanda and Joe Lyons, for reading and critiquing earlier drafts of Blue Haven. Also, Amanda: as I write this, my book-publishing anxiety is just starting to fester, so thanks in advance for the textual counselling you will surely offer in the coming months.

After my last (and also first) book came out, *Vanishing Hour* (VH), I received an outpouring of support that not only touched my heart, but encouraged me to keep writing. Though I started jotting down a list of formalized names, I quickly realized this list was both incredibly long, and not inclusive enough. So, if you: a) were planning to throw me a kick-ass book launch (that was unfortunately cancelled due to the pandemic); or b) volunteered to DJ at said book launch; or c) sent me congratulatory flowers that smelled like spring; or d) were among the first to read VH, and share your thoughts with me, or the internet; or e) attempted (successfully or unsuccessfully) to feature VH at your book club; or f) invited me to participate in your virtual book club (hey ladies!); or g) purchased book copies for yourself, friends, or relatives; or h) have been trying to make time in your insanely busy schedule to read my manuscripts, and contribute a red-haired protagonist; or i) simply offered me a smile and congratulations: I see you, and I am *so, damn, grateful.*

Family is everything, truly. To those I've inherited: Gerbert, Dorothy, Tracy, Paul, Marion, Cathy, Tyson, Max, Sam, Abby, Josh, and Nik—your support, encouragement, confidence, and love keeps the writing gears a turnin'. Grandma Betty: you are an exemplary human being, and I cherish you dearly. To my late grandfather, Robert King, who authored several volumes on the history of our family lineage: thank you for passing on the "writing gene." We miss you.

I count my lucky stars that I've been afforded (possibly through some universal loophole) the most supportive duo of selfless parents a girl could ask for. Mom and Dad: "thanks" doesn't cut it. But thank you, for raising me—for still raising me, and for cheering me on. I think you've read nearly everything I've ever written, from chicken-scratch letters in kindergarten, to *real published books* (and the many, often painful, attempts in between). I hope I make you proud.

Much love and gratitude to my sisters, Emily and Sarah, for being avid and enthusiastic chairs of my small fan club; for drafting the hypothetical, A-lister cast of my book-turned-movie fantasies; for being thoughtful and wonderful and encouraging friends; for giving me 3.5

adorable nieces (Austin, Skylar, Cooper, and Baby G). Simply, for believing in me. It means everything.

Dear Husband: per my last Acknowledgements section, I *still* love you oodles. I'm terribly sorry this book didn't end up featuring the number of superheroes you requested. That said, your other contributions were most helpful. Thanks for allowing me to yammer on for hours about the stories playing out in my imagination. You've married a creative, articulate, and sensitive soul, with a flair for control and a healthy sprinkling of anxiety—which can't be a walk in the park. Nevertheless, thank you for walking beside me, in writing, and in life.

To my daughter, Andi: Holy shit, I love you. You've deepened my empathy, driven me slightly bonkers, and taught me more about love in the past four years than all my years combined. You are the reason—my reason. Of all the stories I've ever written or published, the ones we make up together (even late at night, when you're supposed to be sleeping!) will always be my favorite.

Lastly, I started writing this book thirteen years ago. It was the first book I ever attempted, and after a few grueling months and twenty-eight thousand words of mostly jargon, I pressed pause. I didn't have an ending; *hell*, I barely had a plot, but I saved my half-wit manuscript in a folder, and moved onto other stories—one of which is now published, many not. Still, the basic premise for *Blue Haven* stuck with me, and I thought of it often.

Over a decade later, I revisited those twenty-eight thousand words, and here we are. All of this to say, kudos to the writing community for doing what you do, when the odds feel slim and the weight of work overwhelming. Thank you for *writing*, despite it all. I wish you both the perseverance to continue, and wherewithal to enjoy the ride. Writing is, after all, not a destination, but a journey.

About the Author

Lisa King is a fiction author and researcher whose work has been published in numerous academic journals. She holds degrees in psychology and neuroscience from Western University. In her spare time, Lisa enjoys family outings, ample coffee, and unapologetic napping. She lives in London, Ontario with her husband, daughter, and wonky-eyed cat. She is the author of one previous novel, *Vanishing Hour*.